HIDE AND SEEK

Emily thought she knew the man she married.
Hawksleigh was titled, wealthy, handsome, gallant,
and above all honorable from the tips of his polished
boots to the top of the dark hair that helmeted his
noble head.

But soon she discovered how much she did not know
about this man who refused to touch her . . . this
man whose sleep was tormented by nightmares . . .
this man who was strangely tied to a mysterious foreign
beauty.

Emily had to uncover the hidden truth about him—
even if this unmasking turned out to be her
undoing. . . .

BARBARA ALLISTER is a native Texan who ejoys
reading and traveling. An English teacher, Ms. Allister
began writing as a hobby after experimenting with
techniques to use in her creative writing class.

The Frustrated Bridegroom

by
Barbara Allister

A SIGNET BOOK

SIGNET
Published by the Penguin Group
Penguin Books USA Inc., 375 Hudson Street,
New York, New York 10014, U.S.A.
Penguin Books Ltd, 27 Wrights Lane,
London W8 5TZ, England
Penguin Books Australia Ltd, Ringwood,
Victoria, Australia
Penguin Books Canada Ltd, 10 Alcorn Avenue,
Toronto, Ontario, Canada M4V 3B2
Penguin Books (N.Z.) Ltd, 182–190 Wairau Road,
Auckland 10, New Zealand

Penguin Books Ltd, Registered Offices:
Harmondsworth, Middlesex, England

Published by Signet, an imprint of Dutton Signet,
a division of Penguin Books USA Inc.

First Printing, August, 1990
10 9 8 7 6 5 4

For my editor,
Hilary Ross,
who is both wise and understanding

1

The two horsemen paused at the top of the rise. They looked down at the valley where people worked in the fields. The taller took a deep breath, enjoying the rich fragrance of ripening grains and fruits. "Harvest. Sometimes I wondered if I would ever see it again," said Captain Anthony Hawksleigh so quietly that his batman almost missed the words.

"Different from Spain. That it is," the other man agreed while glancing curiously toward his master. The captain seemed more relaxed than he had been in months, looking less like the bird of prey his friends and enemies called him. Getting out of uniform had helped, the batman decided. Although decidedly not regulation, the dark blue jacket and riding breeches the captain had bought when they landed made their return from the Peninsula a reality.

They sat there for a few minutes more. Hawk stretched, setting his muscles rippling beneath the ill-fitting jacket. His horse stood perfectly still, controlled by the man's long legs. "Only a few more miles, Lester. Then we will be home. Home!" he said, a smile in his voice. Then he laughed out loud, took one more look around, and sent his horse plunging down the rise. His servant, always cautious, followed him at a slower pace, a smile lighting his face as well.

Soon they galloped down the winding road that led to the manor. Once in sight of the house, Hawk paused briefly to enjoy the sight of warm gray stone washed in the afternoon sunlight. Taking off his hat, he ran his fingers through his thick dark hair, trying to smooth his windblown locks. His dark brown eyes noted every change that had been made in the three years he had been away. But even the changes could not hold his attention long. He spurred his horse toward the manor, his family, and, soon, very soon, he promised himself, Emily Cheswick, his fiancée.

He thought of the last time he had seen her, the day he had told her good-bye. Her hazel eyes, more green than brown, swam with tears rather than brimming with the laughter he was accustomed to seeing there. Her light brown hair had gleamed in the sunlight. As he had so many times before, Hawk reveled in his memories of her, of the way Emily fitted in his arms. As tall as he was, Emily matched him perfectly, her head reaching the top of his shoulder. During her Season she had not been enough in the classic mode to be known as a Beauty, but few people forgot her striking features. Because of her height, usually a disadvantage for a young lady, she was known as an Original. To Hawk, she was his promise for the future.

By the time he arrived at the manor, both a groom and the butler stood waiting for him as though he had been gone only days. "Welcome home, Captain," the butler said calmly, but the faintest hint of a smile lifted the corners of his mouth. "Your family and Miss Emily are in the small salon." He held the door open.

Hawk felt his heart began to beat faster when he heard Emily's name. He took a deep breath, closed his eyes for a moment, and walked into the hall where, when they were children, he and his brother had spent hours sliding on the slick marble floor.

"Do not put your hopes on what the farmer thought he saw, Emily. Remember how many times you have been disappointed," Hawk heard his brother call. Hawk had only a moment to register the fact that Emily was running toward him. Then she was in his arms, all thoughts of propriety far from her mind. Hawk tightened his arms around her hungrily. She returned his kisses, her arms wound tightly around his neck and her toes just touching the ground.

"He will remember us soon, Mama," his brother said wryly, trying to hide the catch in his voice. "Even Hawk would not be so lost to good manners as to ignore us forever."

Hawk laughed, loosened his hold on Emily, and let her stand beside him, his arm still wrapped around her waist.

"I am sorry, Mama." He kissed his mother's tear-streaked cheek and hugged her tightly. "Emily distracted me." His fiancée glared at him and glanced at his mother nervously, embarrassed at her own behavior and not at all certain that the very prim and proper Mrs. Hawksleigh would approve of her actions. Hawk's mother smiled at them indulgently, a few more tears trickling down her face. Hawk pulled out his handkerchief and wiped them carefully away. He smiled at both of the women.

"Anything else and I would have wondered if you were really my son," his father said, a look of pride on his face. He looked into the brown eyes so like his wife's, took his son's hand, and pulled him into his arms. For a moment Hawk was startled; then he returned the embrace.

"You cannot avoid me any longer, older brother," Andrew said in a mocking voice that was completely in contrast to the pleasure on his face. Like his father, he too embraced his brother. As soon as the first greetings were over, they moved back into the small salon, no one willing to let Hawk go even for a short time to change out of his travel-worn clothes. Andrew, direct as usual, asked, "Now, tell us what you are doing in England and why you have not written in some time."

"We were so worried about you," his mother said softly.

The hand holding Emily's tightened painfully. She looked up, startled. Hawk's face wore a look of suppressed anger and frustration. She laid her other hand over his, smoothing the back of his hand as though her actions would wipe away the frown that creased his forehead. Just then the door opened, and the butler, a footman, and a maid entered with a tea tray. "Cook begs you to forgive her, Captain. She did not have time to prepare your favorite peach tarts," the butler said apologetically as he watched the other servants arrange the tea things on the table in front of Mrs. Hawksleigh.

"Peach tarts. I have almost forgotten how they taste. Dawson, tell Cook that tomorrow will be quite soon enough. Being at home with my family and Miss Emily is enough for today." Hawk smiled at the butler, his face losing its angry, pinched look. For the next few minutes the conversation was lighthearted and general, detailing the news of the county and the nation. But Mr. Hawksleigh and his younger son exchanged glances, glances that Hawk read correctly.

Soon the clock chimed five. "I must go," Emily said quietly, disappointment written in every line of her face.

"Send a note that you are staying here for a few more hours," Hawk urged. Emily shook her head, her face downcast. "Then I will drive you home," he said, his tone revealing his determination not to be separated from her so soon.

"Take my curricle. It should be waiting, because I planned to take Emily home," his brother urged. "Watch the pair, though—the one on the right has a stubborn streak."

"Another impulsive buy, little brother?" Hawk asked, his voice teasing.

"These I raised from foals. Did the training myself. Let me know how you like them," Andrew said defensively. He stood beside his brother, his light brown hair a contrast to his brother's. Three years younger than Hawk, Andrew was as tall, but his eyes were hazel like his father's and his skin much fairer. For the first time in several years, Andrew felt very young.

"Then I am certain I will have no trouble. You have a way with horses, Andrew. That stallion you sent me two years ago was a good horse." Hawk's eye darkened with remembered pain. "He was shot out from under me two months ago."

"Hawk! Were you hurt?" Emily said, big tears brimming in her eyes.

"Son," his mother gasped, her face paling and her hands clenched.

His brother and father gripped his shoulders comfortingly, their hands tightening firmly. "We will discuss everything when you are ready," his father said firmly. "Now you must return Emily to her stepmother before the lady forbids her our home." His words held a disturbing message, one Hawk was not ready to translate.

"Perhaps I should send a maid home with you, Emily," Mrs. Hawksleigh suggested.

"They will be in a curricle, Mama," Andrew reminded

her. "There is no place for a maid. Besides, I am certain Hawk took Emily driving many times in London. And they did not always take a maid with them then, did they?" Hawk and Emily exchanged an amused glance but held their tongues. "Well?"

"I suppose you are right," his mother finally said. Quickly Emily said her good-byes, donned her bonnet and cape, and let Hawk hand her into the curricle.

"Remember to tell your stepmama that I need you tomorrow," Mrs. Hawksleigh said as she stood at the doorway. "Emily, we must plan a party to celebrate Hawk's return." As though she could not bear to let him out of her sight, Mrs. Hawksleigh kept her eyes on her son. "Anthony, you come straight home."

"I will tell her," Emily promised, her face shadowed by doubt. Then they were on their way, the crisp air bringing roses to their cheeks.

As soon as they escaped from the watchful eyes that lined the road and pulled onto the public highway, Hawk pulled over. Holding the reins firmly in one hand, he put his other arm around Emily and pulled her close. For a few minutes they simply looked at each other; then they kissed, frantically, hungrily, as if afraid the other would disappear. "Oh, Emily, I have missed you," Hawk whispered against her mouth. Then he pulled her closer, kissed her again.

Reveling in sensations she remembered only from three years earlier, Emily murmured, "Me too," allowing his tongue to slide between her lips. One of her hands slipped beneath his coat, and his arm wrapped her closer to him. "Hawk," she said breathlessly. Lost in their own world, they were oblivious of the sound of a vehicle pulling up beside them.

"Emily Ann Cheswick! I knew no good would come from letting you go jaunting about the countryside. When Lord Babbington said he recognized you, I told him he was mistaken. But I see he was not," an angry voice interrupted them. "I told you you had to be home on time so Mary Ann could leave. Well, I will know better than to believe you again. And how could you behave with such impropriety?" The lady in the other carriage turned her attention from

Emily, whose cheeks were now almost white, to Hawk, who
controlled his temper only because the person addressing him
was a lady. "If you think you can take advantage of my stepdaughter to gain her dowry, sir, you had better think again.
She is promised. Though whether her fiancé will want her
once he hears of her behavior today is doubtful," the petite
blond added in an undertone to the gentleman sitting on the
horse beside her carriage. He laughed.

Emily pulled further away from Hawk, retreating into the
corner of the carriage, her face pale and her hands shaking.
Startled by her reactions, Hawk picked up her hand and gave
it a squeeze. She smiled at him and then lowered her eyes
again. He turned to the couple in the curricle beside him.
"Mrs. Cheswick," he said, his voice calm but stern, "I
believe you will discover that my feelings are unchanged.
I love Emily and plan to marry her."

Mrs. Cheswick had continued her denigrating chatter. His
words, however, stopped her light, prattling voice. "Captain
Hawksleigh?" she said, her voice almost a squeak instead
of the musical tones she tried to emulate.

"Whom did you expect?" he asked coldly, waiting for
Emily to tell her stepmother to leave her alone. Emily simply
shrank further back into her seat. Hawk stared at her in
amazement.

Mrs. Cheswick smiled saucily. "Of course. Naturally
Emily would not be so lost to proper behavior to behave this
way with anyone but her betrothed." Her voice was ironic.
"We will just have to beg Lord Babbington to keep the story
to himself." She exchanged mocking glances with the
gentleman. Then she looked at her stepdaughter, her glance
promising that Emily would hear more of her tirade when
she arrived home. "Emily, I must insist that you go home
immediately. Captain, you will understand if she does not
invite you to supper. I am promised elsewhere, and it would
not do."

"My family expects me home shortly. And I will see Emily
in the morning when she comes to help my mother plan a
party to celebrate my return," Hawk said firmly. "I plan
to see Emily often," he added, watching Emily's stepmother
carefully.

For a moment anger lit the woman's face. Then she smiled sweetly.. "A party. How wonderful. Tell your mother I will be happy to release Emily from her usual duties. I will look forward to receiving my invitation." Arranging her hat firmly on her blond hair, Mrs. Cheswick nodded. Then her escort cracked his whip and they rode away.

"Hawk, I must go home. Please," Emily said, her hazel eyes filling with tears. Hawk looked at her closely, noting the disturbed look on her face. He settled her bonnet on her light brown hair again and tied the ribbons in a clumsy bow.

"I haven't gotten better at this in three years," he said thoughtfully. He kissed her again softly. "Sit closer to me," he demanded, pretending to forget her stepmother's interruption. Emily sighed thankfully and nestled close behind him.

"What is wrong with Emily?" he demanded hours later when the family gathered in the small salon again. Surrounded by a bevy of servants during supper, they had discussed inconsequential things: new babies, marriages, family scandals. His family exchanged glances, each waiting for the other to begin. "Mama?"

His mother sighed. "We wrote to you when Mr. Cheswick died, Anthony. Things have not been comfortable for Emily since then."

"What does that mean, 'not comfortable'?"

"Just what it means, brother. Her father left that feather brain in charge of most of the family finances. Emily has to beg for every farthing she gets."

"Do you mean Mrs. Cheswick lost everything?"

"Not her," Andrew said scornfully. "She never takes chances with her money."

"Andrew, do not repeat gossip!" his mother said reprovingly.

"It certainly is not gossip to tell Hawk that his fiancée's stepmother dismissed all the old servants, pensioning off those she could and letting the rest go. You hired enough of them yourself, Mama," Andrew said, getting up and crossing to the mantel.

"He has you there, my dear," her husband added. "Anthony, all we know is what the county knows and what little Emily tells us. And she refuses to say much."

"I know she is expected to clean and cook and watch her little brother," the younger man said angrily. "She is not even allowed to come here unless we ask her well in advance. And she has stopped hunting or going to parties. That woman has turned her into a drudge."

Mrs. Hawksleigh watched as her elder son's face darkened with anger. "Come here, my dear." Mrs. Hawksleigh patted the gold striped settee on which she sat. Hawk sat down, his face shadowed. "From what I can learn, her stepmother has cut back on servants in order to save money. Emily has said nothing to me, but she has increasingly grown more withdrawn, quieter."

"Did Mr. Cheswick play ducks and drakes with his fortune?" Hawk asked, his face reflecting his concern.

"Would it make any difference if he had? If you plan to call off your engagement—" Andrew said angrily.

"Call off my engagement? What kind of man do you think I am?" Hawk was up and facing his brother, anger reflected in every muscle of his body.

"Anthony! Andrew!" their father said sternly. Both men stepped back.

Then a rueful light lit the younger brother's face. "Always let my tongue run away with me," he said mockingly. "Forgive me?"

"Forgiven." Hawk held out his hand. They shook hands and then laughed. "But I need more information. Andrew, tell me what you have found out."

"Apparently as soon as Mr. Cheswick's estate was settled, Mrs. Cheswick started reducing her staff. During her year of mourning, it was understandable. Since they would not be entertaining, they did not need an underbutler or three assistant cooks. But when she pensioned off the butler and the housekeeper, people began to talk."

"Andrew, you are exaggerating. Her story that they wanted to retire and open their own inn was convincing," his mother said reprovingly. "My dear, we did not know the exact state of affairs for months. Since then, we have made certain that Emily spends as much time with us as her stepmother allows. Because you two are betrothed, we could insist that she be allowed to visit."

"But nothing you said was enough to convince Mrs. Cheswick to allow Emily to come to London for the Season," her husband reminded her.

"Her year of mourning was not over," Mrs. Hawksleigh said quietly. She glanced at her elder son. "I did try, Anthony, but her stepmother refused."

"And then she appeared alone as soon as the year was up," Andrew said bitingly. "When we asked Lucretia Cheswick where Emily was, the lady said she had stayed behind to keep her brother company." His brother raised an eyebrow. "I left London and came to see her. Her stepmother could not refuse me entrance if she were not here."

"What do you mean, refuse you entrance?" Hawk asked, his face stormy. "We have run tame in that house for years."

"Not anymore, brother. And when I came here in May, I discovered why. Mrs. Cheswick had gone to London, leaving Emily and her brother alone in the house with only one servant, an elderly maid. Oh, I know you thought I was joking when I told you I found Emily cooking and cleaning like a scullery maid, Mama, but I was not. Emily made me promise I would not reveal the truth to anyone. And since you and Father returned from London, things have been better. They have a cook and someone to clean, as well as a nursery maid who comes in each day."

"You must realize, son, that Mr. Cheswick appointed his wife Emily's guardian and trustee until her marriage," his father said placatingly. "We had no legal rights. All we could do was welcome her into our home whenever she came."

"You could have written to me," Hawk said angrily.

"And what could you have done? Come rushing home from the Peninsula?" his brother asked. Hawk ran his hand over his face as if he could wipe away his problems. He closed his eyes for a moment.

"Emily would be so embarrassed if she thought we knew what had happened. She is so proud," his mother added quietly. She crossed to her elder son's side. "Now you are home. It will be your responsibility to care for her. You will have time to marry before you return to the Peninsula?"

"Yes." The word was bitten off as though it left a bad taste in Hawk's mouth. "I will talk to Emily tomorrow,

Mama, if I can get her to answer me. She is so different—quiet, almost shy.''

"Mrs. Cheswick is looking for another husband. No, do not try to make me be quiet, Mama," Andrew said determinedly. "Apparently having a stepdaughter like Emily is a threat to her ambitions. She plans to snare a lord this time. And according to my little friend, she is afraid gentlemen will like Emily more than herself. So she keeps her out of sight.''

"If the exquisite she had with her this afternoon is an example of her taste, Emily will do well to quit her camp quickly," Hawk said. "But what does that have to do with the change in her?''

"Emily does not confide in me, Anthony," his mother said regretfully.

"Well, I have never heard the lady say anything kind to or about Emily in over a year," Andrew said harshly.

"I will get a special license, get her away from there. We can be married within the week. Isn't there a bishop in our family?''

"Must you leave so soon, then?" Mrs. Hawksleigh asked wistfully. Hawk looked at his mother, puzzled, and shook his head. "Good. Hawk, you do not want to begin your married life hastily.''

"Hastily? We have been engaged for over three years, Mama.''

"You know what I mean. We must proceed properly. We will have the banns read for the first time this Sunday. Let's make certain that we give the county nothing unpleasant to gossip about. I will speak to Mrs. Cheswick myself tomorrow and suggest that she visit the dressmaker immediately. If we approach her correctly, her pride will insist on it. Emily's family must pay for her bride's clothes if she is not to feel like a poor relation." Mrs. Hawksleigh smiled. "Since you are home, everything will be much better for Emily. I will say good night, my dears, and go make some plans. Do not spend the entire night talking.''

"Bless you, Mama. I will do as you suggest. I think I will leave anything having to do with Mrs. Cheswick to you," Hawk said, a smile lighting his eyes for the first time in hours. His mother kissed his cheek and hurried from the room.

"We will be more comfortable in the library," his father said, tugging on the bellpull. "Dawson, we will need fresh glasses and the brandy." He noticed his elder son's eyebrows going up. "Do not pull that face with me, Anthony. This brandy, at least, has a customs stamp on it."

"I wonder how he managed that?" Hawk asked Andrew as they followed their father down the hallway.

"I know better than to ask," his brother replied.

Soon they were comfortably ensconced in the deep red leather chairs of the room that had been his father's domain for as many years as Hawk could remember. He had been sent here for punishment when he had hit his tutor, and had trembled in fear for minutes as he waited for his father to raise his head. He could still hear his father's quiet voice ask, "What happened, son?"

Lost in his reverie, Hawk was silent. His brother poked him with an elbow. He jumped. "Father asked what happened in Spain, Hawk," his brother said impatiently. "And do not try to fob us off with a lie."

"Andrew! Your brother will tell us when he is ready." Mr. Hawksleigh held out a glass of brandy to his elder son and then poured a smaller amount for himself. "How long will you be able to stay in England, Anthony?"

Hawk laughed bitterly. Then he said, "For the rest of my life, as it now stands."

"Have you sold out?" This time it was his father's voice that was sharp.

"No! My orders say I have been invalided home. I will not be able to return until I am given permission."

"Invalided? You were wounded?"

"What happened? When? Should you have been riding? If you had let us know, we would have sent a coach for you." His brother's and his father's comments swirled around him.

"I am all right. At least I think I am," Hawk said, his voice still bitter.

"What do you mean, you think you are?" his father demanded. "We will have Dr. Graves in tomorrow to check you over thoroughly. I do not trust those military doctors."

"No."

"What do you mean, Hawk? You have to see someone. Old Graves has known us most of our lives," his brother said, trying to cajole him into accepting.

"And he would say exactly the same thing that the doctors in Spain said. There is nothing wrong with me, nothing that they can find, at least."

"Explain." Andrew jumped up, refilled his own glass, and offered more to his father and brother. They refused. "How can they send you home as an invalid if there is nothing wrong with you?"

Realizing the inevitability of the confrontation, Hawk sighed, took another sip of brandy, and began. "Two months ago I was sent behind enemy lines. In one of my letters I think I told you that Wellesley gave me a special courier's job." They nodded. "Because of my dark hair and eyes, I was able to go places others could not. And I speak Spanish and Portuguese. That year we spent in Lisbon when I was a boy stood me in good stead many times, Father."

"You were a spy!" his younger brother almost shouted. "What stories you can tell!"

His brother shot him an angry look. "Andrew, hold your tongue," his father snapped. The younger man took one look at them and sank further down in his chair. "Go on, Anthony."

Hawk took a deep breath and closed his eyes. He opened them quickly. "I was a courier, nothing more. I took messages between our allies and Wellesley." He took a gulp of brandy as if postponing the inevitable.

"Yes." The word hung in the air as if written in fire instead of spoken in his father's quiet voice.

"I was captured." Hawk's voice was emotionless, flat.

"But you are safe . . ." His father held up his hand, silencing his younger son. Andrew looked from Hawk's utterly blank face to his father's. The studied calm on the latter told him more than he wanted to know. All three of them sat quietly for a few minutes more.

"When I was rescued, I had been beaten rather badly and was unconscious—and stayed unconscious for two days. According to the doctor, I had been found just in time. Another beating might have killed me," Hawk said, his voice as calm as though he were reciting a list of crops planted in the spring.

"My boy," his father said huskily, surreptitiously wiping a tear from his eyes. "No wonder they sent you to England."

"You do not understand." This time Hawk's voice rang with anger and frustration. "I was not sent to England as a reward or as a person who needs care. I was sent to England because I cannot be trusted!"

"You lie!" Andrew was on his feet, his hands raised as though to fight off an unseen enemy. "Tell me you are lying!"

"Andrew, sit down!" his father commanded, using the tone that had made him famous for keeping the peace wherever he was. "I am certain there is more to the story than we have heard." He sat quietly, waiting for his elder son to continue, only the rigidity of his back and the serious look on his face revealing his nervousness.

"Thank you for your confidence, sir. It may be misplaced." Hawk sighed. "I have racked my memory, Father, and I still cannot remember anything about my capture. I remember leaving the Spanish lines and heading back. I remember the shot that killed my horse. Yes, Andrew, the stallion you sent. Then all is blank." He lifted his glass to take a drink, but his glass was empty. Too emotionally tired to do anything more than sit there, he stared at the glass as though mesmerized.

Andrew pulled himself from the chair and grabbed the bottle, refilling all three of their glasses. He sat back down without saying a word, as if he feared to break the silence.

"Was the position overrun by the French? Did the Spanish lose the battle?" his father asked cautiously.

"No, by the time they found me, that skirmish was successful. The French took the beating then."

"Then what is the problem?" his father asked quietly.

"Wellesley said he could not be certain of me. I am not at all sure he believed me when I said I could not remember. If the doctor had not told him that blows to the head can cause a person to lose all or part of his memory, I think he would have had me shot. I would probably have done the same thing if I were in his place."

"Hawk!"

"Anthony!"

"A commander must protect his men. After my injuries had healed, Wellesley talked to me, told me of his dilemma. We agreed. There was little good I could do in staying. He sent me home to England until I can remember what happened during the day I lost," Hawk said quietly, his voice trailing off into silence. "If I ever remember."

"The more reason for you to see Dr. Graves tomorrow. No, son, you must. There's no need to tell him everything. Tell him about being unconscious; tell him you cannot always remember things. He is not a gossip, and he may be able to help," Mr. Hawksleigh said firmly. "With your marriage to Emily set, you want to be fully recovered as soon as possible. He will understand that."

"Yes, Father," Hawk said, too exhausted to argue anymore. "But you are not to tell Mama everything."

"You may trust my discretion. Anthony?"

"Yes, sir?"

"What are you going to tell Emily?"

"Everything. But in my own time, Father," Hawk promised.

That night Hawk slept in his own bed for the first time in years. He had postponed going up as long as he could by talking to Andrew in hopes that he would finally be able to sleep through the night. But the dreams that had plagued him since his capture returned.

In the early-morning hours Andrew woke with a start. He sat up in bed, listening. He heard the deep, gut-wrenching moans again. Grabbing his dressing gown, he walked into the corridor; the sound was coming from Hawk's room. He cautiously opened his brother's bedroom door and crept inside, certain he would find someone torturing Hawk. He looked around cautiously. The moans were coming from the bed. A litany of "No, no, you can't. Don't!" came from his brother.

"Hawk! Hawk? What is it?" As soon as he reached the bedside, Andrew saw that his brother's eyes were closed. He reached over to touch him, but Hawk pulled away. Andrew reached out a hand to shake him and then jumped back when a voice behind him said, "Don't touch him, sir. Let me do it." Recognizing his brother's batman, Andrew stepped back. "Captain Hawksleigh, the general wishes to see you immediately," Lester shouted.

"Are my boots here?" Hawk asked as he sat up in bed and ran a hand over his face. Then he noticed the bed hangings that surrounded him. "Another of those dreams, Lester?" he asked wearily. He lay back down exhausted.

"Yes, sir. Your brother is here also." The batman handed his master a damp cloth and stepped back.

"Sorry to disturb you, Andrew. I hope you can go back to sleep," Hawk said ruefully. "Maybe I should ask Mama to find me a room farther away from everyone."

"And deny me a chance to pay off those debts from when I discovered that book about ghosts? I slept with you for months," Andrew said as though what had happened were perfectly natural. He exchanged a look with Lester, said good night, and walked to the door. He motioned Lester to follow him. When they were in the hall with the door closed behind them, he asked, "Will he have another one tonight?"

"Not ordinarily. If he does, he usually wakes himself up before the noise begins."

"When did they start?"

"After he was captured. As soon as the doctor said he could return to his own tent, the captain came to me. That night they started." Lester rubbed his hand over his weary face. "Thought he was improving. He hasn't had a dream since we landed in England."

"Does he ever talk about them, tell you what is going on?"

"Not him. Can't seem to remember anything. But . . ." The batman hesitated and then said hurriedly, "Do not try to touch him during one of them. He'll do you harm, he will. He knocked me to the floor one night, he did, without even opening his eyes."

Andrew frowned, pinching the bridge of his nose as if trying to rid himself of a headache. Then his expression changed to one of dismay. "Emily! Lester, he is going to marry Emily Cheswick in three weeks' time. What should we do then?"

2

In spite of her stepmother's interference, Emily was happier than she had been in years. Hawk was home. During their journey to her house, she had kept her eyes on him as though afraid he would disappear again. He had often looked at her instead of the road, caught her staring at him, and smiled.

When they arrived, Hawk helped her from the curricle. Emily looked up at him and smiled. Surveying the area quickly, he realized they were alone. Quickly he kissed her once more. "Until tomorrow," he promised. He watched as she opened the door and slipped inside. Then he jumped back into the curricle and drove off, leaving a breathless and happy lady behind.

She practically danced down the hallway, coming to an abrupt stop in front of the woman who stood with her arms akimbo, blocking the doorway. "I was to leave early this evening. When Mrs. Cheswick finds out how late you were, I am certain she will have a thing or two to say," the maid said threateningly. In the last year she had learned how to make Emily uncomfortable.

For once she was disappointed. "My stepmother already knows," Emily said with a hint of hauteur. She resisted the temptation to stick out her tongue at the other woman. Then she added, "You will need to be here early for the next few days, Mary Ann."

"I only take orders from Mrs. Cheswick. When she tells me she needs me, then I will come," the maid said menacingly.

"Be here very early tomorrow," Emily repeated firmly. "Where is my brother?"

"In the kitchen. The young master had decided he wants

chicken for supper," Mary Ann said with a smirk. "Cook is ill again."

With care Emily kept all emotion from her face. "You may go," she said.

"Yes, miss." Surprised by Emily's firmness, the maid turned and hurried down the back stairs.

As soon as she was certain Mary Ann had had time to make her retreat, Emily walked down the stairs to the kitchen. "Jonathan, where are you?" she called as she looked about the empty room.

"In here," her six-year-old brother called. "Cook showed me how to make little men from scraps of pie dough. Come see what I have done."

Emily entered the small room and saw her brother perched on a high stool, wrapped in an apron that she supposed had once been clean. "Aren't they good, Emily? Cook said they were. But that Mary Ann just laughed at me. Then she sent Cook away. But they are good?" he asked as he jumped down and drew her closer to the table.

"They are excellent. Where is everyone?"

"Mama is out. And Mary Ann told everyone else that Mama had given them an extra afternoon off. I do not like you to leave me alone with Mary Ann, Emily. Where were you?"

"At the manor. Jonathan, guess what happened today!" Her face alive with color, Emily glowed. "Hawk came home!"

Her brother's face puckered with thought. "Who is Hawk? Do I know this person?"

"You were only three when he left, little brother. But you will meet him again soon. He used to put you up in front of him on his horse and ride you around the stableyard."

"He did? Will he teach me to ride a horse? I am too old for a pony, Mama says. Will Hawk teach me?" Jonathan brushed the lock of blond hair that had fallen in his eyes out of the way. "I will be good. When Mama and I visited Grandfather at Christmas, the groom said I had good bottom. Do you think Hawk will teach me?"

"Won't your friend Andrew be jealous if you give his duties to another gentleman?" Emily asked, enjoying the way excitement lit her brother's face.

"No." Jonathan stamped his foot. "Andrew will not teach me anymore. He said I am a spoiled brat."

Emily looked at him, her eyes staring straight into her brother's blue ones. "And what did you do to make my friend Andrew say that?" she asked calmly. Her brother hung his head and mumbled something under his breath. "I did not hear what you said," his sister replied. "Shall I tell Hawk that you cannot get along with his brother?"

"Hawk is Andrew's brother? The one who has been with the general on the Peninsula? Did he tell you any stories? Is he wounded? Did he capture any spies? When is he coming? You *will* let met meet him?" The words practically fell over themselves as the small boy babbled on. "Andrew says Hawk is the bravest person in the world. Do you think so? Is he coming here tomorrow? I must tell Mama that I want to meet him. She will let me meet him, won't she?" Long used to his mother's changes of fancy, Jonathan knew not to plan on his mother's approval before it was given.

"We will ask her. Now, let us see what Cook left for supper."

"I wanted chicken, and Mary Ann offered to kill one. She asked me if I wanted to watch, but I said no. That doesn't make me a coward, does it?" His sister shook her head as she looked around the pantry. "Good. I told Mary Ann that it didn't." He took his sister's hand. "Cook made a meat pie for our dinner." He stopped and looked up at his sister. "I do not like Mary Ann. I wish Mama would dismiss her."

"Tell your mother," Emily said absently as she picked up the meat pie the cook had left. "You can carry the apple tart to the table."

"Are we going to eat upstairs? I would rather eat right here. I missed my tea. Mary Ann said I did not need any." His sister looked at him as he carefully picked up the apple tart. "She said that an apple tart was enough for tea. Cook made me an extra one, you see. But I was hungry."

They climbed the stairs, Emily balancing a tray with the meat pie, fruit, cream, and their drinks, and Jonathan carrying the apple tart in front of him like a prize. "Then you will enjoy your supper. Shall we serve ourselves from the sideboard?" she asked, making him feel important.

"Since we do not have a footman, we must," he said, his

perfectly formed nose sticking up in the air. ''I told Grandfather that we did not have one, and he told Mama to hire
one immediately. But she hasn't. She has not fired Mary Ann
either, even though I told her to.''

And she is not about to do so, not and have to hire someone
else at three times the wages she pays Mary Ann, Emily
thought. She simply smiled and filled her brother's place.
''Tell me what else you did today. Did you finish your
lessons?''

After her brother was asleep in bed, Emily sat in the small
sitting room that adjoined her bedroom, reliving the day. The
room, slightly shabby now, had once been stark white. The
silk covering the walls had mellowed to a soft white, still
a perfect complement to the rose-pink damask of the settee
and draperies. The rug with its soft blues and pinks had been
brought from Persia. When she was younger, Emily had sat
with her sewing, making up stories about the adventures the
rug had seen. When Hawk was gone, she dreamed of his
return. Now he was home.

Too excited to sit down any longer, she began to walk
around the room, letting her hands drift idly over the silky
smooth fabric of the settee or the highly polished wood of
the chair. Her fingertips tingled just as they had done that
afternoon when she touched Hawk, running her hands over
his rippling muscles. Her heart raced. She closed her eyes
and ran her tongue softly over her lips. She shivered with
excitement. For a time she allowed her emotions full rein.
A flush rippled up to her face as she remembered Hawk's
mouth and hands, the feel of his shoulders under her hands,
the way his muscles had rippled as he pulled her closer.

''Hawk is home,'' she whispered to herself. But he will
leave again; you will see. The words echoed through her
mind in her stepmother's voice. She had heard them often
enough.

''He will never marry you. Why would such a handsome
man want a beanpole like you? Going off to fight Napoleon,
ha! He simply wanted to escape his engagement to you. It
is not as if you are beautiful, my pampered stepdaughter.
How could anyone be considered beautiful when she stands
taller than most men in the county? Really, you make a

spectacle of yourself every time you agree to stand up with a man who is shorter than you. I will never understand how you were so popular in London. I suppose your aunt's friends felt sorry for her when they saw you towering over everyone.''

The words had poured out for years whenever her stepmother was alone with Emily. The first years, Emily had been able to ignore them. Her father had towered over her and laughed at her worries about being tall. Her aunt, herself Emily's height, taught her to walk regally, holding her head up high. And in her second Season, there was Hawk.

She had known him for most of her life. But the last few years he had been away at school or traveling with his father. She smiled as she remembered the gown she had worn, a pale lemon-yellow tunic embroidered about the neckline, around the bodice, and down the front of the skirt with green ivy and yellow rosebuds and worn over a slip of the palest green. ''The color of the first leaves in spring,'' Hawk said. She sighed.

Then she gasped. Hawk said he would return early the next morning. She hurried to her wardrobe, already certain what she would find. In despair she lifted out her few suitable dresses, knowing they were hopelessly out of style. The short sleeves and rounded necklines were beyond her ability as a seamstress; therefore, she put those problems behind her as she considered her choices. The pink was such a thin dress that Emily knew she would be cold all day even if she wore a shawl, and the lavender, her newest dress, reminded her of her father's death and the year of mourning. She finally decided on the periwinkle blue. She had recently changed the collar to a more fashionable, higher one and added a long-sleeved pelisse made from a width of the previously full skirt.

Checking on her brother once more, she discovered that his nursery maid had returned. Relieved of that responsibility and free to concentrate on herself, she sat down in front of her glass and began brushing her hair. He is so handsome, she thought. More handsome than that night in London. He had asked her for the first dance, and although she had been saving it in hopes that someone else would ask her, she had agreed. To both their surprise, the dance flew past. He had asked her for another, but they were all promised. When he left a short time later, all the excitement of the evening had disappeared.

But Hawk had called on her the next morning, she remembered, a smile lifting her lips. In his regimentals he had been the most handsome man in the drawing room. Before long his friends had been making bets on whether she would accept him, and on how long Hawk would wait before he asked. After those few stolen minutes in someone's garden, he had written to her father for an appointment. With her father's permission in hand, she and Hawk had arranged an interview with her aunt. Then the engagement was announced. Certain that the marriage would soon follow, Emily had welcomed Hawk's kisses and caresses eagerly, anxious to become his wife. Then he had received his orders. He and her father had discussed the situation and decided that it would be best to wait until he returned before they married. And so she had been waiting for three years. But the hunger of Hawk's kisses that afternoon had convinced her that she would not have to wait much longer.

Emily's bedroom door crashed open. Her stepmother, slightly disheveled, stood there glaring at her. "I hope you know that you have made me the laughingstock of the county, Emily. The story of your behavior this afternoon was the talk of the party."

"Then Lord Babbington must have enjoyed your discomfort. You and he were the only ones who saw us," Emily said sharply, surprising even herself.

"So confident are you? We shall see how serious Captain Hawksleigh will be when I tell him that he does not have my approval. And you know what that means. No dowry!" her stepmother said maliciously. From the time of her marriage she had resented the tall girl only a few years younger than herself. Emily had wrapped her father around her finger. He never said no to her, Lucretia Cheswick thought angrily as she stormed out of the room. Well, Miss Father's Darling had better not plan on leaving anytime soon. Few men would accept a dowryless girl. Emily was necessary to her comfort, and Lucretia did not plan to lose her housekeeper or her son's governess.

Her bravado gone, Emily collapsed into a chair, her shoulders shaking with tears. When he lay dying, her father had told her to trust Hawk. Her fiancé would make everything all right. But her stepmother was the one in charge now. As she had so many times before, she sobbed, "How could he have left her in control? How could he?" Finally she undressed and crawled into bed, still shuddering with sobs.

When Hawk arrived the next morning to drive Emily to his family's home, he realized immediately that something was wrong. His knock was answered, slowly, by a large woman whose neat outer appearance was belied by her odor. "Mrs. Cheswick ain't seeing no one today," she said before he could open his mouth.

"I am not here to see Mrs. Cheswick. I am here to take Miss Emily for a drive," he said firmly, pushing past her into the hallway.

"Are you Hawk?" a small voice shouted from the top of the stairs. Hawk looked up to see a small blond figure hurrying down the stairs as fast as his legs would carry him. He held his breath for a moment until the boy reached the bottom safely.

"Yes, my friends call me that," the man said gravely, hiding a smile while he noted the way the little boy almost ran to meet him.

Jonathan slid to a stop. "Should I call you Captain Hawksleigh? Andrew does not. Neither does Emily."

"So you know Emily and Andrew, do you? Then I suppose you are a friend of theirs. You may call me Hawk."

"Andrew's my friend. He was teaching me to ride until he called me a spoiled child. Emily is my sister," Jonathan said, determined that the facts be given correctly. "Perhaps you would like to teach me instead," he suggested, opening his blue eyes widely and looking wistfully upward.

"Jonathan, return to the nursery immediately. You know that you are not allowed down here at this time," Lucretia Cheswick said sternly. "I must tell your nursery maid to be more strict with you."

Hawk watched all the excitement in Jonathan's face disappear. "Yes, Mama," the boy said in a colorless voice so like Emily's lackluster tones of the day before that Hawk wanted to demand an explanation.

"Do not send the boy away on my account, Mrs. Cheswick," he said quietly. "I am enjoying his company."

"It is not on your account, but on his own. He is missing his lessons." Jonathan opened his mouth to disagree, but she glared at him sternly. "Return to the nursery immediately, sir."

"Hawk, will you come and see me—"

"Go, Jonathan. And no more talking," his mother commanded. After one resentful glance, he was on his way. "I apologize for my son, Captain. Did you wish to see me?" Mrs. Cheswick smiled up at him, noting his broad shoulders and dark eyes. Of course, his skin was burned rather dark, but one could not have everything. And he was so handsome, so handsome that he made her forget her goal. Certain of her own petite blond good looks, she led him into the small morning room she had made her own, sure that no one would prefer her stepdaughter when he could have her lovely self. "What did you wish to discuss?" She smiled up at him, turning her head to one side so that her one dimple would show to advantage.

Hawk cleared his throat uneasily. Had she been anyone other than his fiancée's stepmother, he would have made his disapproval of her very evident. He cleared his throat nervously, watching her carefully. Then he remembered the note in his pocket and blessed his mother. "My mother wanted me to give you this." He handed it to her, watched her open it, and then saw her face darken with anger for a moment before she got her emotions under control.

"So your mother and father want me to go with them to the rector to arrange for the banns to be called." Lucretia opened her blue eyes even wider. "Do you not think this action is somewhat hasty?" Her voice was sweet, with just an edge of doubt.

"Hasty? Mrs. Cheswick, Emily and I have been engaged for three years. Had it not been for my orders, we would have been married long ago," Hawk said, marveling at the audacity of the woman. He had not believed his family's words of warning at first. Now he was not certain they had told him everything.

"Yes, yes, you would have. But so many things have changed. You have been gone so long. Perhaps you and Emily will find you no longer suit one another. A hasty marriage may lead to an unhappy life," Lucretia said sweetly as she lowered her long eyelashes darkened with kohl and lifted them again. She sat in her favorite chair, a dainty thing in gold and ivory designed to fit her small stature. "Sit down, and we can discuss it."

Hawk moved across the room to stand by the window leading to the garden. "What is there to discuss? I wish to marry Emily immediately. She and her father accepted my suit. Are you telling me that she has changed her mind?" Men under Hawk's command in the Peninsula would have told her to be wary when that look came into his eyes. He straightened his shoulder and pulled down the sleeves of his chocolate-brown coat.

But Lucretia Cheswick had forgotten the meaning of caution. "Since her father's death, many things have changed. The matter of the marriage settlements will take some time."

"No." The blunt word hung in the air between them.

"What do you mean? As the person in control of the family finances, I will certainly be the one to make the decision about the settlements," Lucretia reminded him complacently.

"No. Before I left for the Peninsula, her father and I discussed the matter. Because I wanted to be able to marry her whenever I received leave, we signed the settlements then. When Mr. Cheswick died, his man of business assured my father that they were still valid."

"Why wasn't I told? My husband left Emily in my charge until her marraige." The word brought her up short, her face livid. She glared at the tall man who stood before her.

"Perhaps you should discuss it with your man of business," he suggested coldly.

"Know that I will," she said menacingly.

Then the door opened, and Emily entered, her eyes going from the stern face of her fiancé to the reddening one of her stepmother. "Joanthan said you had come, Hawk. I will be ready to leave in just a few minutes. I must give Jonathan his lessons."

When Emily had awakened that morning, she had felt as

depressed as she had the night before. Then her resolve firmed. She would talk to Hawk, tell him about her step-mother's opposition. Her decision made, she had quickly dressed and arranged her hair. She had almost finished when Jonathan ran in with his news.

"May we expect you for dinner, then, Mrs. Cheswick?" Hawk asked politely, as if the words of a few minutes before had never been spoken. Still too upset at having her plans tossed aside to think clearly, she merely nodded, turning the situation over and over in her mind. Her eyes narrowed. She would find out the truth and turn it to her advantage. "Emily," Hawk said quietly, "I will go up to see Jonathan with you." He held out his arm.

Soon they were away, protected from the light mist by the closed carriage. As soon as the door closed behind them, Hawk pulled Emily close. He carefully pulled the bow on her bonnet free and placed the hat on the seat in front of them. He tilted Emily's face up, for her chin was lowered and her eyes downcast, and commanded, "Kiss me good morning." A flush of excitement making her face glow, Emily hesitantly leaned toward him and brushed his lips with hers. "Hmmm. I see you need further instruction," he drawled as he pulled her closer. She blushed and tried to bury her face in his shoulder. "Emily," he said softly, breathing in the freshness of her curls. She looked up. Keeping his eyes on hers, he kissed her, lightly at first, and then hungrily, as though he were starving and she were manna.

The short journey was long enough to rediscover the joy of lips meeting lips, of hands reveling in the feel of the other, of hunger swelling almost beyond the bounds of propriety. When the carriage hit a bump in the road, Emily pulled her lips away from Hawk's and took a deep breath. Her pelisse was undone, and his hands searched her sides for the laces to her dress.

"Hawk, no," she said softly, moving off his lap and to her own corner. "We must not." She reached up a finger to smooth one of his eyebrows. He captured it and brought it to his lips. "What would your mother say if she could see us?"

"That Andrew would take you home from now on. Then

she would organize our lives until we were never given a chance to be alone until our wedding day," he said, half-laughing.

"Just look at me. I am so rumpled that she is certain to know what happened," Emily complained, but the look on her face told Hawk that she had enjoyed their interlude as much as he had.

"Oh, Emily. I have missed you," he said, his face serious. "If I had not had your letters . . ." She settled her bonnet on the curls she had finger-combed into position and smiled at him. "I wish I could have been with you when your father died," he added solemnly.

Her eyes filled with tears. Then she quickly blinked them away. "You are home safely. That is all that matters," she said firmly, marveling how having him at her side made all the world seem more beautiful.

"What matters now is arranging our marriage. Emily, that stepmother of yours had the ridiculous idea that we needed to postpone our marriage until we had some time to become reacquainted," Hawk told her. His tone told her more than his words what he had thought of that idea. "We have known each other most of our lives. Fortunately, my family prepared me for her objections." He leaned back in his own corner, his face serious. "Emily, why did you not tell me what that woman has been doing? Why did you stay? Your aunt would have welcomed you."

"But not Jonathan. After my father's death, my aunt asked me to live with her. When she refused to allow me to bring Jonathan with me, I turned her down; she washed her hands of me. And what could you have done? You were in the middle of battle; you did not need my problems to deal with." Once again Hawk saw the sparkle and fire that had been so much a part of the Emily he had left behind three years before. But it was a sparkle that memory of her stepmother could easily dim. She bit her lip and then rushed ahead. "Hawk, my stepmother disapproves of our marriage. She refuses—"

He put his finger to her lips. "Hush. It is all right. There is nothing she can do to stop it."

Before Emily could ask him to explain, they were at the

manor. His mother, her face anxious, rushed Emily into her morning room. "Is she coming? Did she agree?" she asked, showing Emily to a seat on the settee. Awash with the morning light, the room glowed golden, turning Emily's eyes from green to brown. Hawk looked at her for a moment, puzzled by a thought lying just out of reach in his mind.

He took his seat beside Emily and reached for her hand, rubbing his fingers over her palm. "You should ask me, Mama. I am the one who talked to her."

"Well, is she coming to dinner? I must send word to the rector immediately."

"Yes."

"She is?" Emily asked, not certain he had gotten the information correct. "Last night she said—"

Hawk cut her off. "This morning she read Mama's note and said she would be here. Maybe she changed her mind." He had no intention of worrying Emily about the problems her stepmother had been ready to cause or the way she had cast out lures to him that morning.

"Then Emily and I must get busy. The party should be early next week, don't you think, my dear? Then I am certain there will be a round of parties among our friends. Such a wonderful time for a wedding. How many people should we expect? Your aunt, of course, And your stepmother's father. Hawk, take yourself off. Find your father and brother, my dear. Emily you sit at the desk and begin a list." Realizing from the absentminded tone in his mother's voice and his fiancée's rueful glance that he would be superfluous for some time, Hawk followed his mother's suggestion.

"Already deserted, Hawk? I knew Emily had more sense than to marry you," his brother teased as Hawk walked out into the hallway. For a moment Hawk stiffened; then he relaxed and laughed.

"Mother captured her," he said.

"Oh, the poor girl. Has Mother mentioned a list?" Andrew asked. Hawk nodded. "Then she will be busy until dinner. Did you talk to Emily's stepmother?" he asked in a more serious vein.

"Yes. Thanks to you, I was prepared. That lady will cause Emily and me trouble if I let her," Hawk told him, his face stern. "Was she always like this?"

"Not when Emily's father was alive. Apparently he kept her on a firm rein. And when her father is here, she is different. He came last spring to oversee the planting. He's a good man, loves that grandson of his."

"Jonathan. He told me you had been teaching him to ride until you called him a spoiled child. What did he do?" Hawk asked as they walked out toward the stables.

"Decided he could ride my new stallion. Hawk, that horse still gives me problems. I turned my back for a moment, and there he was, climbing up on that brute, the blasted horse standing stock-still. My heart nearly went into my boots. I was shaking all over when I pulled him down. Told him if he ever tried that again, that was the end of the lessons. That afternoon he was back up there. That is when I called a halt," Andrew explained, running a hand through his hair. "Maybe by next week he will have learned his lessons from his mistake."

"He sounds just like another horse-mad little boy I once knew," Hawk teased, marveling how his little brother had grown to be a man in the years he had been gone.

"Father never let me get away with disobeying him or the grooms. You know that, Hawk. And Jonathan has only his mother and sister to guide him. And you cannot depend on his mother. That woman has no sense. Instead of letting the boy keep his pony, she sold it. Said the groom's salary was more than she could afford. Her father roared when he discovered what had happened." Andrew led his brother down the center of the stables. He stopped in front of an open stall where a fine-boned bay nibbled at her hay. "What do you think?"

"Rather a light weight for you. More Jonathan's style than yours," his brother said carefully, not willing to hurt his brother's feelings.

"Not for me. For Emily. I thought I would give him to her for a wedding present. What do you think?" Andrew asked, his face thoughtful. "Since Mrs. Cheswick sold most of the horses, I have provided Emily with a horse whenever she let me. As my sister-in-law, she will have no reason to refuse."

"An excellent idea. This is a lovely lady." Hawk entered the mare's stall, patted her neck and ran his hands down her legs. "From her height, I would suspect that you had chosen this mare especially for Emily," he said thoughtfully.

His brother's face reddened. "She rides so well, it is a shame she cannot ride whenever she wishes," Andrew said as if ashamed. "Blast it! She never gets lost following the dogs."

Realizing that his brother had said more than he intended, Hawk let the comment pass. "Show me the rest of the horses," he suggested.

By the time the bell rang, calling them to luncheon, Hawk and Andrew had selected several horses for Hawk to try. "I keep the others near Newcastle," Andrew explained. "Father bought me an estate when he saw how much I enjoyed working with them. Had a horse last year that was a winner. But most of my riding stock is still here. With me at school most of the time, it seemed more practical. And this year Father insisted I be introduced formally." Both of the men frowned.

"Dashed formality. Still, a little town bronze never hurt anyone," his brother said. "I suppose you were bored the whole time you were in town."

"Gentlemen," their father greeted them as they walked up the stairs. "Make your changes quickly. Your mother sent word that our guests have arrived. Blasted country hours!" They nodded.

A short time later, they were all gathered around the dining table. Hawk, seated across the table from Emily, studied her carefully as she retreated, becoming the quiet, retiring lady of the evening before. Without neglecting his table partners, he watched her, noting the way she laughed until she looked up and saw her stepmother watching her. Then her face would lose all its warmth and excitement. His mouth narrowed ominously, and he waved the footman serving the eels away. Then he deliberately forced himself to smile casually.

He was not laughing later that afternoon as they tried to make the arrangements for the wedding. His mother and Emily proposed an idea; Mrs. Cheswick disagreed. Finally Hawk had borne as much as he could. He stood up. "Rector, you have said that three weeks from Monday would be an acceptable date." The elderly man, longing for his late-afternoon nap, nodded. "The banns will have been called three times. We will marry then. The next thing to decide will be whether it will be a morning or afternoon wedding." Hawk dared Mrs. Cheswick to argue with him. She opened her mouth and then shut it quickly when he asked, "Emily?"

"A wedding breakfast is traditional . . ."

"Then we will have a morning wedding. Will ten o'clock be suitable?" Everyone nodded. "Mrs. Cheswick, will you host the breakfast? If you choose not to do so, I am certain my mother would be happy to oblige."

"And make me the talk of this area? I will manage. Of course, it will not be as lavish as what you might prepare, but as my husband is no longer living . . ." She dabbed her eyes with her handkerchief.

"The guest list?" Hawk asked his mother, much as he had demanded reports from his men.

"Emily and I have kept it simple. No more than a hundred or so at the breakfast; of course, that does not include the celebration on the grounds for the workers of our two estates," Mrs. Hawksleigh explained calmly. Emily watched in delight as her stepmother's eyes grew larger and her face turned an unbecoming shade of puce.

"A hundred or so? And a celebration on the grounds?" she gasped.

"Just family and our closest friends. I am sorry the crowd will be so sparse. But Emily has such a small family, only her aunt and a cousin or two besides you and your family, of course." Mrs. Hawksleigh took a breath and hurried on. "Emily suggested that Jonathan be her page, her only attendant. I understand pages are all the go in London. If we had time . . ." Before Mrs. Cheswick could do more than gasp, Mrs. Hawksleigh hurried on. "Will you be able to go into town with us tomorrow?"

"Town?" Lucretia asked, wondering how she had misjudged Mrs. Hawksleigh all these years. The woman was a martinet. "With a wedding breakfast for two hundred to plan, I shall be too rushed to go anywhere." She waved her hand languidly. "So much to do. Fortunately Emily will be there to help."

"Not right away." Mrs. Hawksleigh sat up in her chair, her back straight. "She must arrange for her bride's clothes. I shall be delighted to escort Emily to the dressmaker's. Last night my maid and I selected several fashion plates of costumes we thought would be delightful on Emily. I want you to look at them and tell me what you think, my dear." Hawk's mother smiled sweetly at her future daughter-in-law and ignored the frown that grew on Mrs. Cheswick's face. "After having all sons to dress, I shall positively delight in dressing a daughter. And Anthony, Andrew, and Jonathan must accompany us." Mrs. Cheswick started to say something, but Mrs. Hawksleigh interrupted before she had time to say a word. "I know exactly what you are going to say, Lucretia. Do not worry. I would not offend your sensibilities by offering to pay for Emily's and Jonathan's bridal clothes. I will have the bills sent to your man of business." She sat back in her chair, delighted in the results of the day.

Hawk and Emily exchanged a glance and then looked away to hide their amusement. Lucretia Cheswick sat back in her chair, her face wiped free of any emotion, although her eyes blazed. Emily took a deep breath as though she had been struck. Hawk, feeling her back tense under his hand, reached down and took her hand, giving it a comforting squeeze. She relaxed a little, wishing she never had to leave his affectionate presence.

3

The news of Hawk's return took the countryside by storm.
Always popular, he found himself the center of his friends'
and their parents' attention. Invitations began with a trickle
at first, but when Emily's and his banns were called the next
Sunday, he felt he had been caught up in a social whirl that
threatened to pull him under.

Emily too felt trapped by the situation. She loved Hawk;
there was no doubt in her mind about that. But after almost
two years away from society, she was not certain how to
behave. Her stepmother did nothing to help the problem.

The carriage ride home the evening they had made the
wedding arrangements had given Lucretia a chance to shred
Emily's confidence even further. "This can still be
canceled," Mrs. Cheswick had said threateningly, thinking of
the letter she had sent to her man of business that morning.

Those threats were dashed, although Lucretia was careful
not to let Emily learn what the reply to the letter had said.
It had confirmed what Hawk had told Lucretia. Her husband
had ensured that no one could interfere with his daughter's
marriage, no one but Emily herself.

Her face set in angry lines none of her admirers would
have recognized, Lucretia Cheswick began her next
campaign against her stepdaughter. "We shall be paupers
by Christmas, Emily. How your father could arrange your
affairs so shabbily, I do not know. He could not have meant
for you to be so reckless in your spending. Do not allow
your future mother-in-law to persuade you to purchase any
more gowns. Why a great clodpole like you needs so much
finery is beyond me. Your bridegroom will take one look
at you and hurry back to the war, leaving you behind to

become the laughingstock of the neighborhood. What will you do with these gowns then? It is not as if they become you. At least you could take my suggestions so that I will not be embarrassed when we appear in public together." Mrs. Cheswick's litany of complaints echoed through the coach or a room whenever they were alone. Blocking them out was impossible.

After being bombarded by denigrating remarks for almost two years, Emily often doubted herself, wondering if her stepmother could be right. She wondered too whether Lucretia knew something about Hawk's return to the war, something he was keeping from Emily to protect her. Hoping to discover the answer and relieve at least a few of her worries, she tried to find time to talk to Hawk alone.

Although his mother kept him busy, Hawk found time to spend with his father and brother. He had been stunned when his father asked him into the library a few days after his return and announced, "I am giving you this estate, Anthony. You will need a home that is all your own, one where you and your wife can make your own decisions. Little chance she has to make any decisions, living with that woman."

"But, Father, you and Mother—"

"Will be living on the estate outside London. Since you have been away, I have grown increasingly involved in affairs of government, especially the Exchequer. With the problems facing us at this time, I feel the need to be closer to the capital. Before you returned, your brother had agreed, reluctantly, to oversee the outlying estates." Andrew walked in at that moment. "Sit down, son. Tell you brother what we have discussed," his father ordered.

Anthony and Andrew exchanged rueful glances. Andrew sat down and crossed his legs, checking once again to see that the new mixture of boot polish and champagne that Lester had showed his valet gave a better shine. "About what?" he asked carelessly.

"About your running the estates so that I will have more time for London," his father said impatiently.

"Why? With Hawk home now, he can take care of everything. Then I will be free to concentrate on my horses," the younger man said casually. "Maybe I can find a Barbary mare to make the strain faster."

"Andrew, stop talking nonsense. You know that a trip to Arabia is out of the question at this time." The older man frowned. "I will not give you permission."

"Anthony, tell him to let me go. He did not stand in your way," the twenty-one-year-old said. He frowned.

"Andrew, stop teasing Father. You know the only reason he allowed me to buy my colors was Uncle George's will. At times I wish he had refused." The despair in Hawk's voice softened both the other men's faces.

"You will remember, my son," his father said, crossing to stand behind him, his hand on Hawk's shoulder. "You must give yourself more time. Why not sell those colors? You will have enough to do with managing the estates and your fortune. Your Uncle George only demanded one year in the army. You gave almost four, three in the Peninsula. And think how happy Emily will be to hear that you plan to remain in England."

"If Uncle George had left me the funds he left you instead of the estate of Yorkshire, I know exactly what I would do," Andrew said, his frown disappearing. "I would buy the new blood stock I want and forget about the war."

"Forget about the war?" Hawk closed his eyes and reminded himself that his brother had not seen the destruction he had witnessed. Still his voice was anguished as he said, "I will never . . ." Then he laughed bitterly. "I cannot remember, and you want me to forget."

"No, son." His father's fingers bit into his shoulder. "We want you to go on with your life. Let your mind and body rest. You will remember someday." He glared at his younger son, who was just opening his mouth. Andrew shut it hurriedly.

"When? It has been months. What if I never know?"

"You always told me not to worry about the future, big brother. Have you forgotten your own advice?" Andrew asked, making his voice light. "Think about Emily and your marriage instead. You have only a few days of freedom left." Hawk's face brightened at the thought. They all laughed. "What should I get you and Emily for a wedding present?"

Hawk stood up, looked his father in the eyes, and then said ruefully, "You will never be able to outdo Father's gift." He held out his hand. His father took it and then put his arms on Hawk's shoulders and gave him a pat. "Thank you, sir. Emily, I know, will enjoy living within easy visiting distance of her brother."

"And your mother and I will enjoy being close to London." His father gave his son's shoulders a squeeze and turned away, wishing he could eliminate the anguish in Hawk's face. "We will return to London for the rest of the Little Season as soon as the wedding takes place. Andrew, do you go with us?"

"No, I'm for Newmarket and then Yorkshire. My trainer thinks those Yorkshire moors may be just the place for several of my horses. Do you want to go with me, Hawk?" Andrew asked, and looked faintly startled by his father's crack of laughter. Then Hawk smiled, and Andrew realized what he had said. "No, I do not suppose you do. Emily might be somewhat distraught if you mentioned it to her," he said quickly, laughing at himself.

"I have no intention of leaving Emily alone again for a very long time," Hawk said earnestly, his face reflecting his love for the lady he had known for so many years. "That is, if I ever get to see her again."

"What do you mean? Just last night . . ." Then Andrew saw the look his father and older brother exchanged. His face flushed. "Oh. Well, Hawk, you should have known that Mama would not forget polite behavior for always. I recommend—"

"I recommend that you two find something more worthwhile than taking up my time. I have dispatches to read. Hawk, see the bailiff. Start doing your own planning. And you, young Andrew, would be wise to listen," his father said with a stern look on his face and a laugh in his voice.

"Since we are not wanted here, shall we go?" Andrew asked, holding the door open for his brother. Their father watched as they left the room together, their broad shoulders in their blue-and-rust riding jackets filling the doorway. If the laughter of the moment could only last, Mr. Hawksleigh wished. Then he put his worries behind him and opened the first document.

During the next few days Hawk and his brother covered the estate thoroughly, talking to the farmers, checking the soil, discussing plans with the bailiff. Most evenings they were entertained by friends in the neighborhood, or Emily and her stepmother came to make additional plans for the wedding. Although they saw each other daily, Hawk and Emily were allowed only moments alone.

Under Mrs. Hawksleigh's careful guidance, Emily visited the modiste, selecting more gowns than she had ever thought possible. When her stepmother tried to get Emily to add yet another flounce or ruffle, the modiste, alerted by Mrs. Hawksleigh, carefully made her own suggestions, always soothing Mrs. Cheswick with some clever remark about her petite size and about the way the decoration would enhance the older woman's perfect figure. Before Lucretia realized what was happening, she had ordered several new gowns for herself.

Although Emily understood the modiste's actions, the hours she spent hearing her stepmother praised as a pocket Venus began to erode the little confidence she had begun to regain in Hawk's arms. She felt like a giant beside the other women, her head rising inches above theirs. Only her pride and the knowledge that Hawk believed she was the proper height kept her from slumping. But after a week of fittings and shopping, she began to wonder if it would not be simpler if they eloped to Scotland, scandalous as that would be.

Then Hawk and his parents arrived in their carriage to escort her to yet another party, and she took one look at his dark brown eyes and his mouth and melted inside. Most evenings they could only touch hands, murmur a few words as they came together in the figures of a dance, and wish. Both of the older ladies made certain their time together was limited.

For Hawk the time was stressful. He needed to be alone with Emily to tell her what had happened. "Meet me tomorrow morning at eight for a gallop," he whispered as he escorted his fiancée in to supper one evening only a few days before their wedding.

"The modiste is coming for a final fitting of my gown for the wedding. And Sir Horace, my stepmother's father, will be arriving later in the day," Emily whispered, her face revealing her regret.

"Then meet me in your garden. Surely you can steal a

few minutes to spend with me," he pleaded, not at all certain he wanted her answer to be yes.

"In the garden at eight," she promised, her eyes on his and shining with love. Hawk looked at her and took a deep breath. He smiled.

Before he could continue, they were joined by his mother and father. "Smelling of roses and moonlight. It does make me remember when you were courting me, my dear," his mother said as she smiled up at his father and then at them.

"You were just as beautiful as Emily. And I was as impatient to make you mine as our son is with his betrothed," Mr. Hawksleigh said gallantly. Both women blushed becomingly. "Shall we find our places?" Mr. Hawksleigh led the way to where Andrew and his partner waited.

No matter how busy Hawk's days were, his nights were more exhausting because he was not sleeping well. That night Hawk tossed restlessly in his sleep, disturbed by the dreams that had interrupted his rest for months. He awoke, his heart pounding, his throat raw. He kept his eyes closed for a moment, trying to bring the memory to the surface, certain it was in his grasp. Then it slipped away. He cursed and opened his eyes.

"My vocabulary will not be fit for polite company if I continue to associate with you," his brother said. His voice was carefully amused. He did not try to explain why he was in Hawk's room.

"Andrew, go to bed." Hawk sat up. Andrew was standing beside the bed, a candle in his hand and a worried look on his face. "It is nothing new, little brother. I am sorry I disturbed you."

"These dreams are growing more frequent. That must mean something, Hawk."

"But do I want to know what it is?"

"Hawk!"

The older man sat up in bed and ran his hand through his hair. "You know I did not mean that. Bring me a drink. Maybe that will help me sleep."

"You could ask Mama for one of her sleeping potions," Andrew suggested hesitantly as he poured a small amount of brandy into a glass.

"That would not stop the dreams. It would simply make me harder to wake up. The surgeons tried that once. My cries woke the camp. That is when the general decided to send me home," his brother explained as he downed the brandy. "Go back to bed."

Andrew turned and walked toward the door. Then he stopped. "Have you told Emily about these nightmares?" he asked, his face hidden in the shadows.

Hawk shuddered. "Tomorrow," he said quietly, no emotion in his voice. "Tomorrow."

The next morning Emily started the newly hired servants to work. Then she slipped into the garden. She sighed, thinking that only a few short weeks ago she too would have been inside polishing furniture. But with her father's visit imminent, Lucretia Cheswick had thought it prudent to hire a larger household staff, although she begrudged every penny they cost her. As soon as the wedding occurred and Sir Horace returned home, Emily knew they would be dismissed. To protect Jonathan, she would have to find a way to alert Lucretia's father to the problem.

A few minutes before the hour, Emily sat on the bench in the garden, enjoying the scent of the late roses. She raised her face to the sun and closed her eyes. In this garden her friends and she had played many games. Hawk, older by several years, grudgingly had joined them. Andrew and she would hide, and Hawk would look for them. It had been such a happy place then.

She opened her eyes, and there he was, tall and handsome in the early sunlight. She laughed and ran toward him, her joy overcoming her recent shyness. Hawk opened his arms and held her close. "My laughing love," he whispered, his breath sending a strange trembling through her. Then he kissed her as he had the first day he returned, deeply, hungrily. Emily's merry laughter ran out for a moment and then was stilled beneath his lips. In a window above them, the curtain held back by a white hand dropped back into place.

Their interlude was shattered a few minutes later. "Emily, there are many things we must do immediately. My father arrives today. You know how particular he is," Lucretia

Cheswick called. She walked briskly into the garden. The
lovers stepped away from each other guiltily. "Why, Captain
Hawksleigh. No one told me you had arrived. And so early
too." Her glance from one to the other made Hawk shift
uncomfortably.

Emily stepped back further from Hawk. He watched as
the bright, laughing look he loved disappeared. Emily's eyes
dropped to the ground. "I rode over to talk to Emily about
some plans for our wedding journey." His bride-to-be
blushed and glanced up at him under her lashes.

"Well, you must join us for breakfast, I suppose. Emily,
my dear, you will remember that the modiste will be here
shortly. I do not want her kept waiting. My father said he
would arrive before luncheon, and she must be gone by
then." Lucretia's smile was sweet, but her eyes bore into
her stepdaughter. "Come along, now."

"We will join you in a few minutes," Hawk said firmly,
putting his hand on Emily's arm to hold her in place. "I must
talk to Emily first." His brown eyes stared into Lucretia's
blue ones. She was the first to look away.

"Alone?" the older woman began to protest. Then she
watched as those eyes grew harder. "Well, I will send a maid
out. This match has stirred up enough talk as it is." She
turned and flounced back into the house.

Hawk led Emily to the bench. He held her hands in his
and took a deep breath. "Emily, there is something I must
tell you." Her back stiffened as if to prepare herself for a
blow. Then he plunged into his story. Emily's eyes grew
wider, then darkened with fear for him. "I will understand
if you wish to call our engagement off," he said as he
finished.

"Well, no one else would. No, my darling, do not look
at me that way." She smiled and reached up to smooth away
the frown on his forehead. "I have no intention of allowing
you to escape." Her fingertips caressed his lips. One eye
on the gardener and maid nearby, he kissed her fingers,
wishing he could kiss her lips again. "You are mine," she
said firmly. "Your general may have questions about you,
but I do not. You would never betray your country."

"Emily. Oh, Emily," he sighed, his eyes filling with tears

that he quickly blinked away. For a few moments he was totally at peace. He smiled at her, the same smile that had captured her heart forever so many years ago. Taking her hand, he stood up and led her into the house.

After Hawk had left, the morning did not seem so long to Emily. During the tedious fittings, she thought about Hawk and what he had told her. She closed her eyes, wondering at the agony he must have been going through. Even the occasional pinpricks as the seamstress fitted the garments did not capture her attention.

Dressed once again, she hurried downstairs, halting at the top of the last flight of stairs. Sir Horace and a stern-faced woman had arrived. Her stepmother's voice echoed shrilly in the hallway. "I did not invite you to my home. I did not plan to have you stay," Lucretia told the stern woman, who frowned at her. "Papa, you had no right to being her with you."

"Well, Lucy, you had done nothing about engaging a chaperone for yourself. I had to do something," her father explained, dabbing his ruddy face with a large snowy-white handkerchief. Not much taller than his daughter, he was as round as a hogshead of wine. "I told you at Christmas that it would not do for you to live alone. As soon as I received Jonathan's weekly letter that told about Miss Emily's marriage, I knew I had to do something. Mrs. Hardcastle comes with excellent references. She will be the ideal person to be your companion."

"I do not need a companion. I do not care what society thinks of me," his daughter screamed at him. "I will not have you force another person into my life as you forced me to marry Cheswick. Do you understand? I refuse to allow you to take control of my life again!"

Her heart aching, Emily took a deep breath, wondering if her father had known how his second wife had felt about the marriage. Lucretia had certainly played the happy wife as long as Mr. Cheswick had lived. "It explains so much," she whispered. She turned quietly and slipped away to her room, her hands shaking and her stomach in knots. "Poor Lucretia. Poor Father."

By the time tea was served later that evening, the tempest

was over. The stern-faced woman had disappeared. Emily carefully refrained from asking about her. "How long do you plan to stay, Sir Horace?" she asked as she watched him play a game with Jonathan.

The little man wiped his brow carefully, pursed his lips as if in displeasure, and said, "Longer than I wish to. A week or so after the ceremony. Never thought I would see this day, Miss Emily. Lucretia always said it would never come. Happy for you, though, very happy." He looked at the board, tweaked Jonathan's cheek, and made another play. "Lucy and Jonathan are coming to stay with me for a time. At least until after Christmas, aren't you, little man? Give us time to make other arrangements." He spoke in a voice only a little louder than a whisper. His daughter looked at the little group around the table, and her face hardened. She threw down the needlework she had been holding and made her escape.

"Arrangements? What kind of arrangements?" Emily asked.

Sir Horace looked around the room carefully. "That girl of mine has no sense. Told her when your father died that she needed a chaperone. She told me she had you. Gave in then. Not going to give in now. Don't tell me you did not hear her screeching like a cat; I saw you at the top of the stairs. No, do not be nervous. Lucy was so busy being angry with me that she did not see anything," he assured her. He wiped his brow again. "Thinks I never hear anything. But she's gone too far this time. If she doesn't like my choice, then she will have to live with me until she finds her own. No hardship on me, having them with me. Give me a chance to get to know my grandson better. Promised him a pony, you know," Sir Horace looked up from the game they were playing and flashed her an impish smile.

"Grandfather, I am too big for a pony. I need a horse," Jonathan said solemnly. "You said you would speak to Andrew. He has horses I like."

"That I shall, lad, as soon as I see him."

"Jonathan, you know better than to beg for something like a horse!" his sister said reprovingly. "Where would we keep it? Who would take care of it?"

"Hmmm. So what the lad said was true. My daughter has sold all the riding stock and gotten rid of her grooms." He looked Emily in the eyes. She would not give him the satisfaction of looking away, but her face turned red. "Enough of that. Tell me about this young man of yours. Lucy said he has been a soldier. Wouldn't think you would enjoy following the drum. Does he plan to sell out? Where will you live?"

"At the manor. His parents are giving the estate to us as a wedding present," Emily said quietly, ignoring most of his previous questions.

"Is it profitable?"

"You will have to ask the bailiff about that, Sir Horace," Emily said coolly but politely. Her back was as straight as a ramrod. He looked at her and then back at the board.

"No need to get on your high horse with me, missy. I am only thinking of your welfare. More than that daughter of mine does. Would have thought your father would have had some sense than to leave everything in her hands. Just like her mother. Afraid to spend a penny when a ha'penny will do. Well, I will not have it, I tell you." His face grew even redder than before. Both Emily and Jonathan stared at him in alarm. Noticing their concern, he wiped his face again and gave the game his full attention for a few minutes. "I would like to speak to your young man, Miss Emily. Make certain everything is all tight and proper."

"I will introduce you tomorrow," Emily said, wondering all the time what Hawk would make of Sir Horace. "However, Hawk told me that my father ensured my future before he died."

"Should have thought more about his son's future too. We shall have to find you a tutor, my boy." Jonathan frowned, not at all certain he wanted someone else in his life. "Do not look at me that way, little man," his grandfather said sternly. "Your sister has been overseeing your lessons. With a home of her own to manage, she will not have time for that anymore. I will hire someone and pay him myself."

The little boy's face clouded over. He looked anxiously at his sister. "Are you going away forever, Emily?" he asked, his lip beginning to quiver.

"Only as far as the manor. You and I talked about my living there after I marry. Remember?" Emily's voice was soft and soothing. She glared at Sir Horace, who had the grace to blush.

"I *will* see you again? You will not go away forever like Papa, will you?" the little boy begged.

"You will see me often, sweetheart," she promised and ran her hand through his hair. "Now, finish your game. It is long past your bedtime." His grandfather nodded his approval, his face stern but loving.

Soon afterward Emily sought out her own bedchamber, exhausted by the emotions of the day. Other than the time when the dressmaker had been fitting her gowns, she had had no time to think about what Hawk had told her. She stepped out of her soft blue-green muslin and put it aside to be washed, her face thoughtful as she wondered at the pain Hawk had to feel. He had tried to make the situation seem ordinary, but the emotion in his voice gave him away. She straightened, determination in every line of her being. She slid her nightrobe over her head and lay down, drawing her covers about her. Hawk would never have cause to doubt her, she promised herself. And she would help him regain his confidence in himself. She touched her lips softly, remembering his kisses. Only a few more days until she would be his wife.

The same thought ran through Hawk's mind as he lay in bed that evening. Emily had reacted just as he had hoped she would—caringly, lovingly, with worry and anger that anyone had doubted him. And her kisses sent fires raging through him. Maybe his mother had been right to keep them apart. Had he been alone with her often . . . He drifted off to sleep peacefully.

The peace lasted only part of the night. Once again he plunged into the nightmare, this time more deeply than before. His cries brought both his brother and his servant running. Andrew leaned over the bed, calling his name. He touched Hawk's arm. Before he could protect himself, Andrew felt Hawk's hands tighten around his throat. Although he struggled, he could not break free. Lester hurriedly pried Hawk's hands away so that Andrew could make his escape. Suddenly Hawk relaxed, the tension leaving his body. His breaths deepened.

"Should we wake him?" Andrew asked when he could speak again.

"Best let him sleep," Lester replied. Neither man looked directly at the other. They slipped out of the room and returned to their own beds. Andrew lay awake for some time, his hands massaging his throat. He would tell Hawk what had happened in the morning, he thought. But that plan vanished when he saw the relaxed look on Hawk's face.

The relaxed look remained there until the Saturday evening before the wedding. Mrs. Hawksleigh, not satisfied with her first dinner party, had decided to give a ball to celebrate the nuptials. By the time the evening arrived, Hawk had greeted so many uncles and aunts and distantly removed cousins that he had begun to wonder if they all were really his relatives or only people who had wandered in and decided to stay. He had not had a moment alone with Emily since the morning in her garden. He was determined that somehow he would get her to himself that evening. Carefully he scouted the rooms before finding one his mother had left undisturbed. Then he enlisted his brother's aid.

After dinner had been served and before the receiving line formed, Hawk slipped his arm through Emily's. He bent and whispered in her ear. She looked up, a question in her eyes. This evening her eyes were more brown than green because of the unusual rose-beige color of her silk gown. Hawk smiled at her. She smiled back and nodded. He walked away. Making his escape, he left the room. A few minutes later she left also, pleading a need to make a few repairs before the ball began. Mrs. Hawksleigh looked at her knowingly but nodded.

Then Emily entered the paneled room that Hawk had selected. He was there before her. As soon as she walked in, he put his arms around her and pulled her close, his lips plundering hers of their sweetness. "Open your eyes," he whispered against her lips, wanting to see her reaction. Slowly she raised her heavy lashes. The flickering of the single candle glittered in her eyes. Hawk froze. Then he began to breathe heavily, as though he were afraid, and his hands tightened on her arms. Outside a shrill laugh rang out. Hawk's hands tightened more, creasing the silk of her sleeves.

"Hawk?" Emily tried to pull away, but she could not get loose. "Hawk! You are hurting me." He stared into her eyes as if mesmerized. Once again Emily tried to shake his hands free. They were rigid. Realizing that pulling away would gain her nothing, she took a step forward, frightened in spite of her love for him. He took a step back. His hands relaxed slightly. "Let me go," she pleaded quietly, wondering what was happening. She took another step forward. His hands relaxed more. Then the door opened.

"Mother is looking for the two of you. I told you that the most I could promise was a minute or two," Andrew said jokingly, his face carefully turned toward the doorway. "You will have to promise to do the same for me someday." When neither of them answered, he looked at his brother's set face and Emily's wide eyes. "Emily?"

"Go away, Andrew," she begged. "Give us a few minutes more." He hesitated for a moment, his face disturbed, and then left the room. Finally able to get free, Emily took Hawk's hands in hers and brought them to her lips. He tried to pull away, but she held him fast. "Hawk," she whispered, the word a plea.

The word broke Hawk's trance, echoing through his head and heart like a javelin thrown by some ancient spear carrier. His eyes grew anguished. "What have I done?"

"You were only holding me too tightly, my darling," Emily said, trying to reassure him. She rubbed her arms as if she could rub away the bruises she knew soon would appear. She put her hand up to touch his face, but he pulled away.

"What have I done?" he asked again as if to himself. He shuddered as a horrible scene replayed itself in his mind.

"Mama insists that you two join us immediately," Andrew said as he slipped back into the room. "And your stepmother has been asking for you, Emily. You must come at once." He glared at his brother again and was dismayed by what he saw. "You go first, Emily. I will stay with Hawk." She glanced at her betrothed, his face still rigid with horror, and then slipped away from the room, the brightness of the evening dimmed.

Andrew grabbed his brother by the arm and gave him a shake. Hawk pulled away, swung around, and went into a crouch, his fists up. "No, I will not let you—" he said fiercely.

"Hawk. Get hold of yourself. This is Andrew—Andrew, your brother." Finally the words began to penetrate. Hawk shuddered once more. Then he stood up, moving as though he were exhausted.

"Andrew," Hawk said in a trembling voice. "Oh, Andrew."

"Tell me about it later. Now we must get you in that receiving line before Mama comes looking for us." Andrew whisked his brother out the door and away. Somehow Hawk managed to do the right thing, to move correctly. Occasionally, though, he noticed Emily and Andrew watching him, anxious looks on their faces.

That night Hawk got little sleep as he relived the nightmare in his mind. "Please leave me alone. Don't hurt me. Please, no!" The words echoed, growing louder and louder. When he closed his eyes, Hawk could see the petite woman in front of him, her dark hair tousled and her skin bruised, backing away from him, fear in every line of her face and in her voice. What had he done?

4

When Hawk arrived at breakfast the next morning, Andrew was there before him. "We must talk," Andrew said quietly. Hawk closed his eyes for a moment and then nodded. He drank his chocolate and then sat back waiting for Andrew to finish.

"We need to find someplace private," Hawk suggested as they walked from the room and discovered two of their older cousins just descending the stairs. Andrew nodded.

Then their mother appeared. "Hawk, you are not dressed for church. With the last reading of the banns today, you must be present. What would Emily think if her future husband neglected her only a day before the wedding. Andrew, you might as well accompany us also." Feeling almost like a guilty schoolboy reprieved from some loathsome task, Hawk did as she directed.

That day the hearty congratulations and back slaps of his friends grated on Hawk's nerves. He watched Emily carefully and slipped to her side as soon as he had a chance. He took her arm and folded it in his own. With only the slightest hesitation, Emily allowed him to lead her to their carriage. "Tomorrow this time we will be wed," he said softly. The knowledge of her faith in him had given him his only comfort during the long night just past. He helped her into the carriage, his fingers closing over her upper arm to lift her. She winced. "Emily, what is wrong? Are you hurt?"

She glanced at him curiously to see if he were joking. His face was serious. He was so handsome her heart began to beat faster. He, like she, had ordered a new wardrobe. His corbeau-colored coat hugged his shoulders as tightly as his highly polished boots hugged his calves. Standing on the step of the carriage, she was at eye level with him. She smiled wistfully. "A few bruises. You do not know your own strength, my dear." His face grew darker, troubled. "Do not worry about them. My wedding gown has long sleeves."

"I hurt you?"

"You simply held me too tightly, Hawk." Emily recognized something was wrong and stepped down to the ground, her hands on his shoulders. "You did not mean to hurt me. Please do not worry about it."

Her smile and calming words soothed him. He watched her leave, knowing the next time he saw her she would be walking down the aisle toward him, toward their life together. Then he walked back to his family, his face somber. As soon as they arrived at the manor, he pulled Andrew aside. "Change clothes and meet me in the stables." Before long the two were dismounting at their eyrie, the top of a small hill where an old fortress had once stood. Hawk climbed over the remaining wall and stood looking around him. For a time the only sound was the sweep of wind.

Andrew took a seat, his back against a boulder. He fidgeted, pulling the cuffs of his blue riding jacket down and straightening his neckcloth unnecessarily. The wind tossed his hair into his eyes, and he brushed it back impatiently. Not totally comfortable with his role as his brother's confidant, Andrew waited.

Finally Hawk turned around. "What happened last night, Andrew?" he asked. His face was a calm mask that held his fears.

"When?"

"When you came in to get us the first time? What did you see? What was I doing?" Hawk shot the questions at his brother as though they were balls from a musket.

"Well. Hawk, it was dark. And I deliberately avoided looking at you, to keep from embarrassing Emily."

"Tell me what you saw. I have to know." Hawk's face was full of anguish.

"You had your hands on her arms as though you were afraid to let her come too close to you. Emily looked somewhat upset."

"Oh, God. What am I going to do?" Hawk sank to the ground and buried his face in his hands.

"What has happened?" Andrew got up and moved closer to his brother, putting his hand on his sleeve.

Quickly Hawk told him what he remembered: the dark, beautiful woman, her pleas, and Emily's bruises. "What have I done?" he asked again, his face full of despair.

Andrew listened to his story. Then he stood up and wandered about the hilltop for a time, wishing that he could give his brother the comfort he deserved. When Hawk was certain that Andrew had left in disgust, his brother returned. He sat down in front of him. Then Andrew asked, "Where were you? What was happening? Who was the woman?"

"What difference would that make? That woman was afraid of me. I will never be able to forget the look on her face. How can I live with that memory?"

"Hawk, get hold of yourself, man. You were in the middle of war. Do you remember where you were or who she was? Maybe she had betrayed you," Andrew said soothingly, reaching for any idea that would comfort his brother. "Maybe you surprised her, spoiled her plans. Try to remember where you were, what else was happening."

"All I see is her face. All I hear is her voice. The rest is dark." Hawk lay back on the ground, his face to the blue sky, his eyes shut. "Why can't I remember more?" he cried out.

Andrew stood up, the concern on his face vanishing. He gave a whoop. His brother sat up in astonishment. Andrew was grinning broadly. "Listen to yourself, Hawk. You said, 'Why can't I remember more?' You are beginning to remember. Father said it would happen if you gave yourself time, and it has. You are beginning to remember."

"I wish now those memories had stayed lost," Hawk said bitterly, once more seeing Emily wince as he put his hands on her arms to lift her up.

"Nonsense." Andrew's natural optimism rose to the front again. "There is bound to be an explanation. You could never harm an innocent person." Remembering the way war changed people, Hawk remained silent. "Soon even those nightmares of yours will be a thing of the past. You did give me a start the other night when you grabbed me. I should have listened to Lester, I suppose. He warned me not to touch you when you were in the middle of one."

Hawk's voice was suspiciously calm when he asked, "What did I do?"

"Grabbed me by the throat. But Lester got your hands loose quick enough." Andrew sat down again beside his brother. Hawk froze. "Now that you have started remembering perhaps those dreams will disappear."

"Perhaps." Hawk lay there quietly with his eyes closed.

Andrew grew restless. "Are you ready to return to the house?" he asked. Hawk shook his head. "I want to check with my groom about one of my horses. Will you be all right alone?" Reassured by his brother's nod, Andrew swung into the saddle. "Do not trouble your mind. I know you have done nothing wrong. Wait until your full memory returns before you begin to worry. Think about tomorrow instead. By this time tomorrow it will be perfectly acceptable for you and Emily to be alone whenever you wish," he said bracingly. "Think about that instead," Andrew galloped down the hillside.

Hawk lay there as if frozen, his eyes wide open. "Emily," he whispered. He ached for her. He had been counting the hours until he could make her his. "Emily!" he cried out in despair.

The next morning dawned as bright and golden as any bride could wish for. Emily rose early and washed her hair. Her maid, a local girl named Mary, whom she had hired when Hawk had insisted that she needed one immediately and had offered to pay the girl's salary, laid out Emily's wedding finery and traveling clothes before packing the last of the other items carefully away. Then it was time to dress. Emily slid the soft white dress over her head, marveling once again at the softness of the silk. Her stepmother had complained that the gown was too plain, but Emily did not agree. Using lace and ribbons only a shade darker than the white of the dress, the modiste had fashioned a deep ruff and bands of lace that dipped to a wide V above the high waist. The pattern of lace continued on the sleeves, ending in pleats at the wrist to match the ruff. Above the hem, the skirt was decorated with Spanish trim of the same materials. For once Emily knew she was looking her best.

She watched as her maid used the curling wand to create

soft curls around her face. Then she reached for her bonnet, its frame covered to match her dress. Designed simply, it was decorated only with ribbons and a row of lace about her face. The crisp air of autumn gave roses to her cheeks as they drove to the church.

Finally she stood beside Sir Horace, a bouquet of late roses trembling in her hand. He pulled out his handkerchief and patted his face. Then he patted her hand. "A beautiful bride, my dear. That is what you are."

Her stepmother twittered. "And what a pair you make with the bride towering over you like a mountain. Jonathan, stand up straight." Then Lucretia Cheswick entered the church. She had chosen a celestial-blue gown for the wedding, determined to outshine the bride. But nothing could spoil Emily's day. Hawk was waiting for her beside the minister and his father. She had eyes for no one else.

Hawk watched her come down the aisle, her eyes downcast after that first quick look. He felt a tingle of excitement run through him. Then she was beside him, her hand in his. His fingers tightened around hers. Jonathan took his place beside his sister, his face serious as he concentrated on his duties.

The sunlight glinted through the stained-glass windows of the church, forming halos of color around the group at the altar. The guests looked at each other and smiled as they listened to the young people repeat their vows, his voice firm and steady, hers soft and trembling. "Such a perfect match," one of Hawk's cousins whispered to her husband. He merely grunted.

A few days earlier Hawk would have agreed. He loved Emily, had loved her for more years than even he would admit. The feeling of her fingers in his caused the blood to sing in his veins. In a few moments she would be his, his wife to cherish and protect. Deliberately Hawk pushed unpleasant thoughts out of his mind and concentrated on listening to Emily repeat her vows. She glanced up at him as she began. Their eyes met. It was almost as if they were alone. The rest of the ceremony passed in a blur.

Before either of them realized what was happening, the wedding breakfast was over. Emily took her brother in her arms and kissed him. Embarrassed, he pulled away. Then he reached up to hug her again, his mouth quivering a little. "Do not leave me," he begged.

"You are going to visit your grandfather," Emily reminded her brother. "Think how alone he will be if you come with me instead."

Jonathan looked up at Sir Horace, who stood nearby. The older man had heard what the boy and Emily had said and looked appropriately unhappy. "I do not want you to be sad, Grandfather," the little boy said, his chin quivering. He turned back to Emily and Hawk. "You *will* be back?

"Yes." Hawk knelt so his eyes were on a level with his brother-in-law's. "When you come back from your grandfather's, Emily and I want you to come visit us if your mother will agree," he said, his voice reassuring.

"And she will agree," Sir Horace said heartily. "I shall see to that." Not truly satisfied, but placated, Jonathan hugged his sister again and manfully gave his hand to Hawk.

Quickly Hawk and Emily made the rest of their good-byes and entered their carriage.. The door closed behind them, shutting them into their own private world. Emily laughed softly and moved closer to Hawk. He sank back into the corner of the carriage and pulled her close, forgetting his earlier resolve to keep his distance. He loosened the bow on her bonnet and laid the hat on the seat in front of them, along with his. Emily lifted her face to his, her lips pursed. Hawk could not resist their rosy sweetness. He bent his head and kissed her. She nestled close to him, her fingers discovering the interesting ripples of muscles under his jacket. He pulled her closer; his tongue begged for entrance between her lips. He slid his hand down her side to her breast. Startled, she went still. For a moment, he did not realize what had happened. She pulled back just a little. Remembering his promise to himself, he let her go, horrified at his own lack of control. He took a deep breath and straightened his spine.

Emily moved away and sat straight upright on the seat beside him, her cheeks flushed. She looked at him from the corner of her eye. His face was calm, almost emotionless. "Hawk?"

"Yes, my dear," he said in a voice as controlled as his face.

"Am I too forward? My stepmother told me that a husband does not like a forward wife. Is that why you moved away?" Emily asked, certain that Hawk would answer her as honestly as he had when she was six and asked him why he let that other dog get on top of his spaniel.

This time, however, her question caught him off-guard. "No," he said before he thought of the implications. Then he inhaled and then exhaled slowly, giving himself time to get his emotions more firmly in hand. "I mean, we must think of where we are. We are not alone."

His wife sat back, at first satisfied. Then she thought of the other times when they had been alone in the carriage. He had not thought of the servants then. Deliberately she relaxed a bit and sat closer to him. Soon she was nestled once again at his side. But this time he did not put his arms around her and pull her closer. Emily felt as though her head were resting on a boulder. But she was determined not to move. The carriage hit a bump, and his arm went around her to hold her in place. She sighed and crept closer. She closed her eyes. Soon, exhausted by the preparations for the wedding and the many assaults on her emotions, she drifted off to sleep.

Hawk listened to her breathing deepen. As soon as he was certain she was asleep, he wrapped his other arm around her in a desperate hug. How was he ever going to survive? "I love you, Emily," he whispered, his breath sending ripples of sensations through her unconscious form. His face was as bleak as it had been the day the general sent him home to England.

As alert as he had ever been on watch, he stayed awake. When Emily began to rouse, he put her carefully in her corner and sat back in his own. He watched as she yawned and stretched slightly until she realized where she was. Then she sat up with a start and with a guilty look on her face. "Have I been asleep long? What must I look like?" she asked.

"With all the arrangements you have had to make, it is no wonder that you were sleepy. We are almost at the inn where we will spend tonight," he said quietly. "I made arrangements for you and your maid to share a room. The inn is not as private as I might have wished for."

Startled, Emily stared at him. "But you . . . We . . ."
He face flamed red again. "If you think it best," she finally
stammered, a trifle relieved but more disappointed. The
evening before, her stepmother had told her, in great detail, what to expect from the marriage bed. Emily had
listened, wondering why, if the duty were so distasteful, so
many widows hurried to marry again. She had wisely held
her tongue, and slipped away at the first opportunity. Now
she would have to wait longer to discover the truth. Her
natural exuberance bubbling up now that she was away from
her stepmother, Emily started to ask her husband. One quick
look at his face, however, told her the decision was not a
wise one. She sat back quietly.

That night after dinner, Hawk escorted Emily to her room
and said good night. He entered his own chambers, shut the
door, and sank back against it with a huge sigh. After
dismissing Lester, he fell into bed, lying awake for several
hours before sinking into a broken sleep. That night in his
dreams it was Emily who backed away from him in horror,
moaning and pleading with him. He awoke in a cold sweat,
his hands wrapped around a pillow as though it were
someone's neck and he were wringing it.

He froze. Then he threw the pillow across the room, where
it hit a bottle of port on the table and sent it crashing to the
floor. The noise was deafening in the quiet room.

"Captain, are you all right?" Lester asked as he burst into
the room. His fear of intruding on a wedding night was less
than his fear that his master would harm his new bride. The
candle he carried cast a warm glow over the room.

"Go back to bed," Hawk said wearily. "It will wait until
morning." His batman-turned-valet looked at the pillow lying
in the middle of glass and wine and nodded. He closed the
door behind him and walked back to the adjoining room,
shaking his head.

Hawk lay in bed alone, forcing himself to take deep
breaths. Gradually his chest stopped heaving. His eyelids
would droop, but he would jerk them open again quickly.
Sleeping only in snatches, Hawk passed the night reviewing
his sketchy memories, trying to separate fact from fiction.
By morning his head was throbbing as it had done for days
after he was rescued.

After a late breakfast, he and Emily set off again on their wedding journey. Emily, who had been her father's companion at breakfast most mornings, took one look at Hawk's face and gave quiet directions for their meal. She directed the servants to serve him his ale and his beef, but did not say a word until he had taken some sustenance.

Feeling guilty for his less-than-sunny behavior, Hawk asked, "Were the accommodations acceptable?" She nodded. "Mama and my father recommended the place. It seems very comfortable." She nodded again. "Dash it, Emily, say something," he demanded, as though she, not he, had worn a frown that morning.

"What do you want me to say?" she asked, her voice soft and sweet. "Papa always wanted me to be quiet at breakfast. I suppose learning your likes and dislikes is one of the first things I must do."

"Emily! Stop these missish airs. Were your accommodations to your liking?"

"They were certainly not what I expected," she said. She lowered her eyelashes and looked at him beneath them. "I had no idea the estate where we are going to spend our honeymoon was so far away."

Hawk ran his fingers around the top of his neckcloth. "Well, hmmm, yes . . ." he stammered. "Our journey today will not be a long one. I asked the grooms to saddle our horses." She looked confused. "But if you would rather ride in the coach . . ."

"No, no! It will be wonderful to be in the open air." Especially if he planned to sit in his own corner of the carriage all day, she thought. She swallowed her tea and finished the last morsel on her plate. "I will need to change, but it will not take me long."

What was left of the morning passed quickly as they rode in the fragrant autumn air. The uneasiness that Emily had felt the evening before and earlier that morning disappeared as they galloped along the roadside. After his years away, Hawk noticed everything about the countryside and enjoyed pointing out to Emily a late-blooming rose or a bird heading to warmer climates. The crisp breeze and Emily's laughter banished the dark dreams and memories. Even the clouds that began to appear overhead did not dampen their spirits.

Emily, too, enjoyed her freedom. She basked in Hawk's smiles, laughed with him, and relaxed. When he recognized the countryside around the hunting box where they planned to stay for a time, he pulled his horse to a stop. Emily drew alongside. "How would you feel about a race?" he asked.

"How far?" she asked, her eyes sparkling as they had when she was a girl and he had made the same suggestion.

Hawk laughed, happy to see the animation back in her face. "Down the road to the hunting box, over the next hill. Is your horse too tired?"

"Never." Emily leaned forward and patted the bay's neck. She glanced at him beneath her lashes. "But your stallion looks as fresh as he did this morning. The race will be one-sided unless you give me a head start." She smiled at him mischievously.

"A head start?" Hawk looked at her consideringly. She opened her eyes very wide and looked helpless. "And I suppose if I do not agree, you will never let me forget it?" he asked, happily watching her wide brown-green eyes open even wider in mock horror. "All right. To those trees, and not a step beyond," he said, laughing.

Emily settled her hat with its long veil more securely on her head. She twitched the dark green velvet skirts of her riding habit into place and pulled the lace on her cuffs back out of her way. "Give the signal," she called to the groom who had been pressed into service.

Within moments she was on her way, her habit and veil caught by the wind and trailing behind. For the few seconds it took her horse to reach the trees, Hawk kept his eyes on Emily, his face creased with a wide smile. Then he too was off. Gallant though her mare was, before long Emily could hear the pounding hoofbeats behind her. She bent even lower over the neck of her horse. As they thundered down the road toward the hunting box, she was cetain she had Hawk beaten. Then she glanced back. He was less than a length away, and his stallion was not even breathing hard. Once again Emily leaned forward to pat her horse's sweating neck. They pulled ahead for a second. Then Hawk was beside her, pulling on his reins as they approached the hunting box. Emily guided her horse to a stop in front of the house. "You were holding back, Hawk. That is no way to race," she said reproachfully. Secretly she was pleased that he had chosen to finish the race beside her.

He slid out of the saddle and held up his arms to help her from her horse. A faint hint of laughter still in her eyes, she slid from the horse into his arms. Instead of holding her by her arms and carefully stepping away as he usually did, Hawk let her rest for a moment on his chest, her head above his. Then he let her slide to the ground. Emily's eyes widened as an unexpected shiver of delight flashed through her. She caught her breath and let her hands linger on his shoulders, her eyes on his. Hawk looked at her and forgot where he was. He lowered his head. Emily's eyes closed.

"Was your journey comfortable, sir?" a dry voice asked. Hawk and Emily sprang apart, each assuming as calm an expression as they could master. Hawk turned to face the caretaker of the residence.

"Yes. Have our servants arrived?" Hawk asked as he held out his arm to his wife.

"Only those your mother sent early. But everything is in order, as I assured Mrs. Hawksleigh in my last letter." The butler led the way to the entrance, his back as stiff as it had ever been. Emily and Hawk exchanged rueful glances and followed him. "I had forgotten about him when I made plans to come here. He treats me as though I had never grown up," Hawk whispered to Emily, pulling her arm through his.

"Who is he?" Her voice was so soft that Hawk could barely hear it.

He bent his head closer to hers. "Wiggins, my grandfather's last butler. My grandfather left him a pension and the right to choose where he would reside. The first time we came here after he took up residence, he greeted us much as he did today. Father did not have the heart to tell him we did not need a butler here. I suppose he never has. But if you want him to go . . . ?" He paused, pulling her to a stop beside him.

"No! Anthony Hawksleigh, I will not allow you to use me to get rid of that old man. We will manage." She smiled at him, taking the sting out of her words, and swept into the house.

A short time later she watched her maid unpack her clothing, fussing over how crumpled everything was. "Just find me something to wear for dinner," Emily finally said, looking toward the door separating her bedroom from her husband's. After the ease and laughter of the morning, she did not intend to be away from him for very long. "Anything will do." In spite of her statement, she rejected three dresses as being unsuitable before she finally agreed to a beautiful periwinkle-blue muslin with a cashmere shawl in blue and white.

Hawk, used to changing in an instant, entered the small salon long before Emily. The room, although appointed in the best tradition of several years earlier, was rather dark. Hawk crossed to the windows to let in the sunlight. He pulled the bronze velvet curtains back and then let them drop. In the time they had been in the hunting box, it had begun to rain, a slow, lazy gray mist covering everything in sight. Hawk dropped the draperies and moved toward the fireplace, where a small fire worked to keep the chill out of the room. He sat for a moment in a chair close to the fire, but soon grew too warm and moved away. As he placed slowly up and down the room waiting for Emily, the details he could remember about the dream returned to plague him.

By the time Emily joined him, his face was dark with worry and with determination. She stood for a moment in the doorway, waiting for him to look at her. He continued to stare into the fire. Finally Emily walked slowly across the room, her footsteps noiseless. She put her hand on his arm. He swung about, his hand going for his absent sword. Startled, his wife jumped back. His arm dropped. Quickly Hawk fought to regain his composure.

"Emily, is everything here the way you like it?" Hawk asked, more to give himself time to think than anything else. He took a few steps back, his face worried and his voice more shaky than she had ever heard it.

"Hawk, what is wrong?" she asked. She crossed the room and stood before him, her hands on his arms. Although she was hesitant about what she was doing, she kept her voice level. Her eyes locked with his.

He looked down at her and resisted the temptation to kiss

her. Prudently he guided her to a seat on the nearby settee and took a seat in a chair across from her. "Nothing, my dear. Do not let that active imagination take control," he told her. His voice was as light and teasing as he could make it.

Once she would have told him to stop lying to her. But her confidence was too newly bolstered for her to put it to the test, so Emily sat down, her eyes on her husband, and calmly discussed the weather as though it were the most important happening in her world. No matter how she tried to hide it, however, her eyes revealed her knowledge that something was wrong.

Throughout dinner, a long meal protracted by poor service, Hawk and Emily would look at each other and then look away. The servants, noting their nervousness, exchanged knowing looks as they bustled to and from the room. When Hawk refused the poached salmon and roasted capon on the third remove and Emily refused the jellies that Mrs. Hawksleigh had told the cook were her favorites, the footman left the room and hurried to the kitchen. "Best be ready for them soon," he told Emily's maid and Lester. "Won't be downstairs much longer." He winked at the maid, and she blushed.

To everyone's surprise, the evening dragged on. After a few hands of piquet, Emily and Hawk turned to the old favorite, cribbage. "You are cheating again, Emily," Hawk said later that evening as the footman entered with the tea tray.

"You always say that when you lose," she said, laughing. She sat back and automatically fixed him a cup of tea just the way he liked it. "And you did lose," she reminded him. Picking up her own cup, she smiled at him over its edge.

"Nonsense. I would have made it good in time."

"How? Anthony Hawksleigh, you are as big a rogue as you ever were. Do I get my usual prize?" She opened her eyes wide and leaned forward, her lips parted slightly.

"Emily!" Hawk glanced around the room at the interested servants. His voice reproved her.

Blushing furiously, she put her cup down. For the last few hours she had managed to put her tension and her memories aside. Now everything came flooding back. She straightened her skirts, looked at the clock nearby, and murmured, "I had not realized it was so late. I must retire." She blushed again. Her eyelashes swept down her cheek, and she glanced at him from under them.. Seeing how grim his face had become, she lost some of the brightness in her own face. She hurried from the room.

Sitting in front of the dressing table, she let Mary brush her hair. In her lovely nightrobe of ivory silk trimmed with blond lace that Hawk's mother had given her, Emily looked in the mirror, seeing once again the fire in Hawk's eyes as he lifted her in his arms when he first came home. Impatiently she crawled into bed and dismissed her maid. The lone candle on the bedside table flickered in the darkness.

For hours she lay in bed watching that candle and waiting. Hawk was in his room. She could hear his steps. Step, step, step, creak, step, step, step, turn. Finally the rhythmic sound put her to sleep, tears trickling down her face. The candle guttered out.

5

When her maid entered to bring her a cup of tea the next morning, Emily somehow found the strength to keep her face from revealing her emotions. But she knew from the look of pity on Mary's face that she knew what had happened. And soon the entire household would know as well.

Emily hurriedly dressed, choosing a soft rose plaid that her stepmother had condemned as making her look as large as a mountain. She looked in the mirror, wondering if Lucretia were right. For all his kisses, Hawk had ignored her for two nights. Because of Lucretia's talk, Emily knew that was not usual. She glanced in the mirror again and rushed from the room, certain that the early hour would guarantee that she would find Hawk there. A footman was just removing the last dirty dish from the table while another set her place. "My husband?" Emily asked hesitantly.

"Gone for a ride, Mrs. Hawksleigh." Emily jumped. "I believe he mentioned that you would be sleeping late," Wiggons added. Without seeming to move a muscle, he looked at a footman, and the man hurriedly pulled out a chair for Emily. "Would you prefer tea or chocolate, Mrs. Hawksleigh?" the old butler asked as if he were still the ruler of a large mansion.

Emily sank into her chair. "Tea," she said quietly. She glanced around the room, noting the sideboard set as though twenty people instead of two were expected. Suddenly she was as exhausted as though she had not slept for weeks. She watched as the footman placed the tea service and cup in front of her as if the drink that was part of her usual morning routine would restore order to her world. As she poured her first cup of tea, she promised herself that she and her husband would talk when he returned.

While Hawk was riding, trying to escape his despair, and Emily drank her tea, a conference was occurring upstairs. Lester and Mary met in the captain's dressing room. "I was afraid something like this might happen," the valet said as he walked back and forth, making the maid more nervous than she already was.

"She tried to hide it, but I could tell she had been crying. And his side of the bed as neat as it was when I left. It isn't right, Mr. Lester. There must be something we can do. Everyone will be talking. You know what goes on below-stairs."

"I may have a temporary solution, Miss Johnson," the man said solemnly. "You know the Captain was sent home from the war because of injuries he received." Her eyes grew brighter as she began to see the possibilities. She nodded. "Then this is how we must proceed," Lester said quietly.

By the time Hawk returned from his ride, the story entrusted to the upstairs maid who had come to clean the rooms was known to most of the household staff. Had he noticed, Hawk would have seen the maids sigh as he passed them, and one or two dry a tear. "So brave," the youngest parlormaid whispered to a handsome footman as she passed him.

"Glad it's not me," the footman answered, wondering what he would do if the situation ever happened to him. "Wonder why he married her if—"

"Be quiet. Someone might hear you," the maid whispered, looking around the room suspiciously. "They're Quality. More than likely she had no choice." They exchanged glances.

"When are you off today?" the footman asked. Before she could answer, Hawk had entered the hallway, his long strides carrying him past them quickly. Dropping a curtsy, the maid hurried off. The footman rushed to open the door.

The long ride Hawk had taken that morning had done little to lift his spirits. Exhausted after two almost sleepless nights, he dropped into a chair that looked out over the garden. His eyes fixed on the disorder there, his mind replayed the snatch of memory.

It was there that Emily found him. Like any well-brought-up lady of her generation, she had put her own despair aside and arranged the details of the household. She had talked to the cook about the meals for the next few days and complimented Wiggins on his organization. Finishing her inspection of the household, she had wandered down the small hallway aimlessly, certain only she did not want to return to the bedroom where last night she had cried herself to sleep.

Maybe her stepmother had been right. Maybe Hawk had married her only because he could not, as a gentleman, escape. She sighed and wandered into the small library Wiggins had shown her earlier.

Hearing the door open, Hawk turned. He stood up and took several steps toward her, his face solemn. "Emily." The word was merely a breath.

She stopped. Her eyes met his for just a moment. Then they fell. Her throat tightened, and she was not able to say a word. She took a few steps toward him and then stopped. She looked up at him again, her eyes brimming with tears. "Why?" she asked.

He closed his eyes in despair. Then he rushed to her, engulfing her in his arms. "Oh, Emily." For a moment she did not respond. Then her arms encircled his neck, holding him close, feeling the tremors that shook him. His arms tightened around her. "Emily" he whispered in a choked voice. She sobbed and tried to get closer to him.

The door opened. They stepped back from each other, and Emily turned away, wiping her cheeks with her handkerchief. The footman, carrying clean glasses, stopped, his eyes bright and curious. "Shall I come back later, sir?" he asked. He looked from one to the other, taking in every detail in order to tell his friends.

"No." Hawk was curt. He stood watching as the footman replaced the glasses and then left. Emily crossed to the bookshelves and pulled down a book at random. By the time the footman left, they were both under careful control. Hawk walked over to his wife, looked at the book she had opened, and smiled wryly. "Emily, since when did you start reading Greek?" he asked. His voice was deliberately light.

"What?" She glanced up from the page, her eyes wide. The hurt in them was still evident.

He ruthlessly repressed his longing to take her in his arms, blessing his years in the army for the control they had given him. "Greek. When did you start reading Greek?"

She looked down at the book she held. Then she flushed. Turning away from him, she slid the book back into its spot on the shelf. Wishing she could disappear, she stood for a moment before gathering her courage. Then she turned back to him. She smiled, and his heart ached with longing.

"Come." He held out his hand. "Call for your cape. Let us explore the gardens. Father said he had not been here in sometime, and they had been allowed to go wild. While we are here, you can tell the gardeners how you would like them changed."

For several moments Emily stared at him, not willing to let the situation slip away so quickly. But her fears that her stepmother might be right kept her from speaking out. Hawk smiled at her. That was enough. She took his hand, allowing him to lead her from the room.

Their actions that day set the pattern for those to come. Part of the day they spent together, walking about the countryside, hunting or fishing, playing cards, riding. When the air seemed so charged with tension they thought they might catch fire, they separated. Each meal was an exercise in frustration. Each night was a cavern of despair.

After the first few days, Emily did not cry herself to sleep while listening to Hawk pace the floor in the room beside hers. She simply lay there wishing she were brave enough to go to him. One night she slipped from her bed and crossed to the doorway, her hand on the latch. Then the footsteps stopped. Losing her nerve, she slipped back in bed, unaware that Hawk stood only inches from her, his head pressed against the door that separated him from her.

Almost afraid to sleep because of the dreams that plagued him, Hawk pushed his body to its limit, finally turning to long rides in the middle of the night. Emily would lie awake from the time she heard him leave. Where was he going? she wondered. Then she carefully made her mind a blank, trying to blot out her stepmother's words: "Don't expect him to be faithful to you." She would blink away tears until she heard him return, and then drop into a heavy, dreamless sleep.

By the time they returned to the manor, Hawk, Emily, and Lester moved like sleepwalkers. Emily, alone in the carriage for the return trip, slept the day away. Hawk rode across the countryside, pushing his horses until they were lathered, pursued by two demons: his still-incomplete memories and his desire for Emily.

Arriving before the coach, he threw his hat and coat to the waiting footman and demanded, "Where is the post?"

"In the library, sir. May I get you some tea, or do you wish to wait until Mrs. Hawksleigh arrives?" the underbutler asked calmly, although inside he was, he told the housekeeper later, as shaky as any jelly. He had been selected for the position of butler of the manor when the older butler followed his master; now all that remained was the approval of the new master and mistress.

"Wait." Hawk paused. "No, now. My wife will be arriving shortly. But bring it yourself." The man nodded, but his mind was whirling. What could he have done wrong?

Within minutes the tea tray was ready. He nodded to the footman to open the door to the library, and walked in. Putting the tray on a low table, he turned to face his master. "Will there be anything else, sir?"

"Who are you?"

"Clarke, sir. Your butler." The man stood tall and proud, hoping that Mr. Hawksleigh would not contradict him. "Your mother selected me."

Leaving the pile of mail on the table beside him, Hawk rose and slowly walked toward Clarke. Once again the man felt his insides turn to mush. "Have the servants ready to meet my wife when she arrives, Clarke. I will escort her myself." Hawk mentally reviewed what his mother had told him about the importance of making Emily feel in charge of the household. Then he asked as if in afterthought, "And, Clarke, when the luggage arrives, have my things sent to my old rooms. My wife will occupy the best guest chamber. She wants to redecorate the master suite." During the hours on horseback, he had decided that his only chance of sanity lay in putting distance between himself and his wife. Twice in the last few days he had opened the door between them and slipped into her bedchamber and watched her sleep, wrenching himself away only by the force of his will.

"Certainly, sir." The butler opened the door to the hall, letting the noise of an arrival enter.

"Hurry. I do not want her kept waiting," Hawk said sternly. He took a deep breath, pasted a smile on his face, and walked down the hall behind the butler. The other servants, waiting for just this moment, took their places.

Emily allowed her maid to straighten her bonnet and then stepped down from the coach into her husband's waiting hands. "Welcome to your new home, my dear," he said formally, pulling her hand through his arm. He smiled at her.

Straightening her back, Emily smiled back. She knew what was expected. Moving down the line of servants, many of whom she had known all her life, she smiled, asking after this one's son or another's sister, making each feel special. With those who were new to her, she made certain she learned their names and something about them.

"Tea is ready in the library, Emily," Hawk said as she reached the end of the line. "Let Clarke take your bonnet and cloak. After that trip, I am certain you are thirsty."

Emily allowed herself to be led into the warm, comfortable room. She poured a cup of tea for them both. They sat there silently sipping their tea. When she had finished, she put her cup down. "Shall we change for dinner?" she asked, looking through the windows to the twilight outside them.

"I thought we might have something light in our rooms, if you agree," Hawk said. Emily's eyes grew wide, and her heart began pounding against her ribs. "No sense getting dressed again when we are both so tired." He moved toward the door, and she followed, a small smile on her lips. He paused with his hand on the latch. "Emily, I am moving back into my old rooms. I told Clarke to put you in the best guest chamber so that you can have the leisure to redecorate the master suite." He heard rather than saw her reaction, a gasp of dismay. He stiffened his back and turned away. "Good night, my dear. I will see you in the morning." He opened the door and stepped back to let her pass.

For a short time Emily froze, her dismay evident from her face. Then she took a deep breath. "In the morning," she said quietly. Then she swept down the hallway and up the stairs. Hawk gazed after her, heartbreak in his eyes.

That night Emily lay awake as usual. This time, instead of Hawk's footsteps she heard her stepmother's voice: "He does not want you, you great clodpole. He will leave you behind. He is simply too much of a gentleman to call the wedding off. You will see. Who could love a woman who towers over half the men?" Over and over again, the same words echoed. Finally Emily could bear it no longer.

"No!" she screamed. "No! You are wrong! He loves me! I know he loves me!" She threw her pillow across the room and then burst into wild sobs.

Mary entered the room quietly, shutting the door to the hallway behind her so that the maids, already curious, could hear no more. The story they had told the servants at the hunting box might not survive at the manor if they did not act soon. Then she reopened the door slightly. "Call Lester. Tell him I need him," she said softly. Then she crossed to the bed where her mistress lay. She picked up a bottle of eau de cologne and moistened Emily's forehead. "There. You will feel better soon," she whispered. Worn out by her emotions, Emily drifted into a restless sleep.

A short time later Mary heard a soft scratching at the door. "You needed to see me, Miss Johnson?" Lester asked, his face worried.

"Hush! You will wake her. Come. We can be private in here." Mary led the valet into the sitting room of the suite. Quickly she told the man what she knew, finishing with, "We must tell the captain."

Lester shook his head. "Not me. He's already taken my head off once today. His temper's too uncertain."

"He has to know. What if he hears it from Clarke or one of the others? How would he feel then?" Mary raised her sturdy chin. "If you will not, I shall," she said firmly, and started for the door.

Lester put out a hand and pulled her to a stop. "I will go, but what should I tell him?" A worried frown crossed his face. "What if he learns what we have said?"

"Tell him that I asked you to call him, that the mistress needs him," she said impatiently. "Go. Even if he learns what we have done, what harm is there? We did it only to protect her."

"And him," Lester added quickly. Mary nodded and pushed him through the doorway.

Lester took a step and then came back. "Go. Before she wakes or he goes to sleep," the maid said sternly.

The man mounted the stairs, reminding himself that the captain had always been good to him. In the rooms where he had grown up, Hawk sat staring at a glass of wine, a good port his father had laid down some years earlier. He closed his eyes for a moment and then jerked them open as Lester walked in. "You can clear this away. I'm for bed," he said, gesturing to the dishes on the table before them.

"Captain . . . ." Lester took a deep breath. "Captain, Mary Johnson, Mrs. Emily's maid, said to ask you to come to her."

"Mrs. Emily's maid? What has she to do with me?"

"Not her maid. To Mrs. Emily. Sir, she is not herself. Her maid asked to speak to you." Lester spoke the words so quickly that Hawk missed their import.

"Tell her I will see her in the morning. Now, help me with these boots." Lost in his own problems, Hawk had blocked out what his valet was saying.

"Captain, you must come. Mrs. Emily needs you, now!" This time Lester's voice cut through the fog that surrounded Hawk.

His head snapped up, his eyes alert. "What did you say?"

"Mrs. Emily needs you, sir." Before Lester could move, his master was out of the door, almost running down the hall and the stairs.

He burst into Emily's room. "What is wrong? Where is she?" Hawk looked frantically around the bedchamber.

"She just dropped off to sleep, sir," Mary explained. She pulled back the blue satin bed hangings and showed him Emily, tears still on her cheeks, her breath still sobs.

Hawk stood there stunned. He turned and walked toward the fireplace, his arms wrapped around himself as if he would protect himself from further hurt. "Why did you send for me? What is there for me to do?" he asked dully.

"She was screaming at someone, but no one was here," the maid explained, her voice quivering. Hawk turned; his eyes narrowed. The fire at his back made him appear for just one moment surrounded by a halo of flames. In his shirt-sleeves, with his shirt undone, he seemed some giant of legend. Mary stepped back, frightened, although she was trying not to show it. "She needs you, sir. She is so alone."

Hawk caught sight of Lester, standing just inside the door to the chamber. "The two of you go. I will stand watch over her," he said quietly, his exhaustion evident in his voice.

"But, Captain . . ." Lester protested. Hawk waved them from the room. Then he pulled a chair close by the bed, his eyes on his wife's face. Her gown of embroidered lawn lay about her in crumpled folds. Her nightcap had disappeared, and her hair seemed dark across the pillow. Finally he sat down, but the height of the bed made it impossible to watch her. He stood up again, his legs wobbly from lack of sleep. He leaned against the bed, his eyes drifting shut. He jerked himself up again, but his eyes started to close again. He splashed his face with cold water, but even that did little good.

At last he moved the chaise closer to the bed, yet far enough away so that he could see Emily. He sat down to rest for a few minutes. Sometime later a strange sound woke Emily. She started and then froze. Her heartbeats sounded like drums in her ears. She heard it again. A little braver in the flickering firelight, she turned her head slowly on the pillow. Then her eyes widened. She sat up cautiously, not at all certain she knew where she was. The sound was louder this time. And it came from her husband. "Hawk," she called softly. "Anthony?"

He moaned again, twisting as though he were trying to escape from something. "Hawk!" Something in her voice must have reached him. He moaned once more and twisted, sending himself tumbling to the floor. Instantly he was awake, his hand where his sword should be. Then he saw her, and his eyes grew wide. He took a step backward, falling backward on the chaise, his eyes never leaving hers.

She slid from the bed and walked toward him. Her heart beat with happiness, but her head reminded her of the disappointments of the last few weeks. "Hawk?" she asked. He stood up, his face impassive, and waited until she had taken her seat beside him. "Your maid was worried about you, my dear," he said quietly.

"Not that. What do you dream about?" She put her hand on his cheek and stroked it.

He grasped it, pulling it to a stop over his lips. He kissed her fingers and then let her go. He took a deep breath.

"What were you dreaming of just now?" she asked again.

He stood up and crossed to stare into the fire. Just when Emily had decided that he was not going to answer her, he turned around. His face hidden by the shadows, he said quietly, "I am not certain. Emily, what happened to you tonight? You are always so calm, so capable."

She took a breath as though she had been struck. "I fear you idealize me, Hawk," she said bitterly. "Everyone gives in to fear sometime. It has passed." And if it happens again, I will be certain you never know, she added to herself.

He walked over to where she was sitting and took her face in his hands. He looked deep into her eyes. She held her breath, seeing the love in his. Then he turned away. "Sleep late tomorrow, my dear," he said quietly as he walked through the door.

Emily stood up. "Hawk," she cried, holding out her hand toward him. In the firelight, the white lawn of her gown seemed almost golden. He did not turn around. "Hawk, do not leave me like this," she begged.

His shoulders sagged. "In the morning. We will talk in the morning." His voice was ragged, and only a whisper. Before she could disagree, he had left. Emily sank down on the chaise, her face a study in confusion and despair.

6

By the next morning the weather was crisp and cold. Emily,
walking slowly toward the breakfast room, shivered in spite
of the warm merino dress and cashmere shawl she wore. She
had chosen the red dress hoping its color would lift her spirits
as well as keep her warm, but neither seemed to be working.
Reaching the door, she took a deep breath. Then she walked
in.

Hawk looked up from the paper he was reading and stood
up. "You look lovely today, my dear," he said quietly as
he seated her. The lines in his face were more pronounced.
He had begun to lose the tan he had had when he returned
from the Peninsula, and seemed almost pale. His hand
brushed her shoulder and then pulled away.

Emily closed her eyes, wanting to believe that he truly
meant what he was saying. But she was afraid. She forced
herself to thank him politely, a tight smile on her lips.
Accepting food she did not want, she talked of
inconsequential things until the meal was over. As they were
walking out of the room, she put her hand on his arm. He
stopped. She could feel the tension in him. "You said we
would talk this morning," she reminded him.

He nodded, his heart beating like a drum beneath the dark
brown jacket he wore. He led the way to the morning room,
a place his mother had claimed for her own and one he knew
Emily enjoyed. The fire on the hearth blazed brightly. He
walked to the window, noting the frost still on the lawn.
Emily took her seat in an armchair close by. She closed her
eyes for a moment, shutting out the yellows, greens, and
white that made the room sparkle like spring. She clenched
her fingers around the arm of the chair, her fingernails

making dents in the striped yellow satin that covered it. The silence grew. Emily shifted restlessly.

He took a deep breath, closed his eyes for a moment, and then turned to face her. His face, already pale, seemed almost white. "Emily," he said, a note of longing in his voice. He cleared his throat, wishing she did not look so lovely in that deep red. She simply sat there, the knuckles on her hands growing even whiter. "Emily, forgive me?"

"For what? For not wanting to make our marriage real?" She stood up and crossed the room to stare down into the blazing fire. The flames were merely a blur because of the tears in her eyes.

He rushed to her, putting his hands on her shoulders, turning her to face him. "You cannot believe that." But the look on her face told him she did. He dropped his hands to his sides and stepped back. His shoulders were as straight as they had ever been when he was wearing regimentals. "Emily, you know how I feel about you, have felt about you for a long time." His dark brown eyes stared into hers as though he could will her to understand what he was saying. "That day in your garden you said you believed in me. Go on believing, please. Give me more time." He longed to pull her close, to sink onto the settee, to show her what passion meant, but he resisted with every fiber in his body. He stepped back farther, as if distance could decrease his longing for her.

"Hawk, something is happening to us. I am frightened. Hold me. Tell me what to do," she begged. She stepped closer to him, her eyes dark with pain.

He took a deep breath and released it slowly. "Emily, I want to. I truly want to. But I cannot." They stood for a moment frozen as though in a game of charades. The tears trembling in her eyes trickled down her face. She reached up and wiped them away angrily. "I will go away. Andrew has sent me a note about some horses he has for me. I will visit him. That will give you an opportunity to finish redocorating Mama's and Father's suite to suit you. And you have to plan the party for the children, here on the estate," Hawk said, waiting for the protest he was certain would follow.

Just as her stepmother had said. She was being left behind. Emily stared at her husband. Her eyes were dry now. "You knew what you were going to do when you came down to breakfast this morning." The flat statement raised the hairs on the back of his neck. "When will you leave?" He felt his heart sink.

"You must see that I . . . we, cannot go on as we have been. Emily, please, my dear . . ." He realized that she was no longer listening to him. A chill went up his spine.

"I will take care of things here. You visit your brother," she said in a calm, emotionless voice. "Remember, your parents are returning for Christmas. Please be here to greet them." She walked to the door, her emotions carefully hidden.

"Emily!" Her name was an anguished whisper. The door closed behind her. Hawk stared at it for a long time before he sat down, his head in his hands.

The unnatural calm she felt helped Emily get through the next few days. She saw her husband off with a cheerful face assumed more for the servants than for either of them. Hawk kissed her good-bye, but he could feel her freeze beneath his hands.

As soon as he was out of sight, she began redecorating. She set people to stripping the wallpaper from his parents' rooms, ruthlessly disposing of the dark blue and dull gold silk previously covering those walls. For Hawk's chambers, Emily selected a white silk with light gray stripes for the walls, with a matching fabric for the chairs. Her sitting room had Mars-yellow walls with gray latticework and a pale gray ceiling, while her bedroom was painted a gray so pale it was almost white. During her visits to the manor she had never dreamed these rooms would be hers one day. Now that they were, she was determined to make them brighter, more airy.

While some people worked on the walls, others stripped the bed hangings, changing the bed design from a simple rail to the more modern system of pulleys. When they began to hang the draperies on the windows and around the bed, some of the older servants were scandalized by their mistress's use of Chinese-red silk and satin, saying the color was not suitable for the apartment of a gentleman. But by the time Emily added Chinese-red lacquer vases and bowl, and one armchair in the same color to the sitting room, they agreed that the room, although unconventional, looked bright and cheerful.

As the rest of the apartment neared completion, Emily still had not found exactly the right hangings for her own bed-chamber. Finally, after consulting Thomas Hope's *Household Furniture and Interior Decoration*, she found a description of the material she was looking for—yellow satin embroidered in red and gray silk and gold thread. The price made her catch her breath for a moment. Then she steeled herself and made her order. Her husband had told her to order whatever she liked. She flipped through the pages of the book again, this time finding Aubusson carpets in pale gray with a Chinese-red border for Hawk's room and in a yellow and red for her own.

With the entire household at her disposal and London merchants eager for her trade and their share of the family's wealth, Emily moved into the rooms very rapidly. As she lay in bed one evening, she looked around with pleasure. The warm tones of the satinwood and rosewood furniture added the right touches. The wood and the silk of the draperies caught the gleam of the flickering candles, wrapping her in light.

One task completed, Emily gave her full attention to the next, preparing for Christmas. Like her own family, she knew the Hawksleighs kept the old tradition. Each child on the estate must have a gift as well as something for everyone in the house and stables. As she worked, the calm that Emily had wrapped around her began to give way to nervousness and exhaustion. Determined that she would not give way to her despair again, Emily kept herself firmly in hand, relying heavily on her mother-in-law's assistance. Letters flew back and forth between them until all the arrangements had been completed.

When Hawk finally returned, Emily was shaking, although her calm manner fooled her brother-in-law. The air was rich with the scent of puddings cooking as the two men made their way to the morning room. Emily had heard the commotion in the hallway, and waited, her face turned toward the door.

She could not prevent the smile and rush of color that lit her face as Hawk walked in. She watched him walk toward her, her eyes softened by love. During the time he was away, she had decided to live each day as it came, accepting whatever affection he was willing to give her. After the last two years of her stepmother, she was certainly used to making do with very little.

The time away from Emily had given Hawk some control over his emotions. But the sight of her sitting quietly in her chair, her eyes on him, drew him to her side as a flame draws a moth. He lifted her hand, turned it palm-upward, and kissed it. His lips lingered for a moment.

"Forget about me, Hawk. Kiss her," Andrew suggested, his voice amused. Hawk dropped Emily's hand and took a step back. "Well, if you will not, you must permit me to do so." He strolled across the room and kissed her cheek. "He was a bear, not good company at all," he told her in a pseudo-whisper, his eyes on his brother. "He needs you around to keep him in good humor."

Emily looked at her husband. He had spent much of the time away outside, she could tell. His face had more color. Her glance noted the way his dark blue riding jacket hugged his shoulders. Quickly she looked down, afraid that her face would reveal all too clearly her own feelings. "Welcome home," she said, her voice soft and musical. "Shall I ring for tea?"

"Listen to her, Hawk. Sounds just like Mama, doesn't she?" Andrew beamed at her. When Hawk had appeared in Yorkshire, he had wondered. But the looks his brother and his wife were exchanging had done much to quiet his fears. "Did Cook make cream cakes?" he asked as eagerly as he had when he was a boy just returning from school. "My cook does not have a hand with them."

"Emily, you must find a new cook. His only knows how to make stews," her husband said, throwing up a hand to ward off the mock blow his brother sent him.

"You shall have all the cream cakes you like," Emily promised Andrew. "Cook has been preparing for your visit as well as Hawk's return." She moved to the settee and motioned Clarke to put the tea tray on the circular table nearby. Hawk took his seat beside her. Her heart beat faster, and her hand holding the teapot shook. But the simple routine steadied her. She poured their tea, wondering if Hawk had had the time he needed, if their life would now be different.

Later that day, she showed Hawk through their suite, uncertain of his reaction. "This is astounding," he said proudly as he walked through his rooms. "Astounding."

"Why? Do you not like it? Should I have it redone?" she asked, not at all confident that he approved her taste.

"No!" Her face fell. "No, leave it alone," he added hurriedly. "You have done a wonderful job." Her face brightened. "But how did you get it done so quickly?" He stood in the middle of his bedchamber and turned slowly, taking in the contrast between the crisp, clean walls and the vibrant accent colors.

"Everyone helped," she said softly. "You do like it? The carpets only arrived yesterday. If they do not please you, we could send them back." If Hawk had realized what an effort it had taken for Emily to make the offer, he would not have hesitated as long as he did. She caught her breath as he walked about the room inspecting the vases and furniture.

Her husband finally turned. He said, "They are not the colors I would have chosen." Emily's heart sank. "But then, I am not very imaginative. You have done an excellent job, excellent!" She smiled at him, and his heart began to race. In the weeks away he had been certain he could control his emotions; now that resolve began melting away. He moved away quickly, opening the Boulle commode beside the bed.

That night, like the others of their marriage, Emily spent alone. Disappointed but not devastated, because of the control she had developed, she went to sleep. Only the pillow she clung to revealed her loneliness.

When Hawk's parents arrived a few days later, both he and Emily welcomed them heartily. Pulling Mrs. Hawks- leigh into the morning room, Emily listened eagerly to the latest deatils of London fashion and all the gossip. Later she and her mother-in-law visited the tenants, distributing the Christmas baskets.

Unlike his wife, Mr. Hawksleigh was not happy about

visiting the manor. When he stepped out of the carriage, both Hawk and Andrew could tell that something had disturbed him. His normally cheerful face was solemn, and he seemed distracted. Even when his sons pressed him for information, he would only say it was nothing to disturb the family about. And for a short time he would remember to smile.

One afternoon shortly before Christmas, Hawk saw his father walk into the study, a sheaf of letters in his hands and a look as black as a thundercloud on his face. Andrew was out visiting friends in the area, but Hawk had wanted to talk to his bailiff. He put his plans aside to follow his father.

He walked into the study, his footsteps so soft the carpet absorbed the sound. His father was staring at a letter in his hand as though it were a snake about to bite him. "What is wrong?" Hawk asked.

His father started, sliding the letter under the pile of others on the desk. "Anthony. I did not hear you come in." The older man put his hand casually on the letters and turned to face his son. "Did you need me?"

"No. Father, you know if you have had reverses, you can tell me. With Uncle George's fortune . . ."

His father got up and put his hand on his shoulder. "Son, I appreciate the offer, but this is nothing that affects our income." An inch or so shorter than his older son, Mr. Hawksleigh was still a handsome man. His hair was still dark and only dusted with gray. "When you first came home, I told you that I was working with the Exchequer." The older man turned and picked up the letters, running his fingers over the top one as if he could read it with his fingertips. Then he took his seat and motioned Hawk to one nearby.

"Then this is a problem with the government?" Hawk asked, at once relieved and yet still troubled. His weeks at Andrew's estate had given him a chance to think calmly, to divorce himself from most of his problems for a time. He was not at all certain he wanted to plunge into another one.

Mr. Hawksleigh nodded, his face still frowning. "I wish Perceval had more time. We need more help. In fact, when you sell out, I hope you will give us your expertise." His frown grew deeper.

"What good would I be? Oh, you have trained me well

to manage my own affairs, but the affairs of government? What good would a soldier do?'' Hawk asked. He crossed to the table where the glasses and wine were kept and poured himself a glass. His father declined. He kept his eyes on his son. Since his arrival, he had been watching Hawk whenever he had the chance. And he was not certain he liked the changes he saw. Oh, his son had improved physically. The dark circles under Hawk's eyes were faint reminders. He had gained some weight. But the control and ability to predict outcomes that had given his son the name Hawk seemed missing. And no matter what his wife said about the problems of newlyweds adjusting to marriage, as a father he knew something was wrong there also. No matter how loving and considerate Emily and Hawk appeared in public, there was something missing in their relationship.

The room was silent for several minutes. Then Mr. Hawksleigh said, his voice firm, ''Sell out!''

''And admit that the general was right? Never!'' Hawk slammed his glass down on the mantel, cracking it.

''You and I both know that you would do nothing to betray your country. Sell out. You do not need to prove anything to Wellesley. And I need you to help me.''

Hawk's face was gray and his hands shaking. He started to speak, but his voice failed him. He cleared his throat noisily.

His father watched the color rush from his son's cheeks and wished he had never brought up the subject. But he had already gone too far. ''Anthony, have you remembered something? What is it?''

''Nothing.''

''Nothing does not make your face gray. What have you remembered? Son, you can tell me. I am your father,'' he said, his voice soothing and quiet. ''What is it?''

''A woman.'' The words shot out of Hawk's mouth before he could stop them. He looked struck with horror.

''My boy, we all have women in our past,'' his father said with a laugh in his voice, delighted that the problem was such a simple one. ''Your mother reminds me of mine whenever she is displeased with me. Was it someone you knew in Spain, and you are afraid Emily will uncover her? I have found that a wife will avoid the subject as much as a man will.''

Hawk froze. Then he walked over to the large globe by the window, turning it idly until he found Spain. He stopped it there, his finger running lightly over the mountains. When he turned to look at his father again, his face was calm. ''Perhaps we should discuss this some other time,'' he said coolly. ''I will leave you to your work.'' Then he was gone before the elder Hawksleigh had a chance to reply. His father nervously tapped the letters he held, his frown deeper than before as he realized that somehow he had failed his son.

With Christmas upon them, Hawk arranged matters so that his father and he were never alone. As master of the house, he selected the Yule log and dispensed the presents and Christmas money to the servants. Although the crops had not been plentiful, neither he nor his retainers had to worry. Unlike many of the gentry, his wealth was not based solely on the land. In fact, to his bailiff's surprise, he had reduced rents when everyone around him was raising them. Therefore, the gifts were as generous as they had always been.

During the time in Yorkshire, Hawk and Andrew had made a whirlwind trip to York, raiding the stores for gifts for their mother and father, assorted relatives, and Emily. The other presents had been easy, but Hawk had struggled over Emily's. He had purchased silks and a new saddle for her, and still was not satisfied. Finally he found what he was looking for, a long strand of pearls with a soft creamy cast. Perfectly matched, they hung in a long rope with a magnificent gold-and-pearl clasp.

Unwilling to wait until the next morning, when they would be surrounded by family, Hawk waited impatiently through the church service and the supper that followed. When everyone said good night and went upstairs, Hawk followed. He changed into his nightshirt and robe and waited until he heard the door close after his wife's maid. Then he opened the connecting door.

Emily sat straight up in bed. Her heart was beating so fast that she felt as though she were choking. ''What do you want?'' she demanded, and instantly regretted the churlish tone in her voice. "Is there anything wrong?" Her voice trembled.

"No." Hawk lit a candle from the embers and crossed to the bed. Emily lay back down, her eyes never leaving his. "Happy Christmas, my dear." He walked toward the bed and handed her the long, thin leather box.

She sat up once again and took it from him, her eyes sparkling. When she released the clasp and looked inside, her eyes grew wide. "Hawk," she whispered, almost breathless with shock. She looked from the pearls to him. Impatient, he took the necklace and dropped it over her head, watching in delight as it spilled down below her waist. His fingers brushed the tops of her rosy breasts as he adjusted the pearls. Both started and pulled back. "Hawk, they are beautiful," Emily said breathlessly as she ran her hand over them. "Thank you." As unself-consciously as she had kissed him when he had returned from the Peninsula, she reached up and pulled his head down to meet his lips. The kiss deepened as he wrapped his arms around her hungrily. When they drew apart a few minutes later in order to breathe, Emily ran her hands over her pearls. Then she pulled further away, slipped from the bed, and hurried to a wardrobe nearby. She took out a package wrapped in a cotton cloth and brought it to him.

Her departure had given Hawk a chance to gain control. He slid from the bed, going to meet her. "Happy Christmas," she whispered, and held out the package. Hawk looked at her, and she blushed, aware she was alone with him and no one would interrupt them. She smiled at him and then dropped her eyes.

Hawk walked back to the nightstand, where the candle burned brightly. Slowly he unwrapped the package. A dozen shirts of the finest lawn lay before him, each representing hours of Emily's time, and a dozen cravats. A small leather box lay on top. Slowly he opened it. "It was my grandfather's," Emily said quietly, uncertain now whether he would appreciate it. "My mother left it to me. If you do not like it . . ."

Her husband slid the heavy gold-and-emerald ring on his finger. "I like it. Not just because it is from you but because it obviously has memories for you. Thank you." The shirts and cravats he was holding kept him from taking her in his arms. An irrepressible smile flashed across his face. "And I am certain Lester will thank you too. He has complained about my lack of linen. I shall have to remind him these shirts are to be saved for special occasions."

"But they are only simple shirts," she protested.

"That you made for me. Mama could not make a shirt if she tried. She always had a seamstress make them. And later we went to tailors. These are the finest shirts I have ever had," he said proudly. He smiled at her. She smiled back. A silence grew between them. Hawk shifted restlessly. Then, before he was tempted more than he already was, he whispered, "Good night." In a moment he was gone. Emily climbed back into bed, her fingers slipping over the pearls. She sighed and snuffed out the candle. Although she was alone once again, somehow she did not feel the despair that had been her companion for weeks.

When she walked into the breakfast room the next morning, Hawk was already there. Their eyes met. She blushed and lowered hers instantly. He caressed her, noting with pleasure that she wore his pearls. The day was a happy one. Andrew's teasing, her mother-in-law's approval, and the joy of being a part of such a happy occasion made Emily sparkle. To Hawk it was like seeing alive again the girl he had asked to marry him. The only flaw in the day was the absence of her brother.

With Christmas over, Hawk's parents did not stay long. Before they left, Mr. Hawksleigh ran his elder son to ground in the library. He entered silently and stood watching Hawk, his head bent over a ledger. From that moment in the study when he had laughed at his son's concern over the woman Hawk had mentioned, he had known he had made a mistake. He did not intend to leave until he had the situation resolved.

He positioned himself in front of the door and cleared his throat. Hawk glanced up. His father watched his face settle into that politely distant mask he had come to hate. Only with Emily and sometimes with Andrew did that public face disappear. "Son," he said, "I was wrong. Tell me about her."

"About whom?"

"Do not try to fob me off by pretending. I was wrong to dismiss you so callously. Ever since I realized what I had done, I have been trying to find you alone. You have been very successful at eluding me. Tell me about the woman," his father said, leaning back against the door. In spite of his age, he was still a fine figure of a man, lean and hard. The dark green coat he wore fitted as tightly as Hawk's, the fabric straining against his muscles. His voice was quiet but firm.

Hawk laid his pen aside. From his father's stance, he knew that there would be no escape. He had seen it before mostly when he had been sent to him for punishment. "There is nothing to tell," he said calmly, looking back at the column of figures in front of him.

"You lie." Hawk jerked his head up. His father walked toward him, his blue eyes on his son's brown ones, keeping them locked with his. Leaning across the library table, Mr. Hawksleigh said, "If there were nothing to tell, you would not have tried to avoid me. What have you remembered?"

Hawk shoved his chair back and rose, his emotions mixed. Hurt by his father's insensitivity to his problem, he wanted to strike out, to hurt him. On the other hand, he needed to talk to someone, someone who would care. But what if his father were repulsed by him? Their eyes still locked, Hawk took a deep breath. Then he walked to a corner where two library chairs sat close to one another. "I've only remembered a little," he said. His father closed his eyes briefly, sending up a prayer of thanksgiving, and followed him.

As Hawk unfolded the fragments, the older Hawksleigh listened carefully, meticulously sorting the information, trying to sift facts from emotions. "What do you remember about the room?" he asked when Hawk's bleak recital was over.

Startled, his son looked up from the carpet at which he had been staring. "The room?" he stammered, his father's question not at all what he had expected.

"Where you were."

At first Hawk could remember nothing. Then he shut his eyes, trying to visualize the scene he had been trying to obliterate from his memory. "At first it is dark, so dark," he mumbled.

"Dark as in night, or dark because there were no windows?" his father asked quietly, his face calm, although the emotions beneath the surface were in turmoil.

His son looked up at him startled. He started to speak and then closed his eyes again, visualizing the scene. "I am not certain. But when the door opened, there were torches." He stopped, opened his eyes. "Torches. Yes, there were torches," he said excitedly. "I had forgotten that. Torches."

"If there were torches, there had to be other people around," his father said calmly. "Try to remember who they were, what they looked like, what was happening."

Once again Hawk closed his eyes. This time, no matter how hard he struggled, nothing would return. "It is gone," he said finally. He slumped in his chair dispiritedly.

His father sighed. Then he got up from his chair and stood behind his son. "Do not give up. Before long, you will understand; everything will return." He leaned over, putting both hands on his shoulders. "I know you. Even under the greatest of stress, you would not give up your principles." He walked over and poured both of them a glass of brandy. Handing Hawk a glass, he took his seat opposite him once more. "Sell out. Come to London. Emily can enjoy the Season, and you can help me."

Hawk sipped the brandy, his face somber. In spite of what his father had said, he knew all too well that war could change a man, destroy the trappings of civilization with which he cloaked himself. He had seen it happen with others. He sighed. Then he thought of the months in the country alone with Emily. He sat up, his resolve hardened. "What will your colleagues say if you enlist my aid?" he asked thoughtfully.

Mr. Hawksleigh grinned. "Perceval is the only one I will have to mention anything to. And he has been as worried as I about the problem. Let me tell you about it."

"No." Hawk held up his hand, his face serious. "If I decide to come to London . . ." His father's face fell. "If I decide to come, you can tell me then. I will think about your idea carefully and talk to Emily. If she wants to come, I will consider it." He took a deep breath, not at all certain he was doing the right thing.

His father had carefully composed his face. No emotion

showed in either it or his voice. "Will you sell out?"

"Probably. A commander must have confidence in himself to lead his men. And right now I have none. I would do them no good even if Wellesley were willing to take me back," Hawk said, his voice level although sad. "But, blast it, they are dying over there while I sit here safe!" He got up and went to the window, staring out at fields of carnage rather than the cold gardens below. "It is not fair!"

His father simply sat there helplessly, realizing that nothing he could say would reach his son. Suddenly the door opened and Andrew walked in. "Clarke told me you were in here. What about a game of billiards?" The tension broken, his father and brother nodded.

7

Over the next few days the members of the family made their good-byes, drifting home or to other house parties. When the elder Hawksleighs left, his father drew Hawk to one side. "Sell out," he urged again. "Do not hang on to something that causes you so much pain." Before Hawk could answer, his father stepped up into his coach. "I will expect you in London soon," he said as he closed the door.

As soon as they could make their excuses to the remaining guests, both Andrew and Emily sought Hawk out. "Did you tell your father you would go to London for the Season?" Emily asked, confused. "You told me we would not go . . ."

"I told him I would talk to you," her husband said impatiently, not ready to have his decisions forced on him.

"London! Good! Now I do not have to take rooms," Andrew said triumphantly.

"Rooms? What are you talking about?" his brother asked.

"You will not mind if I stay with you and Emily. Mama does not mind the drive to the estate, but I do. I was going to find my own place, but this will do nicely." Andrew rattled on. "Will you have room for my horses in your stable? No, perhaps I should set up my own. But you can never tell about hay."

Emily and Hawk listened to him for a few minutes, slightly bewildered looks on their faces. Emily finally looked at her husband and shrugged as if to remind him that the young man was his responsibility. When Andrew's plans began to grow ever more complex, Hawk finally brought him to a halt. "We have not yet decided to go, Andrew."

"But you must. You could not miss the Season. What would people say?" He paused and looked from one to the other, curiously. Watching the way they carefully avoided each other's eyes, he drew his own conclusion. "Emily is increasing. That is why. Why didn't you tell Father and Mama before they left?"

After one stricken look at each other, Emily and Hawk kept their eyes turned carefully away from one another. Emily moved slowly to a chair and sat down, her hands clenched. The soft rose merino she wore was vivid in contrast to her pale face. Hawk looked at her bowed head and silently cursed his brother's careless words. He longed to go to her, put his arms around her, make the words come true. Instead, he stayed where he was. "No," he said bleakly.

Andrew looked from one to the other, the uneasiness he had dismissed earlier returning. "Oh, I say, Emily, Hawk, well . . ." Her voice drifted off into embarrassed silence. He walked slowly toward the door. "If you do decide to go, you will let me know?" he asked, his hand on the latch. The look his brother gave him told him not to say another word. He opened the door a few inches and slipped through. Outside, he paused for a few minutes, his forehead creased with a frown.

Inside the room the silence grew until Hawk could bear it no longer. "Emily," he said, his voice low and pleading. She looked up at him, her hurt apparent on her face. "Sometimes Andrew forgets himself. I want to apologize for him."

"Why? Your mother asked me the same question shortly after she arrived. As did one of your cousins." She gulped back her anger and tears. At moments like these, Emily wondered if she loved or hated her husband. Being honest with herself, she admitted that if she truly hated him, she would have found a reason to leave the room long ago.

"Mama?"

"What did you expect? They love you and their family. Of course they are interested." And so am I, she admitted to herself, wondering if she would ever have the joy of her own child.

"I never realized, Emily." Hawk took a deep breath. "Why didn't you tell me?" He sat down in a chair close to hers and reached for her hand. She pulled it back and clasped her hands tightly.

"When? And what could you have done?" Emily rose from the chair, determined that her anger would not gain control. When he left her alone while he visited Andrew, she had made several resolutions. She reminded herself of them now and took several deep breaths. Certain she had herself under control again, she took her seat once more. "Hawk, this situation is not natural. Of course your family must wonder at it. Servants do talk, you know," she said as gently as she could. "By the end of their first day here, most of them knew something was wrong."

"Then why did Mama ask you?"

"Because she was hoping I would tell her it was all a mistake. She worries about us."

"I suppose my father knows too," Hawk said, his voice level and flat.

"Your mother and he share almost everything," she reminded him quietly, wishing the same could be said within her own marriage. Hawk got up and walked to the door. "What did he suggest?" Her question stopped him.

"That I sell out." He walked back to where she sat. "Emily, he said that I am letting the past keep me from going on with my life. You do understand why I feel the way I do, don't you?" He sat down again, his eyes on her downcast head.

"No, Anthony, I do not." He gasped, hurting as though he had been stabbed. "I know you are an honorable man who has been through a horrible experience. But by holding on to your commission, you are only punishing yourself and the ones who care about you. Do you plan to return to the Peninsula?"

The question was one he had been considering often. He shook his head.

"Then sell out. Let go of that part of your life."

"I cannot! It is not finished. As soon as I remember . . . ."

"And how long will that take? It has been months. And you still remember little. Will you remember more simply because you have the right to wear your uniform?"

Her words struck the right chord. Hawk sat up straighter. "No." The simple word struck Emily dumb. "Let me think about it, Emily." He stood up again and crossed to stand in front of her. He held out his hand. She took it and let him pull her to her feet. Only inches separated them. She looked up at him, her lips parted slightly. He bent and kissed her. Then he stepped back. "I promise you I will think about it."

As he walked out of the room, Emily put her hand to her lips. Had he looked back, Hawk would have seen the love that burned in her eyes. Instead he shut the door and was gone. Emily sank back in her chair, her face stormy. A word she had heard in the stables slipped from her lips. Even that was not enough. She picked up a pillow and threw it across the room, where it bounced harmlessly off a chair. Looking for something further to vent her frustration on, she picked up a small Meissen figure from the table beside her. She threw it across the room, where it hit the wall, shattering with a soul-satisfying sound. Then she too hurried from the room.

After everyone but Andrew had left, Hawk withdrew more and more from Emily and his brother, spending days on horseback, returning only to sit quietly at dinner, letting the conversation ebb around him. Andrew tried to interest him in cards or in talk, but Emily simply watched him, her eyes solemn. After a discussion with Emily, Andrew too left. "You will let me know if you decide to go to London," he said as he bade them good-bye. "I would much prefer to stay with you than in rented rooms."

"We will let you know," Hawk replied. He stood on the steps and watched his brother drive away. Then he turned and headed toward the stables.

Finally the day came when he appeared at the doorway of the morning room, where Emily supervised the running of the maner. "Are you busy, my dear?" he asked.

Emily looked up, startled. She smoothed the skirt of her gold merino nervously. She had dressed hastily that morning, certain she would be undisturbed. Both she and her maid had decided that the new dress was not a success, but Emily had refused to change it since she was to spend the morning inspecting the attics. But there had been a crisis in the kitchen that had taken the housekeeper away. Taking a quick look in the mirror that hung nearby, Emily decided to dispose of the dress as soon as Hawk disappeared. She looked haggard, and he glowed with good health. She looked at him again. There was something more, something that had been missing for a long time. "Not at the moment. Shall I ring for fresh tea?" She indicated the tea tray on the table beside her.

"Not for me." He stood near the doorway, not certain how to proceed. Had he been as hesitant in the army as he was with his wife, his men would have died in the very first skirmish.

She kept looking at him, waiting for him to make the first move. Since Andrew had left, Hawk had said very little. He had seemed happiest when he was silent. He shifted awkwardly from foot to foot. Finally, feeling sorry for him, she asked, "Is there something wrong?"

"Wrong? No." Hawk walked slowly into the room, looked around, and dragged a chair across the floor so that he could sit in front of her. "I have thought about what you and my father said," he said in a rush. He took a deep breath that stretched his already tight blue riding jacket almost to bursting.

"And?" Emily reached for her needlework to keep her hands from shaking. She took a stitch blindly and then glanced up at him, her hazel eyes clear, though troubled.

"I think you are right." She let out the breath she had been holding and took another stitch. "I will go to headquarters and sell out. When you asked me if I ever intended to return to the Peninsula, that was the turning point," he said quickly. "I knew immediately the answer was no. But it felt wrong. Men I had lived with were still dying there. Was it right for me to be safe?" He got up and began pacing around the room, his long legs in his high riding boots eating up the space. "Then I realized that was not the question at all. I began to wonder if my loss of memory was something I had done deliberately, to get me sent home."

"You sound as though you are accusing yourself of pretending not to remember," Emily said, surprised.

"I think I was." He took another turn around the room and then dropped into the seat across from her again. "It took me some time to realize that thinking of myself as a soldier made the problem worse instead of better. You have been very patient with me, Emily dearest."

She wanted to jump up and down and agree with him, but she merely sat there. She took a few more stitches in the chair cover.

"I am not saying that everything is resolved." Emily's hopes sank again. She forced herself to appear calm. "I may never regain my memory." He thought of the nightmares that plagued him regularly, now worse than before. "But I do not believe I will regain it here."

He is going to tell me he is leaving me again, Emily thought. She bent her head over her needlework and stabbed the needle savagely through the canvas. "What do you mean?" she asked quietly. Her voice was as calm as a light summer's breeze.

"I am going to follow my father's advice. Can you be ready to leave for London in a week?"

"London? Me? Why?"

"Emily, please say you will go with me. I know that it will be dull for you until the Season begins, but I want you there," Hawk said quietly. He picked up her hands and held them tightly. Sitting there waiting for her answer, he wondered how he would survive without her. It was agony to be around her, but as he had discovered when he had gone to visit Andrew, it was even worse to be apart. "Please, Emily."

She raised her head, her eyes wide and sparkling, ready to agree. Then she remembered Jonathan. Her eyes grew somber. "We promised my brother he could visit us when he returns," she reminded her husband. Since Andrew had asked about children, Emily had missed her young brother more and more. And because she did not trust her stepmother, she was determined that the boy would have someone more reliable than Mary Ann in charge of him. Even if Sir Horace hired a tutor to accompany him, there was the possibility the man would not stay when he discovered the working conditions.

"When will that be?" Hawk asked, realizing that the visit was important not only to the little boy but also to his wife. He squeezed her hands lightly and let them go.

"I do not know. Jonathan wrote thanking me for his gifts, but he did not mention his return. Apparently Sir Horace has kept him busy. He rides daily. He is as horse-mad as your brother." She laughed as she thought of the fearless way her brother had climbed onto his first pony. "He might be even worse," she admitted.

"What did you expect?" Hawk asked. "Andrew was one of his teachers. Before he was Jonathan's age, Andrew had put his ponies behind him and was riding Father's stallions. When I think of the risks he took . . ." He leaned back and laughed.

"And you were the perfect child? Always doing what you were told?" Emily's eyebrows went up, and her voice was amused and mocking. For the first time in weeks he seemed the man she had fallen in love with, laughing and lighthearted.

"No. Nor were you, my dear. Remember the time . . ." As one memory led to another, they laughed. The servants passing by the door stopped for a moment and then hurried on their ways, surprised yet pleased by the sound.

The laughter, though all too brief, had done much to relax the atmosphere between Hawk and Emily. "I know you do not want to disappoint your brother, Emily. How do you think we should proceed?" Hawk finally asked, coming back to the matter at hand.

"I could write to Sir Horace. Maybe he could persuade my stepmother to allow me to take Jonathan to London with us." Emily looked at Hawk, wondering if he would agree.

"We might as well have both of them." Emily raised an eyebrow. "My brother as well as yours," Hawk explained, his voice still full of laughter.

"Where will we be staying? With your parents?"

"No. Uncle George left me a house on Grosvenor Square. I leased it out when I was on the Peninsula, but I told my man of affairs to keep it available for us this Season. Oh, do not look at me that way, Emily. Even if we chose to stay here for most of the spring, I knew we would need new clothes. And I did not plan to have mine made anywhere but Weston." Nor did I intend to torture myself by remaining isolated here with you, he admitted to himself. The weeks of his honeymoon and of the time before he left to see Andrew were etched in his memory. Had he not left when he did, he would have crawled into bed with her and perhaps destroyed what little relationship they had left.

Reassured that Hawk never intended to abandon her while he indulged himself in the wiles of London, Emily began to plan. "Why do we need to leave next week, when the Season does not begin for weeks?" she asked, putting her needlework aside.

"I want to settle my status with the army." Hawk got up and walked around the room, too nervous to settle in one spot for very long now that his decision had been made. "Will that be a problem for you?"

"Yes. I hardly have time to write to Sir Horace and get a reply. Besides, we must make arrangements. Which servants shall we take with us? My aunt always arranged for meat, vegetables, and fruit to be sent to town as they became available. Shall you want me to do the same?" Confronted with running a large household in London on her own for the first time, Emily felt uncertain. "If you had only told me about this when your mother was here."

Hawk sat down across from her. He picked up her hands once again, holding them fast. "If next week is too soon, we can take longer. I am certain you can solve any problem that arises." He smiled at her, a rather whimsical look on his face. "Why not allow me to help?"

"You?"

"Oh, not with the food or packing. Talk to the housekeeper about those. I think I shall enlist Andrew's aid and pay a visit to Sir Horace." He leaned back in his chair, still holding her hands, forcing her to lean forward. He gave a slight tug, pulling her from her chair into his lap. "I shall have your brother here in a trice," he promised as he wrapped his arms around her and kissed her beneath the ear. Emily leaned back against him, too startled by his action to do more than sit there smiling.

Although they were not ready to leave in the week Hawk had requested, Emily was not to blame. Her arrangements had gone smoothly. The housekeeper, a meticulous woman, had notebooks filled with just the information Emily needed. Some orders did have to be changed, however, since they would not have a home farm at hand to provide them with staples. At first the house on Grosvenor Square was a problem, as no one knew its size, but a letter to Hawk's man of affairs gave them the information they needed. Choosing Clarke to head the establishment, they sent him and the additional servants to London. With orders to hire additional footmen and a chef, he was to prepare the house for their arrival. Emily watched their coaches roll away and turned to the housekeeper. "Are you certain you would prefer to stay here?" she asked.

The woman was quick with her reassurance. "Someone has to be in charge here and make certain the supplies are sent as they are available. Mrs. Hawksleigh always trusted my judgment in such matters, Mrs. Emily."

"And so shall I," her mistress assured her. "Remember you are to hire additional help here if you need it. Mr. Hawksleigh will speak to the bailiff as soon as he returns."

Five days after Hawk and Andrew were expected, they arrived escorting a very large traveling coach. Before the horses had come to a complete stop, the carriage door flew open, and Jonathan jumped out and into Emily's arms. He wrapped his arms about his sister's neck and allowed her to kiss him. A few minutes of affection were all he could tolerate, though. Soon he wiggled from her arms. "Come and see my new horse. I named him General. He is tied behind the carriage." He grabbed her hand and tugged at her.

"Before you show me your horse, sir, is there not someone else you must introduce?" Hawk asked, ruffling Jonathan's curls and indicating the man and girl who stood by the carriage.

Jonathan returned, slightly shamefaced. "I am sorry. Emily, this is Molly, who looks after me, and this is Mr. Yowell, who is my tutor." He reached up to pull his sister down so that he could whisper in her ear. "Mr. Yowell has been to Egypt and has seen the pyramids. This week he is going to tell me about them. And he has books I will be able to read soon."

Extending her greetings to the two newest members of the household, Emily looked at her husband. The look they exchanged told her there was a story to be told. Then

Jonathan was pulling her away from them, toward Andrew and the horses whose reins he was holding.

"Isn't he beautiful, Emily? Grandfather gave him to me. But without the saddle you and Hawk gave me I wouldn't have been able to ride him. Grandfather had forgotten I needed one. And Andrew gave me the bridle. He helped pick my horse out. Andrew knows more about horses than anyone in the world." The boy was jumping up and down in his excitement as he led Emily around the horse.

After greeting Andrew and making the inspection, she persuaded Jonathan that both his horse and he needed to rest. After seeing all of them were settled in their rooms, Emily returned to the study just in time to serve tea. "Tell me what happened," she demanded. "I was getting worried."

"You should have been," Andrew complained. "We had a terrible time persuading your stepmother to allow him to come. In fact, she called us back three times." Emily looked at her husband. He nodded.

"I was certain there was some problem. Were you not able to convince Sir Horace to help?"

"He was not as willing to let the boy come as he said he would be. He said he was going to miss him," Hawk explained. "If he and Mrs. Cheswick had not been embroiled in an argument, I am not certain either one would have agreed at all."

"What kind of an argument?" she asked.

"Lud, Emily, you should have heard them. Half the time they forgot anyone else was around and went at it hammer and tongs. Didn't they, Hawk?" Andrew pulled out his handkerchief and mopped his brow. Emily and Hawk looked at him in astonishment and burst out laughing. "I told you we should have gathered him up and simply escaped. Now look what I am doing." Andrew's tone was full of horror.

"She wanted him to open his house in London for the Season, but he refused. Something about her not having a companion." Hawk snapped his fingers impatiently. "For the first few days we were there, she refused to come out of her room."

"That did not seem to bother Sir Horace or Jonathan at all. You should have seen them together, Emily. Jonathan

does not try to play his grandfather the way he does you,"
Andrew said comfortingly.

"Or you, little brother. You should have seen the way
Andrew dotes on the child."

"He is a superb rider. It is a talent that needs to be
developed."

"Not at the expense of his lessons. You know what Sir
Horace said," Hawk reminded his brother sternly. On the
journey to the manor the two younger gentlemen had often
conspired against him.

"Do not keep me in suspense," Emily begged. "If Sir
Horace did not want him to go, and my stepmother stayed
in her rooms, how did you manage to persuade him to let
Jonathan visit?" She looked from one to the other
impatiently. Andrew looked away. Hawk shifted nervously.
"What did you have to do?"

"You did make me promise that I would not give up,"
her husband reminded her. She took a deep breath and
waited. "She and Sir Horace are spending the Season with
us," he said in a rush.

All the color slipped from Emily's face. "What did you
say?"

"It was the only way, Emily. We tried everything else,"
Andrew told her.

"It was this or no Jonathan," Hawk said at the same time.
"Sir Horace does not plan to stay all the time. He will make
quick forays into the city to see the lad and then leave."

"But you invited my stepmother to stay for the Season."
Emily stared at both of them, horror in every line of her face.
"In my home. For the Season."

"It may not be so bad, Emily. She is known to be hanging
out for another husband. Probably be too busy to bother you
at all," Andrew said soothingly. "Get her married off
straightaway and be done with her."

"And how do you expect me to do that?" She began to
laugh. "Me find her a husband." Hawk caught his brother's
eye and motioned him to leave. Andrew shrugged and walked
quickly from the room.

Hawk caught Emily by the arms and pulled her upright.
He gave her a shake. She swallowed a hysterical laugh and

looked up at him. "What has she done to you, my dear?"
Hawk asked, smoothing her hair back from her forehead with
one hand while he held her with the other.

Emily twisted away. "You would not understand."

"Tell me," he begged. But she only looked at him silently.
"Emily, I can do nothing to help you if you will not tell me
what is wrong."

"Now you understand."

"Understand what?"

"How I feel. You come home from war, catch me in your
arms, and declare we will marry instantly."

"I did not hear any protests from you when that
happened."

"We marry, and you ignore me, telling me it is for my
own good. Couldn't you come up with something more
original?" Emily looked at him, anger, fear, and pain written
on her face for him to see. "I love you, Anthony Hawksleigh." Tears began to run down her cheeks. He reached
for her, but she pulled away. "You asked me to understand
that you needed time. I have tried to give it to you. When
my stepmother arrives, however, we will have no more."
She used the back of her hand to dash away her tears. "You
know our servants know about our situation. How long will
it take for her maid to learn the gossip and repeat it to her
mistress? The story of your avoidance of me will be too
humiliating for her to ignore. It will be making the rounds
before she is in London a week." She walked to the door,
pulling herself together visibly. "I do thank you for bringing
me my brother," she said quietly. Then she lifted the latch
and walked from the room.

Her husband stood there looking after her. He had known
she would not like his solution, but he had known no other
way. At least she still loved him. And they had several weeks
before Mrs. Cheswick would arrive. Maybe in London . . .

8

Finishing the last-minute tasks before the move to London and spending time with her brother kept Emily busy for the next few days but not so busy she did not have time for some serious thought. Reviewing her reaction to Hawk's news, she had to admit she had behaved badly. But not as badly as she had wanted to. She had wanted to throw something at her husband, something large. Instead, like a ninny, she had given way to hysterics. Well, she did not intend to have that happen again.

Now that she had had time to consider the situation, she had to admit that he had done only what she had asked him to do: make certain her brother visited her. And he had ensured the visit was a long one. Although Hawk had been avoiding her for the last few days, Emily trapped him one morning as he was leaving the breakfast room. Dressed in her soft blue muslin, she used some of the wiles she had learned during her Seasons. She opened her eyes wide and looked up at him, her eyes sad. "May we talk?" she asked, her voice soft and quiet.

He nodded and led the way to his study, preferring to be on familiar ground if she planned to have another go at him. He seated her and then walked to the mantel. Leaning against it, he asked, "What is the problem?" He braced himself for the answer.

When it came, it was not what he expected. "Hawk, my dear, I am an ungrateful boor."

"What?"

"You go to all that trouble to arrange for Jonathan's visit and then have to deal with my ingratitude. I am so ashamed." Her head drooped over her hands, which she was clenching and unclenching. "It is so wonderful to have him here, to know that he is being taken care of properly." She glanced up at him, smiling. "That is worth any price."

"I hope you will remember that when your stepmother arrives," Hawk said dryly, not at all certain what to make of his wife. Since he had arrived home from Spain, her behavior had confused him. When they first fell in love, she was a laughing, irrepressible imp whose wry comments and spirited antics had amused him. Nothing or no one ever bothered her. Now he was not certain he knew the quiet, nervous lady he had married.

Emily rose and crossed the room toward him, a tiny frown on her face. "The thought is not exactly a pleasant one, I admit." He took a deep breath. "But with your help I think we can prevent her from spreading any harmful gossip."

He let his breath out noisily. "What will I have to do?" he asked warily. His wife hid her blushing face in her hands. "Emily, what have you planned?"

She leaned forward and rested her head on his chest. "You will have to be in my room when the chambermaid arrives in the mornings," she mumbled, wondering why she had ever thought the idea would work. He had avoided her since they were married. Why would he listen now? She stood there listening to the rapid beating of his heart, wishing he would say something.

He froze. Then his arms closed around her convulsively, pullling her ever closer. Her hair tickled his neck. He took a deep breath, enjoying the soft fragrance that always clung to her. She felt so wonderful in his arms, he never wanted to let her go. Then all thoughts of the warm, loving body against him faded. He dropped his arms and stepped back. "What did you say?"

Emily's face flamed again. She took one look at his astonished face and turned around. "Never mind. It was only a suggestion." She started to walk to the door, but Hawk reached out and grabbed her.

"You are not going anywhere, madam wife, until you repeat what you just said." He forced her to stop walking and turned her to face him. "Did you just ask me to share your bed?"

Wondering how she had dared conceive the plan, much less tell him about it, Emily looked at the floor, at his highly polished riding boots, at anything but him. "Yes," she whispered. Then she rushed on. "It was only a suggestion. I know you told me there were problems you needed to solve before our marriage becomes a real one, but you do not really have to sleep with me. You only need to visit me once in a while. You could wait until we go to London if you like." She peeked up at him, wishing he would say something.

A broad grin split his face. He reached out and pulled her to him. "Lud, imp, I have missed you," he said, trying to stifle his laughter. He kissed her soundly, lifting her so that her lips were on a level with his. "And I thought you had lost spirit." He kissed her again and put her on the floor safely away from him. It would be too easy to keep her close and destroy his carefully built control. Then he started to laugh again.

She stood there staring at him as though he had lost his mind as the laughter continued to pour from him. She tapped her foot angrily, waiting for his mirth to subside. When he sat down weakly, holding his sides, she said sternly, "It was not that funny. If you did not like the idea, all you had to do was say no."

"Not like the idea?" He was off again. "Oh, I can't breathe," he moaned finally, taking in great gulps of air. "I have not laughed so much in a long time."

His wife waited for him to gain control of himself, noting that the harsh lines on his face had almost disappeared. He looked more like the young officer who had captured her heart years ago. No matter how glad she was to see him relax, she still was waiting for her answer. "Will you agree to my idea?"

Hawk took several more deep, calming breaths. Relax, he told himself, relax. The thought of going into her bedchamber, watching her crawl into bed, crawling into bed with her, began to cause a reaction within him. What would it be like when he was actually there? What would it hurt if he actually made love to her? And if you go to sleep and dream? he silently asked himself. The sight of his handprints on his brother's neck had been enough to convince him that he had to leave her alone until he had more answers. Their memory now made him somber again.

"If you do not like the idea, you could at least tell me," she said. She walked toward the door, her skirt swinging furiously. "I do not understand you anymore."

"Emily, wait." Hawk rose from the chair and walked over to her. She refused to turn around, preferring to stare at the door instead. He stared at the back of her neck, wishing he could trust himself to kiss it and then let her go. He gave himself a mental shake, straightened his shoulders, and said, "I canot say your plan is one I would have chosen." Her shoulders began to droop. "But I will give it a chance."

Her shoulders straightened. She swung around, almost hitting him on the chin. He stepped back hastily. "You will not be sorry, Hawk. I know this will work."

"Emily, you sound like you did when you were a child trying to persuade us to do something you knew your family would disapprove of." He grinned briefly. Then his face grew serious again. "My problems are not the stuff of childhood. Pretense will not make them go away. I will try what you ask for a time, but do not ask more of me than I can give."

The euphoria of his acceptance faded quickly. Once more Emily was the serious lady he had found when he returned from war. "I will try not to." She turned and opened the door. Then she stopped and looked back at him. "But I can be pushed too far too. Let us hope we find some answers before it is too late for both of us." Even after the door shut behind her, her words echoed in Hawk's ears and heart.

When another letter arrived from his father that afternoon, Hawk decided to leave for London immediately. Dragging Andrew protesting along with him, he left for the capital the next morning. The tone of his father's letters had grown increasingly grim of late. And the last one had held a note from Perceval himself asking for his aid. More than once, Hawk wondered what the line "We need someone with your special expertise" meant.

Leaving Lester behind to oversee Emily's journey, he said good-bye to his wife and Jonathan. "You are not to leave until you think Jonathan has recovered from his last journey," he said quietly. "Since Clarke is already in London, you can be certain we will be in good hands. Do not worry about us."

Naturally, his comments caused his wife to think of every disaster imaginable. And when she walked into the front hall just in time to catch Jonathan sliding down the banister, she was packed and ready to leave by morning. Before dawn, the coaches with the rest of the luggage left. Traveling with them were Lester and Jonathan's nursery maid and tutor. Some hours later Emily, Jonathan, and Mary climbed into the great traveling coach. The grooms leading the riding horses accompanied them for a time, but because the men had orders to rest the stock often, they were soon left behind.

Four days later they arrived in London. After the journey, Emily longed for some peace and quiet, some time to herself. Days of her little brother's chatter, especially on the subject of his mother and her running feud with Sir Horace, had made her long to be deaf. Emily knew every suitor her step-mother had received; in fact, she would have been able to recognize them from her brother's specific, sometimes wicked comments. Had she not realized that Jonathan was merely repeating the comments he had head his grandfather make, Emily would have been worried. When Jonathan began, "And, Emily . . ." she had learned simply to listen, nodding her head every once in a while and assuming an interested look. The first day she had listened attentively, but only the news that her stepmother was expecting an offer at almost any time excited any of her interest. "But Grand-father told her not to be a ninny, Emily. Isn't that funny, Grandfather calling Mama a ninny?" She had nodded her head. "She thinks she can catch a marquess, but Grandfather told her to get her head out of the clouds. Emily, there were clouds that day, but Mama was not in them. Is that one of those things that grown-ups say that I'll have to wait to under-stand?" She nodded again. "And, Emily, did I tell you about the cat and kittens?"

As she exited the carriage, Emily resolved to give the nursery maid and tutor a bonus. She stood still for a moment, savoring the feel of firm land beneath her feet instead of the jolting of the coach. She entered the house, pausing to say a few words to Clarke. Sending Jonathan off to the nursery, she looked about her, noting the general drabness of the house, and then met her staff. Speaking to each one individually, she renewed her acquaintance or greeted the new ones. With a final word to Clarke, she left, walking slowly up to her room.

Mary, knowing that her mistress had chosen to drive straight through that day instead of stopping for longer than a change of horses, had a tea tray waiting. Sinking onto the bed, a monstrosity that dominated the bedchamber, she closed her eyes, not even opening them when she heard a door open.

"Clarke said my wife had arrived," a deep voice said quietly.

"She is sleeping, sir," Mary stammered, surprised to see Mr. Hawksleigh in his wife's room.

"I will see her at dinner. Remind her we keep city hours now."

"Hawk, wait!" Emily sat up in bed, or at least tried to. The feather bed and coverlet engulfed her as she tried to pull herself up.

Her husband walked over to the very wide, long bed and peered under the massive bed curtains. "Is that you, Emily?" he asked, watching hands, arms, and a well-shaped leg flail about. He laughed at her efforts for a minute and then put out a hand. "The last tenants must have insisted on soft beds."

"Soft is one thing. Impossible is another," Emily sputtered as she slid free. "Mary, tell the housekeeper to find me a better mattress. If there is none available, I will sleep on a camp bed until she prepares one." Her heart was racing. She took another look at her handsome husband, his dark hair and eyes glinting with laughter, and knew that her reaction had little to do with her entanglement in the bed and much to do with the dark-eyed gentleman in the corbeau coat. His snowy cravat tied in the Waterfall provided a contrast to his tan.

"For a minute there, Emily, I thought you were lost," Hawk said, a mischievous light in his eyes.

"You could have warned me, Anthony Hawksleigh. That bed could house an army or two. Who slept in there, a giant?'' She had been so tired when she first entered the room that she had not taken a good look at the bed. It was unusually low to the floor, and she had not needed a step to get into it; the bedposts rose ten feet in the air and, like the head and foot, were heavily carved. It was a full six feet wide and much longer than other beds. The curtains and draperies were of red velet that had begun to show signs of wear. Emily backed away from the bed as decorously as she could, taking deep breaths that gave her a chance to gain control of her emotions. They also gave her husband an excellent chance to gaze at her heaving bosom.

"And how was I supposed to know about this? The house was leased when Uncle George died. I had rooms that I kept until I left for Spain. Do not blame me for this misfortune,'' he said piously. He watched as she glared at him. Then she sat down on a stool and let her maid straighten her hair. "How was your journey?"

"Tolerable. But I do not recommend traveling with a six-year-old,'' she said, glancing at his reflection in the mirror. He was sitting in a chair nearby, very much at his ease. Emily reached for a bottle of scent and then put it back down quickly, her hand shaking badly. She glanced at him again, resentful because he seemed so casual about visiting her.

"You forget I have had that pleasure. I kept him occupied by having him ride with me. Does he ever stop talking?"

"Not often. Perhaps we should encourage him to think about a career in politics,'' Emily suggested, a tiny smile lighting her face.

"Too bad he was born a gentleman. Lud, Emily, that boy can imitate his grandfather and his mother perfectly. He would make a marvelous actor. Did he tell you—?

"More than I ever wanted to know,''she said hastily, glancing at her maid. Mary had been a captive audience in the carriage, but Emily was not certain she wanted her to be a party to the conversation between husband and wife. Nodding her satisfaction with the hair arrangement, she dismissed the maid. Then she turned around to face her husband. "Do you think Lucretia has a chance to capture her marquess?''

"If she does, that may relieve you of her presence,'' Hawk

said. He smiled at her, wishing he could pull her onto the bed and make love to her until she was as pink all over as her face was now.

"I doubt that. She has said she plans to come for the Season. She will come," his wife said despondently. She looked down at her hands and then up at him again, wishing she knew what to say. "How are your parents?"

"Well. They have asked us to dinner tomorrow evening if you have no other plans." Hawk got up and took a turn around the room, restless now that the maid was gone and they were alone.

"I hope you told them we accept."

"Tentatively. I will see Father tomorrow morning, or you could send Mama a note." He crossed to the door that opened into his own room. He opened it and stood there for a moment. "I am happy that you are here, my dear." He smiled at her and walked into his own room, closing the door behind him.

Emily glared at the closed door for a time. "Men!" she muttered angrily. A scratching at the door brought her out of her reverie. "Come in," she called.

Mary crept quietly into the room, her eyes darting around as if searching out spies. "The housekeeper says she will have a new mattress ready by tomorrow afternoon, Mrs. Emily. She regrets that the late hour makes it impossible to finish today." Mary stumbled over the words as if she had memorized them. Her eyes kept straying to the door that connected her mistress's room with that of the master. "If it is convenient, she would like to have the ropes restrung as well." Emily nodded, her mind still intent on her husband. "If it pleases you, she will prepare another room, or there is a bed in the dressing room."

"That will do," her mistress said absently. The maid smiled and hurried out, carrying a dress to press for that evening. If she hurried, she could catch Lester before he had to help the master dress for dinner.

With Andrew, Jonathan, and the boy's tutor to plan for, Emily kept busy; she had little time to sit and ponder the significance of her husband's actions. Alone on the bed in the dressing room, she did lie awake for a long time wondering what would have happened had she been alone in the room when Hawk had found her.

Rising early the next morning, Emily quickly and skillfully saw the gentlemen off: Hawk to the Exchequer to confer with his father, Andrew to Tattersall's to track down a horse he had heard about the previous afternoon, and Jonathan, protesting loudly, off to his lessons. She dashed off a note to her aunt, Lady Mairmount, to let her know she had arrived. After the strained relationship the last few years, because she had refused her aunt's offer of a home, it was wonderful to have her aunt willing to acknowledge her again. At the wedding she had been almost effusive. Although it was too early for her aunt to be in London, Emily looked forward to seeing her soon.

Then Emily began the real business of the morning, a thorough inspection of the house. Starting with the kitchens, she noted the general shabbiness of the furnishings. And the sight of the attics where the servants had their rooms appalled her. "Hire as many men as possible, Mrs. Henderson," she told the housekeeper. "And order new linens and blankets immediately. My goodness, did no one care that the furniture up there is broken and rickety? We will visit the furniture warehouses this afternoon. Three to a bed may be acceptable in some houses, but not in mine. How those girls have been able to get any work done after sleeping in conditions like that, I will never know. I want everything in the attics repainted. Something light and bright, I think." Emily whirled and headed down the narrow stairs to the third floor.

"But, Mrs. Hawksleigh, those colors are so impractical. They get dirty so easily," the housekeeper protested.

"Then we will whitewash or repaint more often. Are the nursery and schoolrooms as bad?" she asked as she swept into the room where her brother was bent over a table doing his sums.

"Emily, I am almost finished with my lessons. Will you take me for a walk? Or can we go for a ride in the park?" Jonathan asked, his eyes bright and eager.

His sister brushed a lock of hair out of his eyes and laughed. "Later, brat." His face fell. "You may come down to luncheon. Perhaps by then I will have finished my plans for the house and will be free to amuse you," his sister said gently. "How do you like your rooms?"

"They are better than home, but not as nice as at Grandfather's," he said honestly. "I do not like my bed. But there is a chest of soldiers I may play with when I finish my lessons."

"Jonathan," Mr. Yowell, his tutor, stammered, "such comments are not at all the thing."

"Emily asked me," the boy protested, looking to see if his sister was upset with him.

"And so I did." She smiled at him and rumpled his hair. "Would you care to accompany me to a furniture warehouse to pick out your own bed?" she asked. He bounced up and down, nodding vigorously. "Then finish your lessons." He bent his head over the paper again, a tiny edge of tongue caught between his teeth revealing his determination. Emily walked through the rest of the rooms, her face somber.

When the tour was over sometime later, she sat down in a small salon and motioned the housekeeper to sit opposite her. "Has no one made any repairs since my husband's uncle died?" she asked.

"When I came to work here, everything was much the same as you see it today. Captain Hawksleigh was in Spain, the tenants did not have the money to refurbish, and the captain's man of business would not release any money without his master's express orders. There was little I could do," the housekeeper said hurriedly, wondering if she were soon to be looking for a job.

Her recent redecorating experience at the manor gave Emily confidence. She stood up. "Those days are in the past. With the Season almost upon us, we must not delay another day. Start measuring. Send for the painters. When the Season begins, I want this house to sparkle."

That determination kept everyone in the house on the go from morning to night for the next two weeks. Andrew, claiming that the smell of paint was giving him the headache, retreated to his parents' estate. "Send me word when you are finished, Emily," he said, pressing a hand dramatically across his forehead. "My delicate constitution cannot stand the strain." He flashed her a grin.

"You mean you do not like to have your rest disturbed early in the morning," Emily said. She smiled at him, willing to let him escape. "You will return when we are finished, I suppose?"

"If you have not painted my room yellow. Promise me, Emily. No yellow," he said, laughing as he ran down the stairs.

"No yellow," she repeated. She waved to him and turned back to the job at hand.

Even the servants began to avoid their mistress, slipping down the back staircases to avoid her. Emily had been in the linen closet inspecting the tablecloths one day when two maids stopped outside the door. "Coo, I don't know as how this is worth it," the first one muttered.

"But everything's so clean and pretty."

"What good is pretty when you're too tired to look at it? I fall in bed and go right to sleep, I do. Don't even notice the little 'un's snoring, I don't. When you think she'll be through?" Just then Clarke walked up, and the girls scuttled off.

Emily opened the door, a rueful look on her face. Clarke held the door for her, his face impassive. "As soon as the renovations are complete, Clarke, arrange for everyone to have an extra half-day," she said quietly. He nodded majestically. Rubbing the back of her neck, she walked up the stairs to her own rooms, conscious that she too had only to look at the bed and she would fall asleep.

Only Jonathan and Hawk were oblivious of the changes going on around them. Jonathan found life in London almost entirely to his liking. Had he been able to escape his lessons, he would have been happier. But when he finished his lessons, Emily gave him the freedom of the house. He followed the painters about, asking them questions and offering to help until Emily rescued them. Next, he decided to learn to hang wall coverings, covering himself with paste and fabric. His sister had to order a dozen yards of fabric to replace the ones he accidentally spilled the paste on. And when he went to the kitchen to watch them installing the new stove, he was so covered in soot that the chimney sweep took him for his apprentice and almost had him out the door.

Finally Emily took pity on her workmen. She ordered the carriage, and she and Jonathan set off. "But they were going to begin to plaster today, Emily," he protested. "I want to see how they make the ceilings."

"We have two more rooms to plan, little brother. And these are ones I must have your help on," she explained.

"Whose? Andrew's is finished. So is mine. And you have forbidden me to enter yours. That leaves only the guest bed-rooms. Those are not very important," he grumbled. After the years of being alone with his sister, Jonathan loved being around people. "The workmen were going to bring their little brother this time. He is already helping them with their business."

"As you are helping me." Jonathan looked at her, his face revealing that he was not at all convinced. "You know your mama and grandfather are coming for a visit soon." He nodded. "Well, I want to surprise them. You are going to help choose the colors and fabrics for their rooms." Emily smiled. Taking a deep breath, she led him into a fabric warehouse.

"I may choose anything I think they will like?" he asked, pleased with her suggestion. "Just like I got to choose my new bed?" She nodded. He narrowed his eyes solemnly.

Watching him pore over the swatches of fabric, she smiled as he looked carefully at each new sample, putting some to one side before going on. When she had told the owner of the warehouse what she intended, he had been aghast; then, throwing up his hands, he had let her have her way. Now he stood by in amazement as the small boy deliberated over the pieces he had put aside.

"This for Grandfather's room," Jonathan said after he had stared at three pieces for several minutes. The fabric he held out was a figured damask in a rich jade. "I saw a horse this color in a shop last week. Grandfather would like it, Emily. Perhaps tomorrow we could buy it for him," Jonathan suggested, his tone very serious. She nodded, knowing the jade horse he meant. "For Mama . . ." He held out a scrap of fabric in an unusual color. "Like peach preserves." He looked up at his sister, his eyes big. "Did I do well, Emily? Do you think they will like them? Grandfather will, I know.

He likes everything I do. But do you think Mama will like the fabric I picked?''

"You have wonderful taste, little brother," Emily said, astounded at the choices he had made. "She will be delighted." And if she is not, she had better not say one word to hurt you, she added to herself.

"Most amazing," the merchant murmured, adding up the order in his head. "Are the draperies to match?" Emily nodded.

Jonathan had his head tilted to one side, looking at the fabrics he had chosen. "The cushions in Grandfather's room should be gold," he said firmly. "And ivory in Mama's. Now, can we go, Emily? You promised me a ride in the park. And we can stop at Gunter's for ices?" He was pulling at her hand impatiently as she made her last arrangements with the merchant.

"The fabric will be delivered immediately," he promised, bowing them out of the shop. When the door closed behind them, he turned to his assistant and said, "Quality. Imagine letting a child decorate rooms. But I must admit the child had better taste than many adults." His assistant nodded and hurried to fill the order.

As they climbed into their waiting coach, Emily pulled her cloak firmly about her and wrapped Jonathan's muffler around his neck more closely. "No ices on a day like today." His face fell. "But hot chocolate would be very nice. Shall we stop on the way home?"

9

While Emily and Jonathan scoured the town for fabric and furnishings, Hawk sold out. When the last paper was signed, he reported to the Exchequer. There he found his father pacing the floor in frustration. The latest shipment to pay the troops had not reached the Peninsula.

"Has this happened often?" Hawk asked.

"Several times. Oh, not the whole payroll. After the first robbery we learned to deliver it in segments. But Parliament will discover the losses soon, and then we will be forced to fight on two fronts. We have to fight for all money we send to Wellesley as it is now."

"If some of the House of Lords had their way, we would not even be in Spain. Do you think they are behind it?"

"No. They may be pigheaded and blind, but they are loyal Englishmen," his father said with a disgusted tone. He sat down at his desk, picked up a pen, and began to sharpen it. "The robberies confuse me. A large shipment goes through, yet another smaller one is picked off. I simply do not understand." He looked at the sharpened pen and put it down. "I told the prime minster that you had some experience in the field dealing with spies and that you would look around."

"Father! What do you expect me to do? I told you I was just a courier. I know nothing of spies," Hawk protested. "I may have met a few on the Peninsula, but that does not make me one. Besides, won't people be suspicious when I suddenly show up here? How am I to behave? If I were the thief, I would wonder why a person who had been serving with Wellesley had suddenly joined his father at the Exchequer."

"Look around as you walk through here. Positons at the Exchequer, as in any government department, are the result of whom you know. No one is going to think anything but that I brought you in to work with me."

"And when I start asking questions?"

"Wait awhile. Look around first. Get to know people. I will assign you some valid work to do; while you are doing that, you can keep your eyes open." His father leaned forward across the desk. "At no time must people suspect that you are doing anything more. We have managed to bury the situation now. If it comes to light, we will have a scandal on our hands. And if the Opposition were to find out everything, we might lose control of the government."

Hawk inhaled and then let his breath out slowly. "You are putting a heavy burden on me. The Opposition would pull support from Wellesley in an instant if they thought the people would stand for it." He paused and looked at his father, a peculiar expression on his face. "But didn't you say the House was complaining about money already?"

"We have managed to cover the losses with other appropriations. But that cannot go on for long. We have to find out who is at the root of this problem, and if it is simply thievery, catch them. If it is the French, we need to find out who is supplying the information." Mr. Hawksleigh stood up. He walked around the desk until he was in front of his son. "Asking you to look into this problem may not be fair after what you have gone through, are going through still, son. If there were anyone else, anyone we trusted, I would not suggest it." He sighed.

"Does the prime minister know what happened to me in Spain?"

"Yes. I have given him my personal assurances that you did not compromise our operations there."

"Father! How do you know that? Even I do not know what happened." Hawk jumped out of his chair, forcing his father to move back. He paced around the office like a hurricane building strength.

"Son, I trust you. You would never do anything to harm your country," his father said quietly.

Hawk closed his eyes for a moment, remembering the

realities of war. How could he explain what happened to men caught up in those situations? What changes occurred? He looked at his father again, noting the pride and loyalty on the older man's face. "Where have you lost shipments?" he asked. His voice was a dull monotone.

"On the way to a port. And, no, the shipments have not always taken the same routes." Quickly, succinctly, Mr. Hawksleigh gave his son the information he needed.

Over the next two weeks, Hawk followed his father's advice, getting to know people, learning who would have had access to the information, gathering information in bits and pieces. Like any government office, it was a breeding ground for gossip. Slowly he began to amass facts.

In the weeks before the Season began, Hawk spent his evenings at his club unless Emily needed him as an escort. With the town still empty of all but the people involved in government and those few souls determined to get a head start with the modistes and tailors, their engagements were very few. Occasionally they would have dinner with his parents, but most evenings Emily worked on the designs for the house. Unable to join his brother at his parents' and escape the confusion, Hawk chose to take some of his meals at his club with Andrew.

He and Andrew were playing cards after sharing a bird and a bottle late one evening at the end of February when one of the gentlemen at the table asked, "Anyone like to make a wager when the men in Spain will get their next rations?"

"Why?" Hawk asked sharply, afraid of the answer.

"Heard today the Exchequer refused to pay the supplier. Accused them of using shoddy goods and sent the stuff back to them. The troops are liable to be on short rations for some time. I say it will take at least four months before another shipment leaves port. What do you gentlemen think?" Calling for the betting book, they entered their wagers. Hawk shook his head when the book came around to him. Andrew, looking first at his brother, did the same.

"Forgot you had just returned, old man," the gentleman who had begun the betting apologized. "Hope you're not offended."

Hawk looked at the young man, once impeccably dressed but now disheveled. A bottle of wine, now empty, stood at his elbow. Hawk shook his head, and the slight tension around the table disappeared. For the rest of the evening, however, Hawk would look up and find his brother watching him as if Andrew were not certain what to think of him.

The next morning Hawk walked into his father's office, casually waving away the clerk who was trying to intercept him. "Father, how many people knew about . . . ?" he began. Then he stopped. "I'm sorry to interrupt. I will return later."

"No. Please stay. We were just discussing you, Mr. Hawksleigh," the prime minister said quietly. Quickly Hawk took the chair Lord Perceval indicated. "What was it you wanted to know?"

Hawk looked from the prime minster to his father. He straightened his shoulders and asked, "How many people knew of our decision not to accept the latest shipment of supplies for the Peninsula?"

"In our office, about three gentlemen. At the suppliers' office, I am not certain," his father said. "Why?"

Hawk got up and began to pace. "The suppliers certainly would not want their name mentioned, not without being deluged by their creditors. Of course, if they were angry, they might be striking back. The leak could have come from them."

"What leak?" the prime minister asked, his face stern and hard.

"At my club last night men were betting on how long it would take us to supply Wellesley's troops now that we had rejected the latest shipment as shoddy."

"And the most popular bet?" the prime minister asked, his voice cool.

"Two months." The older men exchanged worried looks, their eyebrows raised. "What does that mean?"

"That someone has inside information. Very few people knew the terms of the new contract," his father told him. "And I doubt whether the suppliers would release it. Their representative was as appalled as we were over the quality of the goods."

"Give him a list of names," Perceval said quietly. "Let him look around. No, do not say them aloud. Write them down and let him memorize them. No need to give the tattlemongers any more fodder if we can help it. The names on that list are all good men."

Hawk took the list from his father and read it quickly. His eyebrows rose, and he had to agree with the prime minster. It was unlikely that any of them would betray his office. But someone had. As soon as he had the names in mind, he made his bow and left.

As soon as the door closed behind him, the prime minister said, "You were right to suggest we use him, Hawksleigh. This could be just what we are looking for. Now, before my staff sends for me, what about that other information? As riddled as this place is with ears, my office is worse."

That day Hawk finished the report his father had given him to cover his other activities. Turning it over to his clerk to copy, he walked out, intending to visit the gentlemen on the list his father had given him. He had taken twenty paces down the hall when he stopped and returned. The clerks; he had forgotten the clerks.

"Did you leave something behind, sir?" his clerk asked. Hawk shook his head. He walked slowly back into his office. Pulling out a sheet of paper, sharpening his pen, and dipping it in the nearby inkwell, quickly he jotted down ideas, made estimates. He sat back and smiled. Then he hurried from his office for the second time. This time his steps were decisive, his shoulders straight. He walked into his father's office and asked, "Is he in and alone?"

"Yes, sir."

Almost before the last word was out of the clerk's mouth, Hawk was through the door. "I think I have an idea about how the information on the supplies got out," he said. "Look at this. Almost every document here is copied by a clerk."

"And you think it could be one of them?"

"Yes, and it should be easy to test. Call your men in here. Do it separately. Have them prepare a document to be sent out. If the information surfaces, we will know I am right."

"But that will not tell us who the culprit is."

"Give them each different fake documents. Then make

certain each man is in the prime minister's or your sight until late that evening. You can think of some excuse that will work. Do all these men know about the loss of the payroll shipments too?"

"No! This is a totally different problem. Besides, these men are the most loyal that England has," his father said emphatically.

"I hope you are right. Think about it. Then let me know what you have decided. As you said earlier, we cannot wait long," Hawk reminded him, wishing he had never agreed to take on this assignment. "I will start on the plans."

His face stern, the older Hawksleigh watched his son walk toward the door. "I will speak to the prime minster," he said quietly. "If he agrees, we will begin the next day. If you are wrong . . ."

"Then I will begin again." Hawk walked through the door and shut it firmly behind him. The clerk looked up, startled, and then bent his head over his work, glad that he was not the one who had put that look on the gentleman's face.

Knowing that he could go no further that day, Hawk went home ready to put his dislike of confusion behind him and to keep his wife company. Unwilling to admit that he had missed his daily conversations with Emily, he blamed his need to return to his home on his dislike of the gossip in the clubs.

Although Emily had been busy, she had missed Hawk. Rather than accept his abandonment as evidence of the accuracy of her stepmother's view of herself, she was at first resentful. The more time she had to herself, the more resentment grew. By the time Hawk arrived home for a simple dinner that evening, Emily's anger had built like lava just before the eruption of a volcano. But on the outside, she was as peaceful as Vesuvius before the destruction of Pompeii.

"Tell Cook I will be at home for dinner," Hawk said as he walked past his butler. "And have someone take this to my brother." He held out a note crying off from that evening's pleasure-seeking. "Where is my wife?"

"She and the housekeeper were discussing new china and glassware. I believe they were in the dining room. Shall I tell her you are looking for her?" Clarke stood impassively, but privately he wondered at the master's set face. In the last weeks, the lady of the house had spent vast sums of money; new furnishings arrived every day, keeping everyone busy unpacking and sorting. Although the butler knew the family was wealthy, he wondered if his master's pockets were to let. Spending hours at the gentlemen's clubs usually meant that someone, usually the servants and the family, had to pay.

"Do not interrupt her now, but if you see her later, tell her I will be in my rooms." Hawk noticed a peculiar look cross the butler's face. "What is the problem? I thought the painters had finished in there."

"The mistress had me put the seamstress in there. They are finishing the draperies and hangings."

"I will take care of them," Hawk said firmly, his face a mask of displeasure. "Send Lester up to me." He ran up a few steps and stopped. "Tell him I want a bath," he said, the words chopped off crisply. A purposeful look on his face, Hawk turned and hurried up the stairs.

Sometime later Hawk was sitting in a large copper bathtub, his head tilted back on the rim. The tensions of the last few days slipped away from him as he lay back in the steaming water. He closed his eyes, totally relaxed and almost asleep.

The door that connected Emily's room to his flew open. Hawk opened his eyes and sat up. His wife was advancing on him, her eyes blazing. "How dare you dismiss those seamstresses!" she said angrily. "It will be almost impossible to finish the house before the Season now, and you wasted at least three hours of valuable working time by sending them home."

"You wanted me to let them watch me bathe?" he asked. His face was serious, but his eyes twinkled merrily.

"Watch you bathe?" Emily repeated. Her eyes widened. "Oh!" She whirled around, her eyes fixed firmly on the door to her bedroom. Her face flamed with color. "I will talk to you later," she mumbled, and took a step toward the door. She wanted to turn around, to look at that broad chest covered with dark hair, to reach out and rub her hand down his chest, to . . . her blush deepened. She stumbled on a rolled carpet and fell.

Behind her she heard a rush of water. "Emily, are you

all right?'' her husband asked, grabbing a towel and rushing to her side. He took her arm to help her up.

From the corner of her eye Emily could see his bare feet and legs covered with dark hair. She resisted the urge to look up, at the same time her emotions were urging her not to resist temptation. She allowed him to lift her up, her face carefully averted. When she was on her feet again, she tried to slip away from him, but he held her tight. "Let me go," she said, her voice so shaky she could hardly recognize it as her own.

"Not until I know you did not hurt yourself. Can you walk?'' he asked, finally letting her go so that she could take a step or two. She sidled toward the door. Before she could reach it, he took her arm again. Her eyes grew dark with a mixture of fear and excitement. "I refuse to allow you to escape. I have seen you so seldom lately," he whispered as he held her arm gently.

"Whose fault is that?" she asked angrily. She looked up, her eyes sparkling. "You have spent more time at your clubs than at home for the last week." She noted with disappointment that he had wrapped his towel around his waist sometime after he got out of the tub. She kept her eyes carefully away from his broad chest.

"What did you expect? I have been afraid to step inside this room without an advance guard."

"Do you dislike it so much?" she asked wistfully.

"No." Hawk looked at the natural silk wall coverings printed with a Chinese design in a clear blue. "I am glad to be rid of the painters and plasterers," he added quickly, "but I like the room much better now. And the mattress is a big improvement. When will this house be completely finished?"

"If you had left the seamstresses working, perhaps tomorrow. Just look at that." Emily pointed at the heap of fabric lying on a sheet in a corner. "You sent them away so quickly they did not even have time to fold up the material. Do you know how wrinkled that will be in the morning?" She put her hands on her hips and tapped her foot.

"Aha. Now you sound like I have always imagined a wife would sound, forever complaining about something her nusband has done," he said with a laugh that caused his towel to slip down his hips.

Before she could answer him, the door opened, and Lester walked in, followed by one of the footmen with fresh hot water. Emily thought she would faint from embarrassment for a moment. Then she rushed from the room.

"I am so sorry, sir. Had I known . . ." Lester said apologetically. "But . . ."

"Next time, wait until I give you leave to come in," Hawk said dryly, looking at the door through which Emily had just gone. He turned back to the tub. "Pour that hot water in. I will be late for dinner if I do not hurry." Realizing how lucky they were to be getting off so lightly, Lester and the footman exchanged glances. In a few minutes Hawk was back in the tub. The footman, the cans of water empty, hurried down the back stairs, eager to share his news with the rest of the household.

When Hawk entered the salon later that evening, Emily was already there. The room, refurbished in white and gold, was a striking background for her pomona-green silk dress with green-and-gold netting over the skirt. Her new corset, a fashion once scorned but recently reintroduced, held her back straight and pushed her bosom upward. Her first thought when she put the dress on that evening had been to change it. But her maid had convinced her that it was unexceptionable. When Hawk entered and bowed, Emily knew the dress was a success. He could not keep his eyes off her.

"The room feels rather cool to me," Hawk said quietly. "Shall I sent for your shawl?" He eyed her neckline carefully, remembering the footmen that would serve their meal.

"I have one here," she told him, throwing a light film of green-and-gold netting over her shoulders. The shawl simply accented the soft creamy contours of her breasts rather than hid them.

Hawk groaned so softly Emily did not hear him. "Have you finished your shopping for the Season?" he asked, more to have something to say that anything else. He did hope she had not purchased many more dresses as low-cut as the one she had on.

"Madame Camille is finishing the last this week. She is

amazing. But you do not want to hear about my clothes,''
Emily said, stopping herself before she could gush on about
the beautiful fabrics and designs she had chosen.

Before he could stop himself, Hawk asked, ''Do they all
have necklines like that one?''

Emily immediately bristled. ''Is there something wrong
with this?'' she asked haughtily.

''No, no. It's lovely.'' It was a beautiful dress, and Emily
looked as lovely as she had the night of the ball when he
first realized that she was more than just the little girl who
lived on an estate near his family's home. He simply wished
it did not show so much of his wife. The person who had
decreed that married women could dress more provocatively
than young ladies being presented to the *ton* must not have
cared about his wife. The next few minutes were awkward
ones as Hawk ran his fingers around the top of his crisp
neckcloth, disarranging its carefully arranged folds. He
cleared his throat nervously, wishing not for the first time
that they were still just engaged and his mother were still
playing chaperone.

Emily looked up at him, reddened, and looked down
quickly. The perfectly fitting black coat and breeches molded
his body so closely that she immediately remembered the
way he looked sitting there in that tub, standing there in the
towel. To cover her embarrassment she asked, ''To what
do I owe the honor of your presence? We have no obligations
this evening.''

''Blast it, Emily. Isn't it possible that I might want a quiet
evening at home for a change?'' Hawk said blusteringly.

''If so, you are a different person from the man who told
me he was too busy to see me when I wanted to discuss the
plans I had made for the house,'' she retorted, forgetting
for a moment her determination to avoid looking at him.

''You had everything under control. After seeing our suite
at the manor, I knew I could leave everything to you.''

''You simply did not want to get involved. What would
it have hurt if you had stayed home and told me what colors
you wanted me to use?''

''Father needed me,'' he said defensively. He looked at
Emily, sitting primly on the gold settee, and wondering why

he had been avoiding her. "Besides, your judgment is much better than mine," he added, smiling at her coaxingly.

Unable to resist that heartwarming look, Emily returned his smile. The silence in the room grew as they gazed into each other's eyes. Hawk took a step toward her. "Dinner is served," Clarke said as he opened the door. Both Emily and Hawk stepped back from each other, only the looks in their eyes giving away their yearning. Emily laid her hand upon Hawk's arm so that he could escort her in to dinner. It was only with great effort and his knowledge that the servants already had a wealth of gossip about them that evening that made Hawk keep his control instead of sweeping her into his arms and up the stairs.

During dinner they exchanged pregnant glances. At first Emily would drop her eyes shyly when she caught him staring at her. By the end of the meal, neither could remember what had been served. Eyes locked on the other, each went through the motions of the meal. When Clarke brought the port to the table, Emily rose. Hawk left his seat, following her into the salon.

"Do you truly want tea?" he asked suggestively.

"What?" Caught in the process of sitting down, Emily froze for a moment and then dropped into place. Her eyes were a stunning green and filled with surprise.

"Aren't you getting tired?" he said again. From the moment she had burst into his room that afternoon, he had had only one thought in mind: taking Emily to bed. All his previous objections had vanished. The sight of the tops of Emily's breasts rising and falling above the neckline of her green dress had driven every rational thought from his head. He yawned suggestively and stretched, his muscles rippling and pulling his jacket to its limits. He sat down beside her, his hand running caressingly down her arms.

Emily's eyes widened and grew brighter. She leaned toward him, giving him an even better view of her. "Oh!" She put a hand over her mouth as if stifling a yawn herself.

"Send your maid away," he whispered. She nodded. "Go," he urged. She rose and slipped from the room, stopping just before she went through the door, as if afraid he might vanish or change his mind. He simply smiled at her.

She had not been gone two minutes when Hawk heard a commotion in the hallway. The door to the salon few open. "Hawk, Father sent me to get you. You must come immediately," Andrew said. "He even made me break an engagement for dinner to come and get you. What is going on?"

"Now? He wants me to come now?" Hawk demanded, rising angrily.

"Are you deaf? That is what I said. He has some bee in his bonnet about something. There's someone else there too—I saw his coach but couldn't see his crest. Wish you would tell me what is going on." Andrew sat down and crossed his legs, inspecting his white stockings for the slightest sign of a rip or of dust. "Too boring, not knowing everything."

"Now?" Hawk repeated. When Andrew nodded, he walked to the secretary and pulled out a sheet of paper and a pen. Dipping his pen into the ink, he wrote a few lines. Then he crossed to the bellpull. When the butler arrived, Hawk handed him a note and said, "Have a maid take this to my wife. And send someone for my cloak."

When he was ready to leave the house, he said, his voice rough with anger, "This had better be important, Andrew."

Emily had gone upstairs in a daze. When a maid entered with Hawk's note, she was sitting in front of a mirror waiting impatiently for her maid to finish brushing her hair. Discarded nightdresses lay flung around the room like leaves tossed by a storm.

"What is this?" she asked as she took the note gingerly.

"It is from Mr. Hawksleigh," the maid said quietly.

Emily's heart dropped. "From my husband?" she asked gingerly. Her hand froze in the act of taking the note. She looked at it as though it were dipped in poison. But she could not postpone accepting it for long. Once it was in her hand, she quickly broke the seal. Then her personal maid and the housemaid jumped as she picked up a Meissen figurine and slammed it onto the floor. "This is the last time," Emily said between clenched teeth. "I had better read of the country falling to pieces in the morning or my husband needn't expect me to believe him again," she stormed, adding a few words she had learned from listening to her husband and his brother. The housemaid edged toward the door and made her escape. Mary pursed her lips and waited for her mistress to calm down. She tucked her into bed and got ready to make her own exit. "Remind me in the morning to write to my aunt. She is expected in town tomorrow, I believe," Emily said, her voice thoughtful—too thoughtful, her maid believed. "And tell Jonathan's tutor to have him ready to accompany me tomorrow afternoon. If Hawk thinks I will go on sitting around here waiting for him, he has much to learn. And my aunt is just the one to help." Emily lay back on the bed, an unholy smile on her face as she contemplated various means of working out her anger.

10

After a long ride through the darkness, Hawk finally brought the most violent of his emotions under control. He had waved Andrew on to his party, telling his younger brother that since he had managed to get home from the Peninsula by himself, he could certainly reach his father's house alone. Hawk tortured himself during the ride with thoughts of Emily's reactions. The darkness also brought memories of his dreams, memories he had conveniently put to one side when he was with Emily.

When he finally walked into his father's study, Hawk still felt frustrated, but he was resigned. The sight of the prime minister brought him up short. He bowed.

"Sorry to bring you out unexpectedly, Captain. Your father assured me that you would not mind," Lord Perceval said. Hawk shot an angry look at his father, but the older man ignored it. "Are you sure about this plan?"

"As sure as I can be without testing it," Hawk told him.

"Hmmm. Three days is a long time." The older Hawksleigh looked at his friend, having heard his arguments earlier. His son would have to defend his proposal by himself.

"If we try with all three at once, how will we know which one is truly guilty? Besides, how can I watch three at the same time?" Hawk asked. He had hesitated over the time line for his plan himself, but he could honestly see no other way.

"What if you were not the only watcher?" the prime minister asked. "It would solve some problems for us. I can call the gentlemen into a meeting with me, a meeting that will last well into the evening. They will think nothing of it if they all are present. If I call them in one by one . . ." His voice dropped suggestively.

"Whom would you get to watch with me? I thought part of the problem was that you did not know whom to trust," Hawk said. He walked over and took a seat across from his father. He crossed his legs and removed a tiny green thread from the leg of his breeches. Wistfully he rolled it around his finger.

"The situation is different. I was introducing you into the Exchequer as a permanent staff member. These people will be around only temporarily and then move on to another problem," his father said quietly. He leaned forward, his face sober, willing his son to understand and accept.

"Spies," Hawk said quietly.

"Agents," the prime minister quietly corrected him. "They have all proved their worth many times before. Those people will never realize anyone is watching them." He glanced at the older Hawksleigh. "I have decided that I want you at the meeting too." The older man's face hardened and his fists clenched.

Hawk jumped up, his face dark with anger. "I suppose you have decided that I cannot be trusted," he said harshly. "I told Father that might be the case." He towered over the two of them for a minute. "You will have my resignation in the morning." He started toward the door.

"Sit down!" The words cracked through the air and brought Hawk to a sudden halt. He dropped into the closest chair, his face still a dark mask. "Stop jumping to conclusions!" Perceval added. "You cannot remember two days out of your life. Good grief, man! There are men who have never left England who have forgotten more than that because they continually drink themselves into a stupor. And if you did give away anything, what value would it be to the enemy now? Stop wallowing in self-pity and get to work. I want you at the meeting because you have information we need. And my agents have more practice following men than you. They know the seamy side of London; you do not."

The words hit Hawk like a storm of hailstones. At first he could only draw his emotions in to keep them protected. Then the words began to dent his mind. "Then you do not—"

"I would never have allowed you to begin work for the government if I had doubts about you. The only reason

Wellesley sent you home was that you had lost confidence in yourself. You did not think I would allow the situation to go uninvestigated, did you?" the prime minister asked. "I take better care of the country than that."

Both Perceval and the older Hawksleigh took breaths of relief when Hawk smiled and relaxed in his chair. "Son, I told you that we trusted you," his father said gently. "The report you finished is excellent. Your clerk brought it to me late this afternoon. And your information about this other problem has been invaluable. Stop worrying about Spain and find out how the payroll shipments are being lost."

"No one is talking about them. It is almost as though no one knows they are missing," Hawk told them.

"Well, someone knows something. Keep on looking," Perceval ordered. "Now, back to this other matter."

By the time the three of them had discussed the situation completely, it was very late. Declining his father's offer of a bed, Hawk climbed back into his carriage. The prime minister's words echoed through his head. Had he been the cause of his own problems? Had he been consumed by self-pity? As the wheels rattled along the road, Hawk analyzed his actions, finally coming to the conclusion that the prime minister might have been right. Emily had been saying the same thing for months, and so had his family.

"Emily." The name slipped from his lips as soft as a sigh. The memory of her in that low-cut dress had his heart racing. He wedged himself into the corner of the carriage and drifted off to a restless sleep punctuated by dreams. Unlike the dreams that had disturbed him for months, these were disturbing in another way. He had just finished unhooking Emily's dress, pulling it from her shoulders, when the carriage came to a stop.

"Cor! Is he on the go?" asked the groom, a young lad from a farm near the manor who was making his first visit to town. He stared in the carriage door as if Hawk were the fire-eater at the village fair.

"Get on with you. Hold those horses' heads," the coachman ordered. Then he climbed down from his perch. "Mr. Hawksleigh, sir, shall I call a footman to help you up the stairs?'' he asked, pulling his cap off his head and twisting it in his hands.

"No. I can find my own way," his master said, his voice clear and firm. "You and the lad head to the stables. Sleep late in the morning if you can." Hawk got out of the carriage, stretched, and walked steadily up to the door. Before the knocker had a chance to sound more than once, it was open.

"Cor! He's a smooth one," the boy said once the door was shut. He waited until the coachman was once more on his perch and let the horses go. He climbed up to his own spot.

No sooner had the groom taken his place than the coachman reached out a long arm and cuffed him lightly. "That's to help you remember to keep that mouth shut. The master was in a good mood tonight, else you might be out looking for work now. Watch what you say around Quality." The groom rubbed his cheek, a resentful look in his eyes, but he nodded.

Inside the house, Hawk made his way up the stairs to his bedroom. He frowned when he saw Lester asleep on a camp bed in the room, his long legs doubled under him to keep them from dropping off the end of the bed. The click of the door roused the valet from his sleep. Waking quickly, he stood up, helping Hawk from his coat. "Haven't I told you not to wait up for me, Lester?" Hawk asked pleasantly. The valet nodded and removed his master's boots. "Then what are you doing here?"

"Clarke thought there had been some emergency, sir. I decided that you might need me. Better that I stay here than have you rouse the house when you returned," Lester explained, as he slipped the rumbled neckcloth away from his master's neck.

"There is nothing wrong. Go on. Get to bed. I will need you in the morning. Father insists that I be at the office before ten. You will not have much time for sleep."

"Nor will you, sir." Instead of doing as he was told, Lester finished unbuttoning Hawk's shirt, slipping it off. He held out a nightshirt.

"I will finish the rest myself," Hawk said firmly, sitting in one of the new chairs. For the first time in the last week or so, he noted the distinct changes his wife had made. The upholstery on the chair matched in color the blue in the wall hangings. The wood, carved to resemble bamboo, was only a shade darker than the silk of their background. His bed and his windows were bare, and here and there around the room were new pieces of furniture. "Good night, Lester," Hawk said firmly before closing his eyes.

He waited until the valet had blown out all but the candles burning beside the bed and had pulled the door shut behind him. Then Hawk walked slowly across the room to the door to Emily's bedroom. He hesitated for a moment and then opened it. Only the flicker of the fireplace lit her room. He walked back to his own bed and picked up a candle. Then he crossed to her bed. Emily lay there, the covers drawn up to her chin, one hand curled under her cheek, which showed the marks of tears. He put out a hand to touch her, but she turned away from him, rolling onto her other side and burying her head further in the covers.

Hawk smiled ruefully. He began to walk around the bed, back to his own room. But he could not keep from looking at her, her face so quiet, so lovely in sleep. Just for a moment, he promised himself as he put the candle on the table beside the bed and slid in beside her.

Emily, exhausted from the emotions of the evening, did not react when he drew her close. Even his kiss did not wake her. Hawk grinned as his own eyes drifted shut. He took a deep breath. Then he too went to sleep, one arm thrown around her, keeping her close to him. As he had on many occasions before, Hawk began to dream. This time, however, the dream had barely begun when the maid, a coal bucket in her hand, slipped into the room to make up the fire. She glanced toward the bed and dropped the bucket.

The sound brought Hawk straight up in bed but did not rouse Emily. "I am sorry, sir. Had I known . . ." The maid, young and easily embarrassed, mumbled her explanation.

"Go about your work. But be quiet. Your mistress is still asleep. And tell her maid that Mrs. Hawksleigh wishes to sleep late this morning," he said quietly, wondering how long it would take the story of where he had spent the night to make the rounds of the household. He doubted whether anyone would believe how innocent his sleep had been. He waited until the girl left and then regretfully slipped from the bed and back into his own room. His fire was burning brightly. Glancing at the clock above the fireplace, Hawk realized he had an hour or more before he needed to be up. He yawned and slipped into his own bed.

When Emily finally awoke that morning, it was very late. She stretched and sat up, feeling more refreshed than she had for weeks. Then she looked at the other side of the bed. The pillow was rumpled and the sheets and comforter thoroughly mussed, while the ones on her side were scarcely wrinkled. Her eyes widened, and she looked toward the door that connected the two rooms. She frowned as she noticed the extra candlestick on the table beside the bed. Then, with a word that would have shocked her husband if he had known she knew it, she was out of bed. She yanked the bellpull.

As though she had been waiting just outside the hall, Mary entered the room almost immediately, a tray of chocolate and bread and butter in her hands. "Good morning, Mrs. Hawksleigh," she said, her eyes wandering about the room, seeking evidence of the information the young housemaid had imparted to her before breakfast that morning.

"Why was I allowed to sleep so late?" Emily demanded, tapping her foot. "I thought I told you to wake me early."

"Mr. Hawksleigh sent word that you wished to sleep late this morning, ma'am." The maid took one look at the angry face of her mistress and hastened to add, "I am sorry. But I thought your orders had changed."

Emily's face softened. "You could not have known. When did my husband send down that massage?"

"When the maid built up the fire here this morning. You were still asleep, I believe."

Emily's face flamed. She turned to stare at the bed as if she could read the story it had to tell. She felt no different than she had last night. And according to Lucretia, she would feel something. How dare he, she thought to herself. How dare he embarrass me so! But a little voice inside her whispered quietly that what she was so angry about was the fact that he had not awakened her.

"Where is my husband now?" she asked. "Is he still at breakfast?"

"Mr. Hawksleigh left some time ago. I believe he had an early meeting with his father," the maid said quietly as she laid out her mistress's undergarments. "Do you wish a bath before you dress, Mrs. Hawksleigh?"

"No." Emily walked over to her rosewood desk and took a seat. She thought for a moment and then wrote hurriedly. "Have a footman take this to my aunt, Lady Mairmount. Tell him to wait for a reply if she has arrived in town. Then return at one."

"Yes, ma'am." He maid was gone only a few minutes. When she returned, Emily was pacing the floor, the chocolate and bread totally forgotten. "Would you prefer something else to eat, Mrs. Hawksleigh?" she asked.

"No. I am not hungry. Did the footman leave immediately?" Emily roamed around the room, taking long strides that stretched the hem of her night robe to their limits.

"Yes, ma'am. Do you wish to dress now?" Mary asked rather timidly, not at all comfortable with her mistress that morning. "Your new plaid morning dress has arrived from Madame Camille. I have just pressed it."

"No. I want something less frivolous. Has the honey-colored velvet arrived?"

"Yesterday."

"Good. I will wear that with my new cloak lined with fur. And the muff and bonnet that match. At least my aunt will not be able to complain about my clothes this time."

Mary hurried to find the required items and returned to lace Emily into her corset. They had just finished when a scratching sounded at the door. Emily snatched up a dressing gown and put it on. "Come in."

"I am sorry to bother you, Mrs. Hawksleigh. But the seamstresses have finished the draperies and hangings for Master Andrew's room. They want to know if you wish them to return to the master's bedroom," the housekeeper explained. Like Emily's maid's, her eyes searched the chamber for the evidence she was looking for, noting with satisfaction the rumpled condition of both sides of the bed.

"Get them to work immediately. Everything must be finished as soon as possible. Have those last two deliveries of furniture arrived yet?"

"This morning. The footmen have put the last piece into

place. The painters are finished. When the last of the draperies are hung and the new china and glassware arrive, the house will be complete once more." The housekeeper beamed in satisfaction at her mistress. The last few weeks had been the most exciting as well as the most exhausting time of her career. She straightened her shoulders proudly and waited for further commands.

"Is there something else?" Emily asked, wondering why the woman did not leave.

"It is Master Jonathan's tutor, ma'am. He wishes to know what time you wish to have Master Jonathan ready for his outing."

All her plans the night before flooded Emily's mind. "Blast," she whispered to herself. The other two women in the house exchanged knowing glances. "Tell him I will send him word later. And get those women working."

"Very good." The housekeeper curtsied, her black skirts rustling crisply. Emily walked to the desk once more. The housekeeper raised her eyebrow and looked at the maid. Mary waved her from the room, mouthing, "Later."

"See if that footman has returned, Mary," Emily ordered as she sat down at the desk and picked up her pen again. She dipped it in the ink and began to write. Her maid hurried from the room. When the woman was gone, Emily dropped the pen and stared at the random marks she had made. Picking up the paper, she tore it into shreds. Then, too restless to keep her seat, she stalked around the room, coming to stop beside the bed. She ran her fingers over the pillow that had held her husband's head. Then she picked it up and threw it on the floor, resisting the urge to stomp on it.

"He has not yet returned." The maid's voice caused Emily to jump.

"Then I shall take Jonathan out. Send word to his tutor that Jonathan will accompany me to the lending library and then to Gunter's. He is to be ready within the half-hour. Then return and help me into this dress." Once again the maid darted out of the room. Not for the first time that morning, Mary wondered just what had happened the previous evening. Her mistress, usually so thoughtful, was certainly demanding that morning.

Like the maid, Jonathan too wanted to know what had happened to change Emily's plan. "But you sent word that we were going to visit Lady Mairmount, Emily. Why are we going to the library? And you told me last week that it was too cold for one of Gunter's ices. And it's colder today than it was last week. Look at my breath." He blew out, and the air in front of his face frosted over.

While Emily dealt with Jonathan's questions, Hawk was sitting in a meeting. He had risen early that morning and now fought against yawning. He had to admit, however, that his thoughts were more on Emily than on the problems of making certain that government funds did not go to purchase shoddy goods.

As the hours grew later, Anthony Hawksleigh grew more and more restless. When dinner was served, his father managed to take him to one side. "These people are not stupid. If you continue to stare at the door, they are certain to suspect something. Pull yourself together."

"But what if something has gone wrong?" Hawk asked, thinking of problems he had not envisioned when he first proposed the plan.

"That is a chance we had to take. The information we decided to release was not particularly vital," his father reminded him. "Now, act like you care about what is being said," he ordered, as though Hawk were twelve once more.

Hawk stiffened. Then he lifted his head and stepped into the dining room as though he were heading into battle. And battle he did, against sleep. The youngest member of the group, he had soon become used to being ignored. Only the prime minister addressed him by name, the others seeming to stumble over what to call him. "Master Anthony" made him sound as though he were Jonathan's age, but "Mr. Hawksleigh" meant his father.

They had retired to the library for more discussion when the moment Hawk had been waiting for arrived. The door opened. The butler pressed a note into Lord Perceval's hand. He scanned it quickly and then looked up, his eyes finding Hawk's. He nodded and put the note in his pocket. He stretched. "Gentlemen, this can wait until tomorrow. We have something more serious to discuss."

"What?"

"Has something happened?"

"Is it the king?"

"We have found the source of a leak at the Exchequer, gentlemen. My agents have him in custody. If you will excuse me, I need to interview the man, find out whom he has been reporting to," the prime minister explained. "Captain Hawksleigh, would you care to accompany me?" He walked out of the room, Hawk only a few steps behind.

"What is going on here, Hawksleigh? Why did Perceval invite your son instead of one of us?" the oldest gentleman present asked.

"I am certain his lordship has his reasons. He has talked to my son several times since Hawk joined the Exchequer. He always wants to talk about Spain," Mr. Hawksleigh said, playing down his son's importance in the operation. No use jeopardizing Hawk's further usefulness.

"Hmm. Forgot the lad had served with Wellesley. That explains it. Well, I'm for home. My wife will be furious with me. Was supposed to escort her to the theater tonight. Bit early in the year for her to go alone. Too many Cits, you know." One by one the gentlemen called for their carriages. When the last guest was gone, the elder Hawksleigh took a deep breath and headed up to bed. The morning would be soon enough to face the bad news.

While Hawk was sitting listening to men argue about paying for goods, Emily had taken Jonathan on his outing. By the time they returned to the house, the footman had returned with a note. Quickly Emily read it, noting with satisfaction the invitation to afternoon tea. She glanced at the clock and sent the footman around to alert the coachman again.

As early as she thought was appropriate, Emily hurried up to the entrance of her aunt's home on Berkeley Square. Her aunt's butler showed no surprise at this early visit; so Emily decided her aunt had mentioned that she was expected. "Lady Mairmount will be down directly. May we offer you some tea while you wait?" the butler asked, delighted to see her again. Her Seasons had been exciting times for the household staff.

"That would be lovely," Emily replied. She took her seat, wishing she had brought the latest book she had borrowed that day from the library, or a piece of handiwork. Waiting for her aunt tended to be time-consuming. Tea had arrived and departed by the time her aunt entered the room.

Emily rose gracefully and made her curtsy.

"Very pretty. Those years in the country did not destroy your social skills, I see. Marriage does not seem to agree with you, though. Thought you would be hoop over the moon by now. You're not increasing, are you? A worse way to spend the Season I cannot imagine. Of course, if it is early yet, you won't have to leave until May. And with the right dressmaker. Yes, I should be able to bring that off. No later than May, though." Although she was using her cane to walk, Lady Mairmount stood straight. As tall as her niece, she had not let her height keep her from being the belle of her year. And she had made certain her niece had taken too. Dressed in the latest fashion in a gown of deep blue wool and draped with a myriad of shawls, she was still a pattern card of fashion. Her hair, once a light brown like Emily's, was now gray and styled in artless curls and partially covered with a flirty lace cap. Her blue eyes inspected Emily thoroughly.

"How are you, Aunt Julia?" Emily asked politely. No matter how old she became, her aunt always made her feel as though she were ten and wanting in manners.

"As well as can be expected after that jostling on the roads. Where is that husband of yours? Would have thought he would have come calling with you." She took her seat in an upholstered chair beside the fireplace. "Well, where is he? And shouldn't he be here when you tell me the news, or haven't you told him yet? Don't be afraid, child. Most men puff up with pride once they know you are caught."

"Aunt Julia! It is nothing like that," Emily protested. She moved clsoer to the fire and immediately regretted that she had worn the velvet dress. She had forgotten how warm her aunt liked to keep her house. "Hawk is at the Exchequer. His father has him working on some special project." She sat down across from her aunt, her feet on the floor and her hands folded in her lap as she had been taught.

"Then I was right. Something is wrong. Probably that step-mother of yours. Why your father married her is beyond me. Told him so at the time. Knew that person would make trouble. Well, what is it now? Is she making a play for your husband?"

"No! She is still in the country with Sir Horace. And according to Jonathan—"

"Jonathan? You have your brother with you? No wonder you and Anthony are having problems. Who would want a brat with them on a honeymoon? Lud, I thought you had better sense than that, Emily. Send him home immediately."

"I cannot. Lucretia is joining us shortly." Before she had finished the last word, Emily was already regreting her remark.

"She is what? Emily, I know you have more brains in your head than that! That woman hates you. Saw it at the wedding. Kept shooting angry looks at you. Made herself the talk of the day. And she is going to be staying at your home?"

"It was the only way Hawk could persuade her to permit Jonathan to come for a visit. I had to know he was all right. You know how she neglected him," Emily said, for once allowing her anger and frustration to creep into her voice.

"So your husband arranged the visit," the older lady said thoughtfully. She tapped her cane on the floor as if trying to summon attention. Then she leaned back and pulled her shawls more closely about her. The muted blues, pinks, ivory, and black looked like an artist's palette that had been stirred violently and then left. "That is interesting." Her blue eyes narrowed and then widened. "Do you wish me to talk to him?"

"No."

"Then out with it. Your letter sounded urgent. I pulled myself out of my comfortable bed to see you. Really, Emily, I had thought you better able to manage than this." She tapped her cane on the floor a few times as if to punctuate her remarks. "Get on with it, girl!"

Now that the moment was at hand, Emily had no idea where to begin. Unused to sharing her problems with anyone, she found it hard to come out with it. Nervously she rose and walked around the room, her stride lengthening with every step she took.

For a few minutes Lady Mairmount allowed her to roam. When her patience had just about reached the breaking point—no one had'ever said she had much to begin with—she said sharply, "Tell me! Or do you intend to lay charades and make me guess? Might do a good job with it at that. Let me see. You already said it was not your stepmother. Must be your husband or his family."

"Not his family. His mother has been wonderful to me, and his father is very helpful, Andrew has been living with us," Emily quickly explained.

"So that is it. You wish me to get rid of the brother."

"No. He has gone back to his parents' estate until I finish redecorating the house." Emily twisted her hands, wishing she could quit dithering and bring out the real issue. She took a deep breath.

"Good, girl. Nothing like putting your stamp on a house to make it a home. Anthony got it from his uncle, as I remember. Must have been quite a sight. Men never notice things like worn carpets or faded draperies." Lady Mairmount leaned forward, her gray curls bobbing as she nodded her head. "What colors did you use?"

"A variety. I did the large salon in white and gold. Aunt Julia, you will never believe how much help Jonathan has been. He has an instinct about colors that an Incomparable would envy."

"You mean you allowed a six-year-old child to help you choose the furnishings for your home? What are you thinking of, child? Knew you took some weird ideas in your head. Look how you refused my offer of a home after your father died. Suppose Anthony found out and is ready to commit you to Bedlam." The old lady laughed musically.

"Hawk approves of what I have done. Most of it, anyway. And going about by myself was boring. At least Jonathan amused me," Emily said, her tone defensive. She took her seat again and waited for her aunt's response.

"He is neglecting you, is he?" Lady Mairmount asked in a gentler tone than she had used before. Her eyes softened as she watched her sister's daughter blush and look at her hands.

"Not exactly. He escorts me whenever I ask him to. Of course, with the Season not yet under way, we have not been

exactly overwhelmed with invitations,'' Emily said truthfully.
"And he has been busy. His father sent for him last evening
after dinner, and he had already left by the time I arose this
morning." She twisted her hands nervously. All the disappointments of the months of her marriage flooded her,
filling her with resentment once more. She had been so
certain last night would solve their problems. She
experienced once again the hurt and dismay she had felt when
she had read his note. Then she remembered the imprint of
his head on her pillow and grew angry once more.

"That is not exactly what I meant." A member of a
generation known for its frankness, Lady Mairmount asked,
"How often does he come to your bed?"

The earlier blush that had reddened Emily's face was like
nothing as she gaped. "Aunt Julia!"

"Well, what else am I to think? What other problem would
you bother me with when I have just arrived? Lud, Emily,
what is wrong with you?" The older lady watched in dismay
as her niece burst into angry tears. Digging into her reticule,
she pulled out a handkerchief. "Here, now. Wipe those
eyes."

"Lucretia said he could not love a clodpole like I am. I
suppose she was right," Emily said, sobbing. She wiped the
handkerchief across her face. "But I thought he did. He
kissed me as though he did. Oh, Aunt, it was wonderful to
feel his arms around me. Then . . . then, as soon as the vows
were said . . ." Emily broke into renewed sobs.

"Marriage frightens some young men. Takes them a while
to recover. Surely on your honeymoon he . . ." Lady Mairmount let her voice drift off delicately. Emily shook her head,
trying to get herself under control. "Well, you are no
clodpole, my dear, no matter what that dwarf of a stepmother
of yours says. Always knew she was jealous of you. May
have smiled when your father was alive, but her eyes were
angry. Probably wished she had your figure. She's a bit of
a pouter pigeon. Bound to get heavier as she gows older.
But you, my dear, you will be like me. Keep your figure
as long as you live." Although Emily had not paid much
attention to her aunt's conversation, it had given her a chance
to gain control over her emotions. "Now, child, tell me what
happened."

Emily poured out the story, beginning with the reason for Hawk's return from Spain. "Promise me you will not disclose this to anyone," she begged, realizing that Hawk would be livid if he thought anyone but his immediate family knew the details.

"Who do you think I am, girl? That stepmother of yours? I have kept more secrets than you have ever known. Go on, now." She leaned forward and tapped her cane imperiously.

Getting over difficult ground as easily as possible, Emily told her the rest, ending with their encounter in his bedroom, dinner last evening, and the condition of her bed that morning. "He did not even have the courtesy to say good morning," Emily said bitterly. "What are the servants going to think?"

"Just what you wanted them to. Lucretia will have no doubt about the reality of your marriage now. Isn't that what you wanted?" her aunt asked. Her tone was sharp.

"Yes. No. I want to be his wife, really his wife," Emily said angrily. "Last night I thought . . . Then he left. Blast!"

"Emily! Watch your language! No niece of mine will sound like she has grown up in a stable."

"I am sorry, but I love him so much. And he loves me. I know he does. I am so confused." She leaned her head on the back of the chair, her eyes closed in exhaustion.

Lady Mairmount tapped her cane on the floor a few times thoughtfully. "Yes, I imagine you are. You say he was the one who suggested that you retire early?"

"Yes."

"And he apparently slept with you last night."

"That's right."

"Hmm. Your husband must be a very frustrated man. Shall we see how we can relieve those frustrations?"

"What can we do?"

"Tomorrow you are to . . ."

11

The next few days were busy ones for Emily. The last draperies were hung. The china and glassware arrived. The entire house sparkled with fresh paint and smelled of beeswax. Emily, however, paid little attention to the details of the household, leaving the final arrangements in the capable hands of her housekeeper.

Emily took the first steps to put Lady Mairmount's plan into operation. The morning after their talk, she had written to her mother-in-law and invited her to luncheon. Although she did not intend to lay the entire account before Mrs. Hawksleigh, both Emily and Lady Mairmount knew that Hawk's mother was just the person they needed to accomplish one part of their goal.

Visiting her modiste took more of Emily's time. At first, Madame Camille was taken aback by Emily's request. "But, madame, I could not. You would be thought fast. Society would shun you," Madame Camille protested when she saw the drawing Emily had brought with her.

"It will be a very private party," Emily said, letting her eyelids close just a little and smiling a secret smile. "My husband . . ."

"Ah, now I see. I am sorry I doubted you, Madame Hawksleigh. I should have known. Do you wish a fine cotton or silk?" The modiste led the way into a fitting room and gave orders to have several ells of material brought in. "Have you thought of color?"

"Perhaps ivory."

"Always lovely, of course, but so demure. If you would permit me to suggest . . . ?" the modiste said thoughtfully as she walked around her client. The new style required careful planning. "I see you in something bright, something warm. Yes, that is it. I see you wrapped in a vibrant color, glowing with all the warmth of a summer sun."

"Yellow? Most of them make me look like I am diseased."

"But no, madam. Just wait. You will see," Madame Camille promised, already planning in her mind the delicate folds that would enhance Mrs. Hawksleigh's tall figure. Petite ladies might be in fashion with the *ton,* but the modiste preferred the taller ones.

Leaving the designs in her dressmaker's capable hands, Emily marked off another item on her mental list. She hurried on to her next task.

Her husband found that time hung on his hands. The clerk who had been selling their secrets had been a petty criminal working for one of the businesses hungry for government money. A few seconds of questioning, especially after the word "treason" was mentioned, had him babbling so quickly that they had had trouble taking the information down. His employers would give him a memo to copy; he would make a second copy to sell, just as Hawk had suspected. His employers too had crumbled quickly; they had never believed that anyone would see through their scheme.

Although one problem at the Exchequer had been solved, the larger one remained. Every day Hawk went to work. Every day he talked to a variety of people. He listened in the clubs. But nowhere could he uncover the slightest hint about the loss of the payroll shipments. He followed every lead he could imagine, but none of them gave him more information than he already had. The last two shipments had arrived safely. It was as though the thieves had vanished.

Frustrated by the inactivity, Hawk spent hours thinking, especially about Perceval's comments on the way he had been behaving. Looking back over his actions, he had to admit that a certain amount of self-pity had colored his world. And, being honest, he had to admit that this had had a profound effect on his family, especially Emily. If he could trust himself as his father and the prime minister had, he would rush home to his wife, ready to woo and to bed her. He had realized Wellesley's wisdom in sending him home. However, the dream, although it had grown less frequent in the last two weeks, still worried him. It was too real, too vivid to be easily put aside.

Since that evening when his barriers had been at their lowest and he had crawled into bed with his wife, Hawk had waited for some sign from Emily. He found reasons to go home in the middle of the day, hoping to take her for a ride. She was always gone or busy. He left her messages. They were ignored. As the Season drew closer, Hawk began to look forward to it because he knew that there would be evenings when Emily would want his escort. His brother's casually mentioning Emily's presence for luncheon or seeing her with Lady Mairmount did not help soothe his feelings.

Whereas once he had not slept because he was afraid to dream, now he was not sleeping because he was pacing up and down in front of the door connecting his bedroom to Emily's. More than once Hawk walked toward the door, only to draw back again, wishing his wife had given him some encouragement. He knew he had the right to walk into that room, but unlike some of his contemporaries, Hawk saw marriage as a partnership between people who cared for each other, much like that of his parents. He would not take her unwillingly. Then he would remember the dream. He would throw himself on his bed and lie there until sleep claimed him. His conflict with himself blinded him to the fact that the dream happened only occasionally.

On the other side of the door, Emily heard the pacing and remembered the early weeks of her marriage. Her own nights were wakeful as she planned new ways of occupying her time. She had already visited the theater, made daily visits to the lending library, and haunted her aunt's house with the lady's encouragement. Although she never answered Hawk's notes, she carried them around with her much as she had carried his letters when he was in Spain.

After evading her husband for over a week, Emily walked into breakfast Monday morning as though she always joined him for that meal. Ordering fresh tea, she sat down, looking her best in a light gold woolen morning dress trimmed in ribbons a shade darker. She smiled at him as though she had seen him only moments before. Hawk stood still, his hand frozen around the top of the chair. He had risen automatically when she entered, and now he could not tear his eyes away from her.

"Are you already finished, Hawk?" Emily asked when he continued to stand and stare at her. She was enjoying her chance to look at him too. His hair, longer than it had been when he returned home, was artfully disarranged. Even though he had lost most of the bronzed color he had had when he first returned, his skin was still dark. His eyes reminded her of the rich chocolate syrup the cook poured over poached pears. That morning he wore a simple dark blue coat that fitted his shoulders as though it had been poured on, buff pantaloons that clung to every muscle in his thighs and calves, and Hessians. Realizing that he could read her hunger in her eyes, Emily quickly looked down at the cup she held in her hand.

For Hawk it was enough to break the spell. "No, I had just begun," he told her, reseating himself. "I am surprised to see you, my dear. I was beginning to think I had imagined you."

"Hawk!" she protested, laughing.

"Well, you must admit you have been the elusive wife these last few days. Even Andrew has seen you more than I have."

"I have been busy," she said quietly. Before he could ask her what she had been doing with her time, she asked, "What do you think of the house?"

"Charming. I especially like what you have done with Andrew's room. Has he seen it?"

"Seen it? He insisted on visiting the furniture factory with me. He said he did not intend to sleep in a bed once inhabited by tenants." She laughed softly. "I suggested that he might like to pay for his new furniture, but he reminded me that your Uncle George had left you all the money."

Hawk laughed too. "He could buy his own town house, but he refuses to do so. He asked me what the good was in having rich relatives if they never did anything for you." The footman brought fresh tea. Hawk accepted another cup and then asked, "What brings you to breakfast this morning, Emily?" His voice was quiet and gentle but very firm.

"Aunt Julia is giving a dinner party, just a few select

friends of hers, before the Season gets under way. Shall I accept for us?'' Emily asked. Her voice was level. Not a trace of nervousness showed through. She waited for his answer, not at all certain even at that late date that he would agree.

''What evening?'' As she told him, he watched her face, noting the sheen of excitement in her eyes. Having her in the room with him for the entire evening would be worth even the dullest of dinner parties, and Lady Mairmount's dinners were never dull. ''Tell her yes. But, Emily, you do not have to wait for my approval to accept an invitation.''

''I know that. But Aunt Julia would say something rude and embarrassing if you did not go with me. Remember what she said to my stepmother at our wedding breakfast?''

''Lord, do I! Lucretia's face turned puce. I wonder what happened after we left?'' he asked, his dark eyes smiling.

''We may find out soon. Yesterday I received a letter from Lucretia telling me she plans to arrive by the end of the first week of the Season. And, Hawk, she said she had some interesting news to tell us. Do you think she is engaged?''

''Knowing Lucretia, I would ask first what she thought was interesting. But if finding a second marriage is what has been on her mind, I would not be at all surprised. Has she found a chaperone?''

''No. Sir Horace is escorting her to town.'' Emily giggled. ''Hawk, he says he will entrust her to my capable hands. Those were his very words. I wonder what he expects me to do.''

''Keep her from being thought fast, I am certain, but that is as likely as having your last chance win first at Newmarket.'' He looked at his wife and realized they were more relaxed with each other than they had been in weeks. Perhaps they should have come to town as soon as they had arrived home from their honeymoon. Remembering that fiasco sobered him. He cleared his throat and glanced at the clock that sat on the table beside the door. ''Is there anything else?''

For Emily, too, the enjoyment slipped from the morning. ''No.'' He started to get up. ''Wait! How are we to know the engagements we each have accepted?''

''Have Clarke keep a book. We can give him the

information as soon as we decide. If there are conflicts, we can discuss them," he said rather curtly. After visions of escorting Emily to balls where he would hold her and twirl her around the floor, the thought of each of them going separate ways filled him with despair.

"I will order a book for him today," Emily promised, only the thought of her plan making her feel any better. Dropping a kiss on her cheek when he would rather have clasped her in his arms and hurried upstairs, Hawk quickly made his departure.

Emily sat there quietly for a few minutes. Then determination lit a fire in her eyes. She walked briskly to the morning room that she had made her office and dashed off a note. "Take this to Mrs. Hawksleigh," she told a footman when he appeared. Then she sat back to wait.

Later that morning as Hawk shuffled papers from one pile to another and tried to think of some other avenue of information about the robberies, his father entered his office. "Sir," the younger man said, standing up. "Did I forget something? Was I supposed to be at a meeting?"

"No, nothing like that. Your mother made me promise that I would tell you as soon as possible that she wants you to have luncheon with her tomorrow. And she said she would not accept any excuses. How is Emily? I never see her anymore. You and she should come to dinner later in the week," the older man suggested as he took a seat in front of the desk.

"She is fine. Busy. You know she has been redecorating Uncle George's house. Perhaps you and Mama need to come to us so that you can see it," Hawk suggested.

"Done a fine job, has she?" Hawk nodded and smiled. "Tell her to expect us . . ." He pulled out a slip of paper and consulted it. "Hmmm. We go to Lady Mairmount on Thursday. Perhaps Friday? Better check with your mother tomorrow. She may have forgotten to put something on my list. Check with Emily too. These ladies, how they ever keep track of where they are supposed to be, I will never know. They have more complicated lives than some of our generals." He laughed and slapped his knee at the thought. Then his face grew serious again. "You found anything new?"

"Nothing. It is almost as though they have gone underground."

"Maybe they have given up."

"Something inside me insists that is not so. I hope I am wrong." Hawk leaned back in the chair, his face serious. "Perhaps if I talked to the guards once more, they would remember something, anything."

"We may have to wait until there is another attempt, much as I hate the thought," his father told him. He rose. "I will tell your mother to expect you."

"Just me?"

"She politely told me that I could eat my luncheon at my club."

"Lord, what have I done now?" Hawk asked, searching his memory much as he had done when he was a teenager and had to face his father's and mother's anger.

"You faced the French. Now prepare to face your mother," his father said, only half-jokingly. Hawk groaned.

When he joined his mother in her morning room the next day, Hawk was a pattern card of perfection. Outwardly serene, he looked around for Andrew before realizing his brother was not present. "Just the two of us, Mama?" he asked, giving her a hug.

"We have not had a talk in a long while, Anthony." She patted the place beside her on the settee. Hawk took the seat she had indicated, wishing she would disclose her purpose quickly. His mother, however, meandered through questions designed to put him at ease. "How is Emily? Is Jonathan enjoying London?" Finally she asked, "You do know the Season begins shortly?"

"Yes." As hard as he tried, Hawk could not keep the trace of sarcasm from his voice.

"And Lady Mairmount's dinner party is only two days away?"

"Yes." This time the word was more emphatic.

His mother rose and stood looking down at him. Had he been able to see her feet, Hawk was certain he would have seen her toe tapping an impatient rhythm on the rug. "I never believed that one of my sons would be such a clodpole."

"Mother!" Hawk started to get up so he could face her, but she shoved him back into place.

"This is Emily's first Season as a married woman. Have you thought of that?"

"Of course I have."

"Not very hard. Have you looked at her jewelry, really looked? Of course, she would not say anything to you, but you should have noticed it yourself. Just the other day when Emily was showing me about the house . . . She has really done a remarkable job, hasn't she? And to think that one of her advisers was a six-year-old. That should have been you, my dear. I know . . . I know. Your father is just the same. Hates disorder and confusion."

This time Hawk's voice was soothing. "Mama, what are you talking about?"

"Talking about? Why, just what the town will be talking about. Anthony, it is no secret that our family is very comfortably off. I have always been glad I had only sons. Think what it would have been like for a girl, having to fight off fortune hunters. Poor Emily, that happened to her before you came along."

"What does our having money have to do with Emily?" Hawk asked patiently. Even though his mother's comments seemed random, he knew she had put careful thought into what she planned to say.

"You have been married several months, Anthony. What will people think when they see Emily in those pearls or that emerald set from her mother? You should have already invested in some good diamonds as soon as you came to town. I believe Lucretia Cheswick took one look at Emily's mother's diamonds and had them reset. You can imagine what she will say when Emily goes out with that modest necklace her father gave her when she made her bow to society." The butler announced luncheon, and she took his arm. "I had Cook make all your favorites."

"And I promise that I will buy Emily some diamonds immediately. Lucretia Cheswick will have no chance to make jest with her," Hawk promised, smiling down at his mother. The secrets of his marriage were still safe. He took a deep breath again.

"Not diamonds. But not rubies either. Perhaps coral. Yes. Coral and perhaps topaz or amethyst. Anthony, if you are short because of redecorating the house, I will advance you the funds," his mother said seriously.

"Thank you, but I can afford to buy my wife as many jewels as she wants," he said firmly. "I will ask her to visit the jewelers with me tomorrow."

"No, no. That would ruin everything." His mother stopped suddenly, her face showing the slightest tinge of red.

"Why? Mother, what are you up to?"

"Nothing."

"I do not believe you." He seated her and took the seat on her right hand.

"I want Emily to think you thought of this yourself. You are not to tell her that I had anything to do with it. Surprise her. The jewels will mean so much more if you pick them out." Mrs. Hawksleigh smiled sweetly, running her fingers over the sapphire pendant she wore.

"But I know nothing about selecting jewelry."

"You mean that none of your ladybirds has ever demanded a gift?" his mother asked, totally shocked.

"Mama! You are not supposed to talk about such things like that," her elder son said, the shock in his voice evident. Theoretically, he knew that his mother was awake on every suit, but hearing it from her mouth was something different.

"Really, my dear, you are such a prude. How else can I help you? Simply tell the jeweler you wish to see something for your wife. He will show you what he has. Perhaps you could find out what color she will be wearing to Lady Mairmount's and choose something to go with that. The others you can choose more leisurely."

"You are determined that Emily will disgrace you, aren't you, Mama? I believe you are afraid that the *ton* will find you at fault instead of me," he teased. "Maybe I should visit one of those places that create paste jewels. No one would know. I could buy her a whole treasure chest of those."

"Anthony Hawksleigh, if you think I believe that you would even think of doing such a thing, you are a bigger clodpole than I first thought," his mother said with a laugh. "Remember. This is to be a surprise." She sat back with a satisfied smile. Was Emily going to be surprised! The jewels would make a much better gift than the flowers her daughter-in-law had suggested. For a moment, she wondered what Emily was planning, and then pushed the thought from her mind.

When Thursday arrived, Hawk had found just the right set of jewelry. The moment he saw the necklace, bracelets, and earrings, he had known the coral and diamonds would be perfect on Emily. Her maid said that she would be wearing that color to Lady Mairmount's. But as he sat and stared at the pieces, he began to doubt his choice. Perhaps he should have taken the diamonds. He looked at the necklace again, picturing the stones nestled against Emily's throat, and was reassured. He shut the case, impatient for the opportunity to present them.

Hawk had been dressed for almost an hour, waiting impatiently for a chance to give Emily her present. He wondered why he had not thought of the jewels himself. He could picture her face when she opened the box. "Blast, why doesn't that maid send for me?" he said, pacing about the room. He was alone; Lester, having helped him into the black evening coat and made a last adjustment to his cravat, had left after he handed Hawk his ring. Hawk walked to the door, wondering what was happening on the other side.

Finally the signal he had been waiting for came: a knock on the door to the hallway. Quickly he tapped on the connecting door, opening it before Emily could give him permission to enter. She was standing on the other side of the bed, a cloak in her hands. The soft coral of her dress lit her face with a hint of blush.

Now that the time Emily had been waiting for had arrived, she was cold, so cold she shivered. She could not take her eyes from his. He walked across the room. "These are for you," he said as he came around the bed.

Emily looked at him and then at the case in his hand. "What is it?"

From the moment he had entered the room, Hawk had stared at her, wanting to see her expression as she opened the box. Except for noting the color of her dress, he had not taken in any details. Emily slowly walked toward a table, not quite certain what was happening. She put the black leather box down and opened it. Her eyes widened in excitement. "For me? These are for me?" she asked, a soft sheen of tears in her eyes. Hawk glowed with pride. Then she bent over. He stiffened in shock.

"You are not wearing that dress out of this house," he commanded, noting with dismay that her breasts almost tumbled out of her neckline as she bent slightly.

"Come. Put them on me. Please." Emily smiled at him, the soft, winsome smile that had led him into conservatories and onto terraces while they were engaged. She held out the necklace to him and slipped the bracelets over her gloves.

His eyes darted from her face to her neckline. Maybe the necklace would help fill it in, he thought as he walked toward her. If it did not, his wife would change her gown, or they would not go. He took the necklace and turned her around, fastening the clasp securely. He could not resist the opportunity any longer. His hands brushed her shoulders.

She turned around to face him, her hands tracing the path where the necklace lay. "Thank you," she said in a breathless voice. She leaned forward and kissed him, her lips warm and sweet and slightly open. Then, before his arms could close around her, she whirled and dashed for a mirror. Bending over it, she twisted and turned, looking at the necklace in the glass.

Instead of filling in the neckline as he had hoped, the coral and diamonds seemed to emphasize her creamy breasts, breasts tipped with matching coral nipples he could see quite plainly. "Emily!" he said forcefully.

She danced away, twirling and watching the firelight flicker off her bracelets. "Thank you, darling Hawk. Oh, they are so lovely." So was she, with the firelight glinting through her dress, revealing plainly her long, slender legs, with just a hint of darkness at their joining. She twirled again, lifting the sheer skirt slightly so that he could see her legs covered in silk stockings and nothing else.

He groaned. Moving forward quickly, he captured her, holding her by her upper arms. "Emily, find something else to wear tonight. You are not wearing that dress in public," he said firmly. The thought of anyone else seeing her as she

looked now was too painful to believe. He shook her slightly
to get her attention, and her breasts, once barely held by the
extremely low neckline, tumbled out. "Look at you. What
did you think you were doing when you purchased a dress
even a harlot would have hesitated to wear in public?"

"Don't you like it?" Emiloy asked with a pout. She
ignored the fact that her breasts were exposed to his gaze.

Hawk gulped. He liked it only too well. He could feel
himself reacting. "That is not a gown to wear in public,"
he said, sputtering. He ran a hand through his hair, destroying
the carefully arranged style. He tried to loosen his tie.

"Let me," Emily said, flirting with him. Her fingers
quickly unwound the long piece of starched cloth and let it
fall to the floor. He took a deep breath, surprised that he
could not take in more air. Emily moved closer. She put her
arms around his neck and pulled his head down to hers, her
bare breasts brushing his chin. She kissed him. This time
his arms wrapped around her like a python around its prey.
His lips demanded, and hers answered. Their lips parted,
and their tongues caressed the other's lips.

When they had no air left, they drew away slightly. Then
Hawk buried his face in the creamy flesh only inches from
his face. A thrill ran through Emily, causing a strange ache
deep within her. Her hands circled his head, pulling him
close. Then they kissed again, this time slowly, leisurely.
She pulled back. "You do not think this dress is appropriate,
do you?" He shook his head. "I gave Mary the rest of the
evening off. If I am to change, you will have to unhook me,"
she said quietly, turning in his arms. Her face flamed as she
thought of what she was doing. Then she felt his lips on the
nape of her neck and shivered, forgetting everything.

Hawk's hands shook as he unfastened the copper hooks
down the back of her dress. His kisses followed his hands.
Emily moaned softly. Finally, when the last hook was
undone, she lifted her shoulders, and the coral dress slid into
a shimmering heap around her feet. She turned, her chin held
up proudly. Even though she had planned everything, now
she was nervous, unsure of herself. What would he do?

He closed his eyes and then opened them quickly. He felt
as though he were choking. There she stood in a flimsy shift,
a corset that merely cupped the lower slopes of her breasts

and ended at the waist, and long silk stockings. The necklace, bracelets, and gloves she wore emphasized her near-nudity. No longer thinking rationally, Hawk reached out and took her breasts in his hands. She gasped and moved toward him, one of the thin straps of her shift falling from her shoulder. Once again he kissed the upper slopes of her breasts, caressing her nipples until they formed tight buds that he washed with his tongue. His hands were busy behind her. Soon the corset and shift joined her dress on the floor.

Knowing she wanted to get closer to him, Emily ran her hand over his chest, sending shivers through him. She put her hands behind his head and pulled his lips toward hers. They met hungrily, each seeking and finding passion that built until it threatened to consume them.

Suddenly they were naked on the bed together. Her shyness forgotten, Emily explored Hawk's body, running her hands over him. He explored her. In both, fires raged. Soon touching was not enough. Hawk demanded. Emily responded. They exploded into ecstasy.

Later that evening, much later, they lay in bed satiated for the moment with love and the food Emily had provided. Emily nestled on Hawk's shoulder, half-covering him, one leg entangled with his. He bent to kiss her ear and scratched himself on the necklace she still wore. "Shall I get rid of this?" he asked, letting his fingers caress the skin beneath it.

"Yes." She sighed contentedly. She used the time he was fumbling with the clasp to plant tiny kisses along his jaw and neck.

"Stop that," he demanded, laughing. "That tickles."

"Just like a husband. You are always telling me what to do." She blushed as he bent and whispered something in her ear. "Are you certain we can do that?" she asked, willing to try.

"As easily as your dress came off," he promised. "Did you buy any more dresses like that?"

"One or two," she said, grinning up at him.

"You little minx. You never would have dared something like this when you were living with your aunt." Emily giggled. "Your aunt! Blast! How are we going to explain this to her?" Emily giggled harder.

12

Hawk woke instantly when the dream began. He loosened the arm he had drawn tightly around Emily. He turned his head toward her, afraid of what he might see. Her eyes, sleepy and more green than brown, were open, a sense of wonder and then joy flooding them. She put out a hand and touched his face as though she were afraid he was only a dream.

He sighed and kissed her fingers lightly, sending shivers of delight through her, reminding her of the past night. Even in the soft haze of early-morning sunlight, they could see each other. Slowly, silently, they inspected each other, first with their eyes, then with their hands and lips. Their passion burned brightly, taking them to new heights.

By the time they awoke again, the haze had disappeared and light flooded the room through the open lacework of the curtains on the windows. Emily had scandalized her housekeeper by not installing heavy satin or velvet draperies in her bedroom, but now the choice proved a wise one. "Good morning," her husband whispered. His eyes were dark with passion kept in check.

Emily smiled at him, blushing a little at the knowing look in his eyes. "Good morning," she answered, her voice as soft as a summer's breeze. For a few minutes they simply lay there, adjusting once again to the shared passion, the joy.

Then Hawk yawned and stretched, thrusting his arms outside the covers and baring both his and Emily's torsos. Embarrassed to be nude in front of him in the light of day, she pulled the covers around her. Hawk shivered too and slid under them. "The fire has gone out," she said regretfully.

"I doubt that." He rose on one elbow and looked down at her, enjoying the way her nipples puckered in the crisp morning air.

"You know I didn't mean that," she said. He laughed and lay back down. He pulled her close again, warming her with his body. "I meant the fire in the fireplace."

"Do we have to have a fire?"

"Yes, if we do not want to freeze."

"I can keep you warm." He smiled at her and then leered lasciviously. He pulled her closer, so close that she was molded against him.

"Hawk." Emily's voice trailed off as his lips covered hers. She wrapped her arms around his neck, pulling him closer.

"Are you warm now?" he asked sometime later. She blushed. He laughed happily. "You *should* blush, you shameless creature. Walking around in that dress." He gestured to the coral fluff that still lay on the floor. "You knew exactly how I would react, didn't you?" He gave her shoulders the slightest shake.

"I hoped." She lowered her eyelids and then peeked at him from under her lashes. A tiny smile played across his lips.

"Oh, Emily, I was so foolish. For months I have ached to hold you like this, to feel you respond to me." His face was serious. "To deny myself you was like killing me. I could not sleep."

"I heard you pacing the floor. I wanted to go to you, to beg you to hold me, to let me hold you." She pulled herself higher on the pillows, tucking the covers under her arms. "Hawk, you shut me out. I did not know how to get you to respond, to tell me what was wrong."

"You certainly discovered a reliable method of capturing my attention. But if you ever try to wear a gown like that outside this room . . ." He frowned at her, willing her to agree with him.

"I wouldn't. If you knew how hard it was to let you walk in here," she said, her face flaming as she remembered the way he had looked when she bent over the first time.

"Good." He leaned back satisfied. His stomach rumbled and hers answered. They both laughed. He slid from the bed and crossed to the bellpull. Hastily she looked away from his naked figure. Then she looked back, enjoying the ripple of muscles as he moved across the floor. "I am going to find a robe," he said as he rubbed his arms in the cold air. He opened the door and walked into his bedroom. A moment later he put his head through the doorway. "Come in here. It's warm," he told her.

Gingerly, more because of the cold than because she was embarrassed to have him see her naked, she slid from the bed and hurried into the other bedroom. "We won't be able to hear Mary when she comes," she said as he lifted her and tucked her under the covers. She shivered slightly because the sheets were cold even though the room was warm. The short walk had also made Emily aware of muscles she never knew existed.

"I'll go wait for her," Hawk promised.

"Tell her to have a fire started. And to bring us some breakfast."

Hawk looked at the clock. "Perhaps lunch instead?" he suggested.

"It's that late?" He nodded. "What will the servants think?"

"Exactly what you imagine." She threw a pillow at him when he laughed at the look on her face. "Shall I have her draw you a bath?" Emily nodded. "Since my room is warm, perhaps you should take it in here." His warm look told her that if she did, she would not be alone. "It is my turn now to be voyeur." Because he was standing in the doorway, he heard the scratching at the door. "Do not go away. I will be right back." He pulled the door closed behind him.

Emily lay back on the pillows and stretched. She groaned slightly when her muscles pulled. A smile danced across her lips, and she hugged herself. If she had been standing, she would have been dancing around the room. As it was, she snuggled down in the now-warm sheets and dreamed. Half-asleep, she did not hear the door open again or Hawk walk across the room. He leaned over the bed, enjoying the sight of her brown hair tossed across his pillow, the blue covers and white sheet pulled close around her. At first he started to bend over to kiss her. Then he backed up and sat down.

Lester opened the door, and Hawk waved him away. Not until Mary poked her head cautiously around the still-open door to Emily's bedroom did he move.

"Her bath is ready," the maid said quietly. "Here is her robe." She thrust the garment into his hands and turned away quickly in order to hide her own red face. She pulled the door closed behind her.

"Emily," Hawk said softly, bending over her. Not able to resist the soft coral of her lips, he kissed her, pulling himself away from temptation only at the last moment. As he pulled away, Emily followed, her lips still kissing his.

"Ummmm." She opened her eyes slowly and smiled up at him. She held up her arms, but he stepped away. She pouted at him.

"Your bath is ready," he said, wishing he had never given the order to have it brought.

"A bath? Where?" The suggestion enervated her. She sat up and threw back the covers, her shyness less important than her husband's admiring eyes.

Hawk handed her the dressing gown he was carrying and watched regretfully as she covered herself. "In your bedroom. While you are bathing, the servants are to bring a meal in here. So hurry." His stomach growled again as if to punctuate his words. Emily opened the door and slipped through. Hawk started to follow, but the sound of maids' voices stopped him.

The rest of the day was as magical as the evening before had been. Emily, relaxed and rosy from the hot bath, had dismissed her maid and walked through the doorway as though it were an ordinary happening. The dressing gown she wore, purchased especially for the occasion, was a velvet in the same coral she had worn the evening before. She had put on her necklace and earrings with it, the jewels glowing against her neck. Beneath the dressing gown she wore the sheerest shift she had ever seen. When Madame Camille had shown it to her, Emily had thought the modiste had made it up as a joke. She could hardly wait for Hawk to see her in it. The bottom of the shift, like the one she had worn the evening before, barely covered her bottom. She cleared her throat to capture her husband's attention.

Hawk stood up and moved toward her. His dark hair was still damp from his own bath. His cheeks were smooth and clean-shaven. When they met, for a moment they only stood and gazed at one another as if each were starving and the other were food. Then they were wrapped together, their lips as hungry as though they had been apart for years instead of only minutes.

Finally, gasping for air, Emily took a step back. Then she put her arm through his and nestled her head against his shoulder. "May I intereset you in some food, my dearest?" he asked with a smile as his stomach growled again.

"I suppose I must if I do not want to waste away," she said coyly. She looked up at him, her eyes glinting with fun, silently urging him to respond to her banter.

"Never. You are too valuable to waste." His smile promised much more than his words said. They walked over to the fireplace, where the servants had laid out a profusion of elegant dishes, all designed to be eaten hot or cold. Hawk seated her. Then he poured the wine and handed her a glass. "To a marriage as loving as these last few hours have been," he said quietly and sincerely.

Emily's smile was blinding as she too raised her glass in a toast. The rest of the day was magical, a respite from responsibilities and worry. Both knew it was stolen time; the dinner tray had contained a note from the older Mr. Hawksleigh: he needed to see his son as soon as possible the next day.

When Hawk left her bed the next morning, Emily tried to tell herself that life had to go on, that she would see him again in only a few hours. Even their last passionate embrace and his whispered words of love could not keep her fears away. Anything could happen. But she did not let him know how nervous she was to be away from him. She smiled and said good-bye as she had so many times before.

Later that day she visited her aunt, turning a brilliant crimson when the older lady began firing questions at her. "Well, I know it worked. You missed my dinner party. What did he say when he saw the dress? Is everything all right between you now? Where is he, by the way?" Lady Mairmount sat back, her eyes noting the whisker-scratched skin on her niece's neck.

"It worked perfectly. The dress was a success, although he has threatened my life if I try to wear anything similar outside our rooms," Emily said with a smile. She picked up her teacup, hiding behind its edge until her blush faded. "I could never have managed by myself. Thank you for your help," Emily said quietly when she had herself under control again.

"Pshaw! You would have thought of something similar soon. Glad I was of service," her aunt said as though she were not bursting with pride at having been a help. Then, changing direction, she asked, "Do you go to the Seftons' ball?"

"We are invited. I believe it appears on both our calenders."

"Both calenders? That will never do. Get up and have breakfast with him. Talk about the invitations then. You must accept the same ones. Anything else, and people will be talking. It is your first Season as a married couple," Lady Mairmount said, scandalized that Emily would even consider attending separate functions. "If you cannot discuss it with him, I will."

"No. He is never to know, Aunt Julia, that I talked to you. Promise me!" Emily begged. "I will talk to him this evening."

"See that you do, child. Now, tell me about those jewels Anthony gave you."

"How did you know about them?"

"His mother mentioned them. Very disappointed to hear you were in bed and he had decided not to leave you." She laughed sharply. "Coral," she said. "Tell me about it."

"Apparently my mother-in-law decided flowers were not good enough for her family. She convinced Hawk I needed more jewelry."

Lady Mairmount gave another crack of laughter. "Never looked in your jewelry case, has he?"

"I did not have any coral. You know that. Besides, it was the thought that counted. That and the fact that he gave them to me. They worked much better than any flowers could have. Would you care to join me for tea tomorrow morning to see the set? Mrs. Hawksleigh is coming.''

"So he came across quite handsomely, did he? I might as well, as long as you do not expect me too early. I'll get there by ten-thirty. No earlier.'' Emily kissed her delighted aunt on the cheek and made her escape.

The afternoon hung heavy on Emily's head. Not even nursery games with Jonathan could keep her mind away from her husband for long. With the unerring knowledge of the young, Jonathan knew every time Emily began to slip away in her mind, and he demanded her attention again.

His father's first words had pushed Emily to the back of Hawk's mind. "The next payroll shipment will leave next week, probably on Wednesday.''

"How will it travel? Do you plan to divide the shipment?''

"To send only one would be foolish,'' his father assured him. "The other question is one we must settle. What are your suggestions?''

"Me? Why me?''

"We want a fresh perspective on the situation. Maybe you can find a route we have overlooked.''

"Father, I will be happy to help. But I have never had to move huge sums of money across country. Besides, I have been out of England so long I do not know the trouble spots on the roads,'' Hawk protested. He ran a hand through his hair, dislodging each carefully styled lock. "There has to be someone else more prepared than I.''

His father frowned. He leaned forward, his face stern and serious. "We have someone who knows the roads and the trouble spots. We have another person who can tell us how many horses and how much equipment we will need. What we need you for is to keep your eyes and ears open not only here but also everywhere you go in London. If there is the slightest whisper about the shipment, we want to know.'' Hawk opened his mouth as if to protest, but his father interrupted him before he could. "You will sit in on the meetings. Then, if you hear anything at a ball or the opera or at your club, tell me immediately.''

"Yes, sir.'' Relieved that his role was to be a minor one, Hawk sat back, waiting for more information. He thought once of Emily, regretting the time he was spending away from her. Then he put the thought of her aside once more and listened to the plans.

Over the next few days Hawk and Emily discovered that their time apart during the day made the time together even sweeter. During these days, they canceled all but the most pressing evening invitations they had received in order to spend time with each other, sometimes just talking, at others coming together with passion that surprised and pleased both of them.

As the Season finally got under way, Emily followed her aunt's suggestion carefully. Each morning she joined her husband in the breakfast room. After they had both finished their breakfast, they inspected the latest invitations, selecting those they would attend. Although they would have been invited to most *ton* parties because of their families, now that Hawk was working for the government they found they were also receiving invitations from the political hostesses as well. Advised by his father which invitations were wise to accept, Hawk reviewed them carefully, consulted his list, and made his selections. Most of the others Emily suggested. Had they been less caught up in their own emotions, the young married couple might have had their heads turned by the attention that the *ton* had given them.

From the opening ball given by Lord and Lady Sefton, they captured the attention of fashionable London. Although not oblivious of the gossip the announcement of their names caused, Emily and Hawk enjoyed the social scene much as they had done when they were engaged. Everything was sweeter this time, though. When they left the last party or musicale, they did not have to part.

Only one problem still remained for Emily: her stepmother's arrival. But even she did not seem as formidable as Emily had once thought. As Jonathan had told his sister, his mother had captured the affections of a guest on an estate near Sir Horace's, a gentleman lately returned from abroad who hoped to further a political career in England. Caught up in her own concerns—keeping her fiancé's attention from straying to the younger ladies making their first bows to society that Season, smoothing his path in his search for a position in the government, and buying her bride's clothes—Lucretia Cheswick had little impact on Emily's life.

Her stepmother still had the power to make Emily uncomfortable. From the first moment she had arrived, Lucretia had disapproved of Emily's clothes, her house, and the way she had been treating her brother. "Dearest Emily," she had said when she arrived, her voice sweet and low, "is that one of the latest styles? And such a bright color too." She had taken an inventory of Emily's dress in less than a minute. "I think perhaps you should let me advise you about colors while I am here." She looked at the rich, warm pink with the hint of coral and knew that the soft pastels that were so becoming to her blond beauty would be overpowered next to it. Emily, encouraged by Hawk, had ordered several new dresses in the various shades of coral and red and knew that they became her like nothing she had worn before.

"Thank you, but my husband prefers me in these. How was your journey?" Emily smiled at the shorter woman, noting with pleasure how she drew back in surprise. "Jonathan is very excited about seeing you again. When you have rested, we will send for him and he can have tea with us." Lucretia could do little more than smile and allow herself to be swept up the stairs to her room. She noted jealously all the new furnishings, carpets, and wall coverings, filing each away in her mind so that she could outdo her stepdaughter once her own marriage was an accomplished fact.

"When we were redecorating the house, Jonathan insisted on choosing the color for your room himself," Emily explained as she opened the door. The walls were very light, the pink only the faintest blush. Spring flowers rioted across the fabric of the bed hangings and the draperies, creating the light airy look of a field of springtime against a pale green background. The green was repeated in the satin of the chairs and the flower-filled carpet.

"Jonathan chose this?" his mother asked, feeling just the smallest pang of remorse when she thought of the way she had put her son from her mind. Of course, the room was not what she would have chosen for herself. It should have been much more sophisticated, more in the Egyptian mode. As Lucretia turned around, noting the fine appointments, she smiled and told Emily, "Delightful. Of course, my son would have exquisite taste."

Emily bit her tongue, made a few more meaningless remarks, and hurried away. She closed the door and dusted her hands against her skirt as if she could wipe off the distaste she felt for the woman in the room behind her.

Fortunately, Lucretia Cheswick and fiancé ran in very different circles than Emily and Hawk did. Even during the day, they rarely came together. Since Hawk insisted that Emily and he plan their evenings with only the briefest stay possible at the engagements they accepted—he reminded her they needed their "rest"—even if Lucretia did appear at the same function, there was only a little time to be polite.

Emily was discovering that she enjoyed married life. Having someone to talk to, to love, and to care for made her feel secure once more. To Hawk's delight, she seemed more like the happy, carefree lady he had first fallen in love with. She responded ardently to his every advance, and he discovered new depths of passion and caring within her every day.

Every day was an adventure in sensation, in closeness for the two of them. Slowly they began to reveal their private thoughts and dreams. When Hawk probed for information about the years he was gone, Emily at first protested, laughing. When he pressed, the words flowed out of her like a river in flood stage.

"At first I did not understand, Hawk," Emily said quietly, her face shadowed with remembered grief. "My father was dead. That was all I cared about. He had loved me. I knew that. I felt so alone. You were in Spain. Sir Horace was worried about his daughter and Jonathan. No one but Lucretia told me anything, and she was so pleased with Father's will that she enjoyed gloating. I never saw her shed a tear, Hawk. Not one. I know she and my father had had an arranged marriage, but how could she stand there dry-eyed, glad that he was dead, glad that she had control of his money?" Emily burst into tears, sobbing as she had not for years.

Hawk simply held her and let her cry. She had tried to be strong for Jonathan, he knew. But a person had to grieve sometime. He had seen brave men break down on the front lines, huge men so drunk they were no longer ashamed of crying. "Cry it out, sweetheart. I'm here. Tell me about it," he whispered as his arms tightened around her, one hand patting her back comfortingly. Still sobbing slightly, Emily drifted off to sleep in Hawk's arms. As he lay there awake, Hawk thought of the last few years and acknowledged that for Emily the situation had been almost as harrowing as it had for him, in a different way. He wondered if he would have been as strong as she was if his family had vanished. When you got hurt, you ran home to Mama and Father, he reminded himself. I should have been here for Emily. His arms pulled her even closer, and, snuggled against him, secure in the love and warmth he shared with her, Emily grew calmer and sank further into a dreamless sleep.

Although Hawk's dreams were still a worry to him, he did not feel he could share them with Emily. He had tried more than once, but he froze every time he tried to force the words out. Somehow he knew Emily would never condemn him for his actions in the dream, but he did not want her thoughts of him colored by that memory.

As satisfying as their times together were and as much as they both longed to get away, to be truly alone together, both Hawk and Emily found themselves wrapped further and further in the social and political world of the *ton*. Hawk's days were filled with tracking down rumors. All but the smallest portion of the payroll had gone through safely. It was Hawk's job to investigate each person who had access to the information about the routes. But neither his father nor he could understand why only a small portion had been taken.

Quickly Hawk eliminated the clerks and office workers. They had not known the details. The only people who had known the route seemed to be beyond reproach. Accepted everywhere, they came from the most respected families in the land. All had served their country well. Hawk, the youngest of the group, tried to find other clues, but there were none.

As his worries increased, so did the number of nights he dreamed. More than once he opened his eyes just before a scream burst from his lips. Emily would stir and murmur a question sleepily. "Go back to sleep," he would whisper. "Everything is all right." Then he would lie awake in the darkness, wishing he were telling the truth. Only Emily's soft breath kept him company in the darkness.

Nervous and edgy, he had snapped at Emily one evening when she had looked at his solemn face and serious eyes and suggested that they stay at home. "We are expected," he said harshly. "And you promised your aunt that she could ride with us."

Emily drew back, feeling as though she had held out food to a starving animal and been bitten for her pains. "So I did," she said quietly. "Shall we meet in the drawing room in an hour? I will send a note to Aunt Julia about when to expect us." He nodded and left the room quickly, already regretting his hasty words. Emily sent off the note and walked slowly up to her room.

Totally disinterested in the plans for the evening, she allowed Mary to choose her dress, a deep red the color of raspberries, with a low, square neckline trimmed with knots of ribbon in the same color. While Emily worried about her husband, her maid used the curling stick to create a mass of frothy curls that framed her mistress's face, making her eyes look even larger than usual. Her diamonds and black-velvet-and-sable cloak completed her ensemble.

Hawk paced the floor of the drawing room, waiting for his wife to appear. Angry words trembled on the tip of his tongue when the door opened and she walked in. The sight of her clear, creamy complexion above the richness of the silk gown made him catch his breath. Then he hurried to her side, his headache and worries forgotten in his delight at the picture she made. "Magnificent, my dear," he said as he took her cloak from her maid and wrapped it lovingly around her. Using the cloak as an excuse, he pulled her close, dallying just long enough for her maid to disappear. "Absolutely breathtaking." He bent and kissed her until her lips burned the color of her dress.

As usual, Emily forgot everything in his arms. Forgetting her dress, she took a step or two closer to him. He stepped back, keeping her almost at arm's length. "Hawk?" she asked.

"Your maid expects you to arrive unrumpled, madam wife," he reminded her. "If we do not hurry, that will not happen. Besides, Aunt Julia is waiting."

"You know she will be late. Last time we had to wait a full fifteen minutes for her," Emily reminded him, pouting slightly as he refused to allow her to come any closer. She lowered her lashes and looked up at him flirtatiously.

"I would want more than a quarter of an hour to finish what you want to begin," he teased. She blushed but did not deny it. "The carriage is waiting."

Laughing, she walked out of the room into the hallway. She was not laughing when she walked back into the room several hours later. Her face was white and stark in its pain. "Emily, talk to him," her brother-in-law pleaded. "There has to be some explanation for what Hawk did."

"What explanation could there be for deserting his wife in the middle of the floor and walking over to that dark, petite foreigner? Andrew, everyone at the ball saw him leave me standing there. Then he walked out with her, forgetting that I even existed. And to take the carriage too. If you and your parents had not been present, my aunt and I would have been forced to find a ride home from friends. Think about what interesting conversation that will make over the teacups tomorrow!" Emily sat on the settee and buried her face in her hands, the diamonds in her ears glittering like the drops that spilled over on the rich silk of her gown.

The door to the room opened, and Lucretia Cheswick walked in, smug in all her blond beauty. "Who was that woman, Emily? My dear, you must be simply devastated," she said, her voice a low, catlike purr. Although her face was carefully sympathetic, every line of her body reeked satisfaction. "And married such a short time, too. I suppose that that must have something to do with it. Anthony is such a new husband that he did not know how to be discreet. Poor thing." She crossed to pat Emily on the shoulder.

Emily sat up straight, dashing her tears from her eyes. Andrew at first took two steps back. Then he rushed forward as though to shield his sister-in-law from Lucretia's barbs. "I had no idea that you would be present this evening, Lucretia," Emily said, a biting note in her voice.

"Lord Darlyrumple, my fiancé, insisted," Lucretia loved to say those words. They rolled off her tongue like pearls of wisdom. "The hostess is a family connection of his. I went under protest. I had no idea the evening would be so interesting." She smiled sweetly. "Shall I ring for your maid, my dear? Perhaps a tisane would help you sleep."

Andrew could bear no more. "And perhaps a saucer of milk would help improve your spirits. How dare you insult your hostess, you . . . you . . ."

"Andrew." Emily's quiet voice stopped him as he ranted at the older woman. Lucretia stepped back, her eyes flashing angrily. Used to having the gentlemen at her call, she had never known how to handle Andrew's anger and disgust. "I am certain you want to retire now, Stepmama. You need a good night's sleep to erase those lines that appeared when you frowned at Andrew," Emily said, her voice very soft and quiet. Lucretia froze as though she had been bitten by her favorite kitten. She sputtered a few words. Seeing Emily's determined face, however, Lucretia made good her escape.

Then Emily turned her attention to her brother-in-law. "Thank you for coming to my rescue, Andrew. Now you must go home."

"Home? But what if Hawk comes home?"

"He will. He is my husband, and this is my house," Emily reminded him. She smiled at him, marveling at the love and affection that seemed to ooze through his skin. "Thank you for everything you have done. Good night." She listened to a few more minutes of protests and then took his arm. She led him to the door. "Good night, little brother."

Andrew started, surprised to hear Hawk's name for him on her lips. Then he sighed and nodded. He bent and kissed her cheek. "Good night. But once Hawk explains to you, tell him to explain to me too," he demanded. "Knew my brother could be shatter-brained at times, but this is too much. Send for me if you need me." He took his hat and cape from the footman standing nearby. "Promise me. Knew I should have moved back in. Then I could stay tonight."

"Leave. I will let you know if I need you," she promised. "Go on with your evening. I told you when you followed me to Aunt Julia's that I can manage alone."

"Knew nothing good would come of his going to Spain. Should have stayed here and raised horses like I do." Still muttering to himself, Andrew left. Emily wondered for a minute whether she should have let him stay, and then shook her head. Her aunt's coachman would see that he got home safely, she reminded herself.

Even after she was ready for bed, Emily waited for her husband. Refusing to crawl under the covers, she prowled around her bedroom like a tiger in a cage. Her eyes grew heavy, and the hours chimed on the clock on the mantel. Hawk still did not come. Finally she sat down on the chaise and closed her eyes for just a moment.

13

When Lady Mairmount, Emily, and Hawk had arrived at the ball that evening, he realized that this would be one evening when they would not be able to make the excuses very early. Lady Mairmount, for all her protests of poor health, enjoyed being one of the last to leave.

Using his unfair advantage as her husband, Hawk secured three early dances with Emily, alternating them with his duty dances. He had begged for more as they danced across the floor, but Emily refused laughingly. As they moved through the figures of the last of his dances, Hawk looked toward the entrance to the ballroom. His face carved as from stone, he stopped in the middle of the dance floor, stepping away from his wife.

From the moment Hawk caught sight of the petite dark-haired woman, he forgot about his wife, forgot about the people surrounding him, forgot about everything but his nightmare. He walked toward the small beauty in the black silk gown as though she were the fisherman and he were the fish she was pulling in. Startled by his behavior, everyone stopped talking for a moment. Then a buzz of shocked conversation filled the room. Hawk heard none of it.

His whole world had shrunk to one figure—the woman from his nightmare. In his dreams she screamed and pulled away from him. At the ball she smiled at the lady who stood beside her, some acquaintance of his mother's. As soon as the lady of the nightmares looked up and saw him walking toward her, she turned pale, the faint flush in her cheeks turning to chalk. The fan she held in one hand snapped. She started to make her excuses, but it was too late. He was upon her, taking her hand in his.

He bowed. "Captain Anthony Hawksleigh, *condesa*. I am happy that you too escaped Boney's dragoons," he said quietly. After months of uncertainty, memories flooded him like the Nile inundating Egypt.

The lady in front of him was as pale as freshly fallen snow, her brown eyes huge and frightened. She took a step or two back, drawing her black silk skirts around her as if they were armor. Then, aware of the eyes that made the captain and her the center of attention, she forced a smile. "I do not believe we have been formally introduced, sir," she said quietly. Her voice, though low and musical, was shaky.

As though he had not heard what she had said, Hawk continued very seriously. "I thought you were dead. I tried to help you. You must remember how I tried to help. Your screams have haunted me for months. How did you escape? Were you rescued at the same time I was? Strange no one mentioned you to me." Words gushed from him as though his memory had released a river of words that refused to be damned.

"Oh, Captain. Those memories . . ." The *condesa* raised a hand to her eyes as if to dash tears from them. "I had thought I had put them behind me. I must put them behind me if I am to continue my life." Her hands fluttered helplessly, and she began to sway.

"Here, let me lead you to a seat," he suggested, capturing her arm in a firm grasp. The older lady who had remained near the *condesa* gave a gasp and raised her brows. Realizing that Hawk did not even notice her, she hurried away to a small group of ladies, eager to share what she had overheard.

"No, no! I cannot. I must leave," the *condesa* said frantically, trying to pull away from him but not succeeding. Then her eyes brimmed with tears. "But I have no carriage." She began wringing her hands and shivering as though the chill of the evening air had penetrated the warm room. "What am I to do?"

"Allow me to be your escort," Hawk said firmly, leading her from curious eyes. "I will call my carriage while you send for your cloak." Totally oblivious of his wife and family, now the center of gossip, he led the small dark-eyed woman toward the stairs, forgetting to make his farewells to their host, who stood nearby.

Looking frantically around her, the *condesa* caught the eye of a gentleman standing in the shadows of a doorway at the head of the stairs. He shrugged as if to say there was nothing he could do. Then the *condesa* took a few deep breaths, straightened her back, and walked on. She forced a smile to her lips as she allowed Hawk to escort her down the stairs. The hand under Hawk's tightened slightly around his arm. She lowered her eyes and then glanced back up at him coquettishly. "You are so forceful, Captain," she whispered, admiration, though still tinged with fear, oozing from her as water filters through sand. She took her cloak from the footman and handed it to Hawk, smiling up at him as he wrapped it around her. Hawk, awash with memories of his lost days, did not wonder about her allowing him to escort her home.

Her beauty was in contrast to the vision that drifted through Hawk's mind. In that, her face was bruised, her eyes frightened. In spite of the differences, Hawk would have recognized the *condesa* anywhere. Her face was burned into his unconscious. Now his whole mind focused on her, intent on learning as much as he could about her. Not realizing how strange his actions were to others, he handed her into his carriage and jumped in after her. "How is it that you are in London, *condesa*?" he asked quietly. "How did you escape?" He turned to smile at her. "Do you know that I am not certain I even know your name."

"My name is María del Carmen, Condesa de Ildefonso," she whispered.

Her words triggered memories that had been locked deep in his mind. "You and your husband were trying to escape the French, trying to leave for the Americas. Isn't that right?" He turned to face her, his heart hammering. All the color and excitement drained from her face, leaving her so pale he was afraid she would faint. "Are you well? Shall I have someone go for a doctor?"

The carriage pulled to a halt. The *condesa* looked up at him blankly for a moment. Then she shook her head. "I will be all right once I am inside," she said in a breathless whisper. "The memories are too much for me sometimes." Only the slightest accent flavored her speech.

"I insist that you allow me to stay with you until you

recover," Hawk demanded as the coachman opened the door. Brushing the man aside, he leapt out and held out his hand to her. Taking a deep breath, she pasted on a quivering smile and let him help her from the carriage.

"Always you come to my aid, Captain," she said as she put her hand on his arm and allowed him to hand her up the stairs into the comfortable house in front of them. "I know my cousin will wish to thank you for your assistance to me in Spain and this evening. May I offer you some refreshments while you wait for him?" she asked. Now that she was in her own home, her face regained some of its lost color. She handed her cloak to the waiting footman and turned to face Hawk.

The stark black silk against her white skin made him draw in his breath. She was a beauty. Her warm brown eyes seemed to promise him more than her thanks. He took a deep breath. "I think it would be best if I met him at some other time. You have had a shock. I am certain you wish to retire."

"No, do not leave," she said frantically, pulling him into a nearby salon, her hand biting into his arm like a steel band. "I do not wish to be alone with my memories." She closed her eyes and shuddered dramatically.

Stepping closer to her, Hawk patted her on the shoulder. She looked up at him with her warm brown eyes, and a single tear rolled down her cheek. He gulped, nervous, as many men are when a woman allows her tears to flow. "I suppose I could stay for a short while. I do want to hear how you managed to get to England," he said thoughtfully.

The *condesa* stepped back, just the hint of a smile quivering about her lips. "Let me order some refreshments," she said quietly. "Then we can talk." She crossed to the bellpull and rang. When her servant had come and gone, she motioned Hawk over to a sofa upholstered in a rich red-and-gold brocade and took her seat beside him.

When he left several hours later, he was exhausted. As his carriage took him home, he thought about the evening. But in spite of their hours of conversation, he could remember few specific details about the *condesa*. He had met her cousin, the Conde de Ildefonso. As her husband's closest relative, he had been next in line for the title. As Hawk thought about the man, he felt slightly uncomfortable. The man's answers were too polished, almost as though they had been practiced. And his thanks had been too hearty. Hawk sighed and reminded himself that one did not choose one's relatives. The *condesa* herself seemed almost uncomfortable in the *conde*'s presence.

Hawk replayed the conversations with the *condesa* and her cousin in his mind, once again marveling at the little information he had learned about them. All he knew was that they had chosen London instead of the Americas in order to protect the *condesa* from gossip. The British, who had rescued her, had found them safe passage, and they had lived in seclusion for months before securing entry to the *ton* through political connections.

Then Hawk sat up straight. "They learned a great deal about me," he said, surprised. The carriage drew up to his door. He walked into his house, surprised to see his butler. "You are late, Clarke."

"Yes, sir." The icy tones of his butler brought Hawk up short. The butler, ensconced in his favorite tavern for the evening, had been horrified when one of his friends had arrived and told him the story of the captain and the *condesa*. Although serving one of the most fashionable households in the city, one whose inhabitants were welcome guests in the homes of the most-respected families, Clarke had found himself the focus of the pity of his friends, his household the center of gossip. He had hurried home, hoping that the news was false, but the footman who had been standing bsside the door when his mistress and Andrew Hawksleigh had been talking disabused him of that notion. The butler took the hat and cloak his master handed him, his face as empty of emotion as he could make it.

"What is the matter with you, Clarke? Has someone stolen the best silver?" Hawk asked jokingly.

"Nothing, sir. Will there be anything else?" The butler's voice was correct, though cold.

"Not tonight. I'm for bed." Hawk started up the stairs toward his rooms. Emily was going to be so surprised, he thought. He hurried up the stairs eager to share his newly found memories with her. Clarke stared up at him resentfully.

Quickly he disrobed, pulled his nightshirt over his head and opened the connecting door to Emily's bedroom. Looking first at the bed, he found it empty. Startled, he glanced around the room and found her asleep on the chaise. "Emily, Emily!" She moved restlessly. Too impatient to allow her to wake up slowly, the way she preferred to, he grabbed her shoulders and shook her. "Emily, wake up." She opened her eyes carefully, hoping that it had all been a dream. "Emily, the most wonderful thing has happened!"

She sat up slowly. Even in the flickering firelight she could tell that something had changed about her husband. His hair was tousled, his nightshirt hung off one broad shoulder, and his face was glowing with excitement. A tiny smile crossed her lips. She put up a hand to touch his face. As she moved, the weight of her earrings brushed her cheek. Her hand moved to her ears, and her face grew angry.

As soon as he was certain she was awake, Hawk bounded away, throwing more coal on the fire. Then he dashed back to her. "Emily, the most wonderful thing has happened. I have—"

"Made me the laughingstock of London," she said angrily. At first simply hurt and certain he would have a good reason for his behavior, Emily had thought about the scene at the ball for hours. Now she was angry. She stood up, pulling herself up to her very highest height. Catching him by surprise, she pushed him down on the chaise. "I suppose this incident, too, was part of your finding out about yourself," she said bitterly.

"It was." Hawk struggled to stand up again, reaching out to pull her into his arms. She pushed him away. "Emily, I remember everything!"

"And that makes what you did tonight all right? You left me, your wife, standing in the middle of a ballroom floor while you walked out with another woman!" Emily began to pace the room, her brown curls bobbing angrily. "You took our carriage and left my aunt and me to go home on foot. Had your parents not taken us up in their carriage, I suppose we would be there still." Coming close to him again, she poked him in the chest with her finger. "Or did you remember us and go back to get us? Did my stepmother tell you, as she gleefully told me, that we managed to get home safely without you?''

Hawk's eyes widened in horror as her words sunk in. ''Emily, love—''

''Do not call me any of those sweet names. I know what you think of me. My stepmother was right. A husband who loves his wife does not create a public scandal and leave her to face it alone.'' Her words hit him almost as hard as her hand did. He sat there stunned, letting her hammer away at him, her eyes lit with green fire. ''Go away,'' she said angrily. ''Just go away!'' She turned her back on him and retreated to her sitting room.

He tried to follow her, but she slammed the door in his face. ''Emily, my memory is back,'' he said as calmly as he could, hoping that she would open the door and rush into his arms.

''Good! Then it can keep you company tonight. I do not plan to!'' He heard a crash on the other side of the door and stepped back a pace or two.

''Emily?'' This time his tone was more tentative. He waited for a moment; then he called again, ''Emily?'' He waited a few minutes and then sighed. He walked slowly, heavily toward the door into his bedroom. Once there, he sat in a chair beside his bed and put his head into his hands. ''What have I done?'' he wondered.

The question was still on his mind hours later when Andrew walked into the library, where his brother sat staring into a fire. Even with little sleep, Hawk was handsome. He wore a dark blue coat and buff pantaloons but looked as though he had only thrown them on. His neckcloth, usually pristine, hung in untidy folds. The moment Andrew entered the room, he went after his brother with hammer and tongs. ''So you finally came to your senses and returned home, Anthony Hawksleigh,'' Andrew said angrily. ''How could you desert Emily and her aunt that way? You made her the laughingstock of the entire town. You should have heard the way her stepmother laughed at her. If you were not my brother, I would call you out. I may do it anyway.'' By the time he finished, Andrew was shouting and his face was red. ''Father said to tell you, if I saw you, that you might as well

forget about going to work today. He did not need another
scandal right now.''

Hawk had raised his head. Now he lowered it despondently. ''Andrew, I did not—''

''You did not think. What happened, Hawk? How could
you walk off that ballroom floor and leave with a woman
no one even knew? Do you know what a feast the harpies
had over that? And Emily was their prey. I wanted to sink
into the floor, to apologize for knowing you, much less being
related to you. Had it not been for Mama and Lady Mairmount, I think Emily would have collapsed right there.''
While he talked at the top of his voice, Andrew was pacing
up and down the room. Usually a pattern card of neatness,
this morning he was as rumpled as his brother.

During the hours he had been lying awake in bed, Hawk
had remembered that he had taken the carriage, deserting
them. He winced as he remembered Emily's words. ''Was
my exit as dramatic as you make it seem?''

''Dramatic? As far as the *ton* is concerned, no one else
is worth a mention. You should have done some thinking
before you left Emily there at the mercy of the crowd.
Dammit, Hawk. You know what these people are like with
a scandal, and you created a beautiful one. Emily will not
dare to step foot out of this house for months. There is no
choice but to rusticate and hope that everyone will have
forgotten what happened by next Season. Fortunately, Mama
and Father arrived only minutes before you walked off the
floor. We were able to whisk Emily away almost immediately,'' Andrew said, his voice condemning.

The door to the library opened. ''Clarke said you had just
arrived, Andrew. Thank you for coming,'' Emily said in a
calm voice as she opened the door and came in. Catching
sight of her husband, she stopped, her hand still on the latch.
''You!'' She whirled and stepped back into the hallway.

Hawk was up and had grabbed her before she could
complete her escape. He pulled her back into the library and
closed the door. ''Emily, I did not mean to leave you last
night. Let me explain,'' he begged. She tried to pull away,
but he refused to let her move. ''Please listen.''

She refused to meet his eyes. ''Listen to what? More of

your excuses?'' She twisted under his hands and won free. ''I saw what you thought of me last night! All of London saw! What can you say that will make that go away?'' Dressed in a dark blue dress that made the shadows under her eyes even darker, Emily looked at him through eyes filled with pain.

''Emily, Mama suggested that you and Jonathan might want to visit her for a time,'' Andrew said hesitantly.

His brother glared at him and said angrily, ''My wife will stay with me.''

''I believe that is my choice, Anthony Hawksleigh,'' his wife said bitingly. ''I might as well be with people who remember I am alive.''

''Emily, I did not mean to leave you alone.''

''But you did, just like you did on our honeymoon and for months afterward,'' she cried, forgetting for a moment that they were not alone.

Andrew, his face registering his horror at being in the middle of a discussion that promised to wash dirty linen in public, backed toward the door and then into the hall, almost stumbling over a small group of servants huddled nearby. Taking one look at his face, they scattered.

Inside the library, Emily shivered. ''You can follow him, sir,'' she told her husband. ''I do not want to talk to you now or in the future.''

''Oh, you don't, do you? Well, then, I will take myself off. But we are staying in London. Make no mistake about that. I refuse to run just because people are talking about me,'' he said. Then he stormed out of the library and the house. His worst fears during the darkest night were coming true. Emily refused to let him explain. As he thought about what had happened the evening before, his guilt at deserting his wife began to melt away under his feeling of hurt. He had made a great breakthrough, and no one cared enough to listen.

No sooner had Hawk left the library than Emily made up her mind. Searching out her brother-in-law, she sent him posthaste to her aunt's home. ''Beg her to come to me. I need her advice,'' she told him.

''Why me? After last evening she said she never wanted

to see anyone by the name of Hawksleigh again," Andrew protested.

"She will have forgotten it by this morning," Emily promised, hoping she was telling the truth. She practically pushed Andrew out her door and into the street, still protesting. After a few minutes with Jonathan, Emily changed her dress, choosing one of the smartest and brightest in her wardrobe. No matter what the *ton* thought of her, she did not intend for her aunt or her stepmother, if she happened to leave her bedchamber before noon, to think she was a dieaway miss.

Emily was glad for the protection her red dress gave her when her aunt arrived. Lady Mairmount entered complaining. "Well, have you spoken to that man? What did he have to say for himself? What excuse did he offer? Has he lost his mind?" She paused, her finger tapping her cheek thoughtfully. "Hmmm. I wonder if that would work? If there were not a woman involved . . . Still, I suppose any idea is better than none. We shall simply have to try it. If it does not work, we can come up with something else." Wandering about the room as she talked, Emily's aunt inspected every chair before she finally sat in one close to the fire. She settled her shawls about her in a flurry of blues and roses and a hint of primrose to match the wool gown and pelisse she wore. "Well, what do you think?" Lady Mairmount asked.

"About what?"

"My dear, weren't you listening?" She frowned before she remembered that frowning caused unsightly lines. Quickly she made her face as emotionless as possible.

"I was listening, Aunt Julia," Emily protested. "But what does it have to do with what happened last night?"

"Are you deaf, girl? We will tell a few people—I know exactly whom to tell first—about your husband's horrible experiences in Spain, hinting of course that the reason he returned to England was that Wellesley was worried about his health." Lady Mairmount sat up and took off two of her shawls, letting them drop to the floor beside her. Emily sighed, knowing that before long she would move to another seat, miss them, and demand that they be returned to her immediately.

"What good will that do?" she asked, wondering what her aunt would say if she knew how close to the truth she was getting.

Lady Mairmount raised her eyes to the ceiling and sighed heavily, dropping another shawl on the floor. She stood up and walked toward her niece. Standing beside Emily, she patted her on the shoulder. "You poor dear, last night must have been more devastating than even I dreamed. Just leave everything to me. Before the week is out, everyone will be talking about how brave Anthony is and what a wonderful wife you are to stand by him as you have."

"Aunt Julia, I do not think . . ."

The door to the salon opened with a bang. Anthony Hawksleigh, his face flushed and angry, stormed in, his eyes on his wife. "Clarke told me where you were. You and I need to talk."

"We certainly do, sir. And I hope the first words out of your mouth are an apology." Lady Mairmount walked between Emily and Hawk, her back ramrod straight, her face disapproving.

Hawk stepped back a pace or two. He flushed a brighter red. "Lady Mairmount, I did not see you. I apologize for my rudeness. But Emily and I need to talk. Would you excuse us?"

"No." Neither Emily nor Hawk had expected her answer. Their faces froze in shocked surprise. Hawk opened his mouth, but for the first time in his life did not know what to say. They simply stared at the older lady. "From what I have been able to observe, neither of you has the sense God gave a flea, when it comes to the other. Look what Emily had to do to get you into her bed."

Emily gasped, took one look at her husband, and wished she had never consulted her aunt. Hawk, already red, turned almost purple. He glared at his wife. She could feel his anger but not lift her eyes. Instead, she wished for a hole to crawl into. How could her aunt have given her away like that? "You can wave your magic wand and everything will be all right, I suppose?" he asked sarcastically. His visit to his club had been eye-opening. Only the most rakish of his friends had been willing to talk with him. And one acquaintance had given him the cut direct. Translating their actions as

representative of the *ton*'s opinion, Hawk realized what that
would mean for Emily. He had hurried home, hoping they
could find some solution to the situation he had created.

"No. I am no character out of a fairy tale. This is real
life," Lady Mairmount reminded him. She sank down in a
nearby chair and pulled her two remaining shawls tightly
about her. She shivered slightly. Hawk picked up one of the
discarded shawls and handed it to her. Emily, her hands
buried in the other two, barely noticed. "Maybe we can come
up with something. Who was that woman?" Lady Mairmount
asked in a tone that conveyed her opinion of the lady.

Letting the slur Lady Mairmount had cast upon the *condesa*
slide past, Hawk smiled sardonically. "I have been trying
to tell someone for hours. She was imprisoned with me in
Spain."

"She was in Spain? What was she doing there?" Emily
asked, rising. She slowly crossed until she was standing in
front of him, her hands still clutching her aunt's shawls. Still
angry at him for his callous behavior the evening before,
and embarrassed by her aunt's betrayal of her confidence,
Emily was at war with herself. She was in love with her
husband, had been since she had been old enough to know
what love was, but did not know whether she could trust him
not to hurt her again.

"She lives there. Or at least she did until Bonparte killed
her husband and captured her. Emily, she is the woman in
my dreams, the woman who has haunted me with her screams
for so long." Eager to tell his wife the whole story, Hawk
let his words tumble out. His face was lit with the excitement that she had not seen except in their most private
moments.

"What dreams? Why haven't you mentioned her before?
What do you mean she haunted you? And why was she at
the ball last evening? What is she doing in London?" Emily
asked, her anger taking control for the moment. Lady Mairmount nodded but held her tongue, content for once to be
in the background.

Hawk took his wife's hand and led her to the settee. "I
told you that I did not remember what happened to me when
I was captured." Although for a moment Emily resisted, she

let him seat her, and looked up at him expectantly, hoping he could erase her doubts and disapproval.

"You were captured? Much better. We can blame the French for your state of mind," the older woman murmured.

"Hush!" her niece said impatiently, and turned back to her husband. "I remember." She paused, silently urging him to continue.

"Well, I was not telling the complete truth. I did remember something, something so horrible I was afraid for you." He paused and closed his eyes, giving silent thanks that his worst fears had not been realized.

"I do not understand," his wife said quietly, more moved by him than she wanted him to see. "How could something that happened to you in Spain affect me?"

"Neither do I," her aunt added. "Get to the point."

"All I remembered was that a woman, the *condesa*, was backing away from me, pleading with me not to hurt her. I could not remember any more. I tried. I would wake up after one of these dreams, shaking with fear. One night shortly before we married, when Andrew tried to wake me from my nightmare—apparently he and Lester took it upon themselves to watch over me—I went wild and tried to strangle Andrew. Fortunately, Lester saved him. When I thought about what had happened that night, I knew I had to stay away from you in case I reacted to you the way I did to Andrew."

"A dream. A dream is what kept us apart?" Emily asked, not knowing whether to be angry because he had neglected her or pleased that he had cared enough to worry about her safety.

"A nightmare." Hawk reached out and took Emily's hand, gazing deep into her eyes that now were a clear green. He was bending forward to kiss her when a noise behind him stopped him.

"That is a pretty story, but rather farfetched." Emily drew back from him. Her anger rushed back as she nodded her agreement to her aunt's remarks. Hawk felt a momentary sense of panic. "I do not understand what the woman last night has to do with this dream you keep mentioning," Lady Mairmount said, not at all pleased by his explanation.

"The lady I saw last night was the lady in my dream, the Condesa de Ildefonso. As soon as I saw her, I remembered everything." He grinned at Emily.

His wife's aunt tapped him on the shoulder. "What does that mean, young man?"

"I was not the one the lady was screaming at. I was not trying to hurt her. The French, who had the both of us, had entered the room where we had been kept prisoner. She was afraid of them, not of me!" Once again a beautiful smile flashed across his face, making Emily catch her breath. "I tried to tell you last night, but you would not listen," he told Emily quietly. "Apparently seeing her was the trigger. I remember distinctly now. The French soldiers walked toward us. She cowered behind me, whimpering, screaming. I tried to protect her, but they were too much for me. The last thing I remember before I woke up again in camp was a rifle coming down upon my head." Emily moaned softly and raised her hand as if to touch his face. Then she pulled back.

"That is quite a story, sir. If my niece chooses to believe you, that is her business. Still, it does have possibilities. That blow on your head. I suppose doctors in Wellesley's camp could verify it?"

Hawk looked from his wife to her aunt. Then he stood up, his back as straight as the mast of a ship on a calm day. "If my word is not enough for you, my lady . . ." he began, the look on his face showing his hurt and disillusionment. He looked at Emily pleadingly, but she did not look at him.

"Sit down. All you young people are alike. So quick to take offense where none is meant. It does not matter whether I believe you or not; the *ton* must be convinced."

Emily looked up at her husband, noted the pain in his eyes, pain he tried to hide, and held out her hand. "Come. Sit back down so that we can find some way out of this dilemma," she said quietly, her face still serious.

He sat down beside her and took her hand. "You must know that I would never do anything to hurt you, at least not deliberately," he added, hoping she would believe him. "I do not know what happened last night. I saw her, and for a moment I was back in Spain, in the dark room. All that mattered was that I get both of us out of there safely."

"Very good," Lady Mairmount said. "That is just what we must make people believe happened." She dropped one of her shawls beside her chair and leaned back complacently.

"But it did happen," he protested, looking to see if Emily were willing to believe him. She looked up at him with love in her eyes. Although she knew the next weeks might not be pleasant ones, as long as he loved her she could weather any storm, even those created by her stepmother.

"Do not convince me. Convince society. You knew the *condesa* in Spain but thought she had been killed. Yes, that will work. Now, this is what we must do," the elderly lady began. She took a deep breath, reveling in the chance to display her skill in manipulating the *ton*.

14

For the next few days both Emily and Hawk spent most of their time in the house on Grosvenor Square. In spite of the snide remarks of her stepmother, who on the advice of her fiancé finally removed to his parents' home so that Emily's terrible reputation would not affect his chance of a governmental post, they both enjoyed their time together. For the first time since their disastrous honeymoon, they talked to each other, really talked, telling their deepest secrets and hidden fears.

For Hawk the only problems remaining on his horizon were convincing Emily to stop saying good night at her bedroom door, restoring her to her rightful place in society, and solving the mystery of the missing payrolls. Because of the gossip, he could do none of these things, but he did not let his frustration show.

Even his family began to warm toward him. His interview with his father at the estate outside London had not been pleasant, the elder Hawksleigh making his displeasure clearly known. But his father had listened. Andrew, however, was still decidedly cool, and his mother was clearly on Emily's side.

Still, the situation was proving advantageous in some ways. Now in disgrace and banned from the Exchequer, Hawk was being sought out by people who had once avoided him. Their conversations had proved interesting and informative. After three days of quiet—days Lady Mairmount declared essential to her plan—Hawk returned to his club for luncheon. There he found that the chill of that first morning had worn off some—not enough to make him acceptable to their wives, but enough to make most people acknowledge him. He ate his bird, drank his bottle of wine, and enjoyed a few hands of cards with a dissolute young lord known as one of the most reckless gamblers in all England.

"Avoid the ladies," the man had warned, already deep in his cups, "especially that one."

"Which one do you mean?" Hawk asked curiously.

"The *condesa*," the man said, beginning to slur his words. "She's looking for an older man. Be married by the Season." He smiled roguishly. "But to whom? She's an old man's darling. Just has to make her choice."

Hawk controlled himself with effort, reminding himself that one more scandal involving the *condesa* and him would not win his wife back or restore his reputation. He smiled thinly. "Really? I had not heard."

"Too busy trying to capture her attention yourself, eh, Hawksleigh." The gambler laughed and took the hand. "Luck's changed. Glad you agreed to take a hand."

"Well, I have lost all I intend to for the afternoon," Hawk said firmly, pushing his chair back.

"Always knew you had no bottom. Go on, then. Visit your *condesa* this afternoon and see how many females are there. Then count the older men." The young lord sat back in his chair, laughing. "Care to make a wager?" He was still laughing when Hawk stalked off.

In spite of himself, the man's words had piqued Hawk's curiosity. He took his hat and cane from the footman at the door and hurried home. As soon as he walked into his home, Clarke said, "Mrs. Emily wishes to see you when you have time, sir." The butler's tones were still frosty.

"Where is she?"

"In the small salon." Clarke looked at his master as Hawk hurried down the hall. He allowed the slightest smile to appear on his lips as he thought of the triumvirate that waited for his master there.

"Thank goodness, you are finally home," his mother said as he took a few steps into the room and then halted. "It is almost time to begin making afternoon calls." Dressed in a deep blue afternoon gown, she looked elegant.

"And the *condesa* is at home today," Lady Mairmount added. "Run upstairs and change immediately." Like

Hawk's mother, she too was dressed in her most elegant afternoon gown, a stunning creation of soft violet wool trimmed with sable. She smoothed her gloves over her fingers. When he just stood there, she said, "Well, are you coming with us or must we go alone?"

"Go where?"

"Hawk, my aunt and your mother have decided that we must visit the *condesa* this afternoon," Emily said quietly. Like the other two, she wore an afternoon dress that would raise envy in many hearts. A soft clear red, it should have clashed with the dress worn by her aunt, but it did not. The color gave Emily's face a life and sparkle that it would otherwise have been missing. She was not looking forward to her first venture into society again.

"Why?" Hawk asked, his tone hostile.

"I have done all I can do. The story of your cruel imprisonment and injury is known by everyone who counts. Now we must show that the family is united. We must meet this lady whom you gallantly rescued at such a great cost and make her welcome," Lady Mairmount explained with a slight smile.

"The poor child. What she must have suffered," his mother added. "And after your behavior with her the other evening, she must be devastated by the way society is treating her."

"What do you mean?"

"Anthony Hawksleigh, you know what people are saying about her. She allowed you, a perfect stranger, or so it seemed, to escort her home from the ball, causing you to abandon your sweet, loving wife. And a foreigner too!" his mother exclaimed. Lady Mairmount and Emily exchanged meaningful looks. "Of course, you will escort us when we visit her this afternoon. We need you to make the introductions."

Emily rose and crossed to stand in front of him, one hand on his chest. "Please, Hawk?" She looked up at him, a pleading look in her eyes. Captivated by those eyes, he nodded. "We will wait for you here," she added, and walked him to the door.

As soon as the door closed behind him, her aunt smiled

at her and said, "Very well done. I could not have done it better. Don't you agree, Mrs. Hawksleigh?"

"Perfect, my dear. Simply perfect." She settled back in her chair, a satisfied smile on her face. "It is lovely to have a daughter at long last."

"Are you certain we have to do this?" Emily asked in a rush.

"There is no other way. We want the *ton* to believe that we understand completely about the other evening," her mother-in-law reminded her. "You are certain that she receives this afternoon, Julia?"

"Absolutely. Now, what is keeping that boy? Doesn't he know we must be on our way?" She walked over to the mirror and settled her sable toque more firmly on the gray curls.

Upstairs, Hawk stared into his mirror, trying to tie his cravat. He had already ruined six of them, and this one was not doing what he wanted either. What could his mother and his wife's aunt have concocted now? Finally, frustrated, he turned to his valet. "Do something with this, Lester, before my mother comes bursting in here."

"Yes, sir." Calmly the valet arranged the neckcloth and stepped back. "Is that to your liking, sir?"

"Fine. Now, hand me my hat and gloves, and I will be gone. Lester, when you marry, watch out for relatives."

"Yes, sir." The valet watched his master hurry from the room. Then a smile split his face. He knocked on the door connecting to the next room. "They're off," he said as Mary opened the door.

"Lud, wouldn't I like to be a fly on the wall of that drawing room," the maid said, her face breaking into a smile. "Will she let them in, do you think?"

"Won't be able to keep them out. She probably won't want to. The lady has not been very happy these last few days. Seems she's lost entry to the *ton*'s parties and wants it back," the valet told her. "Wish I could see her face when that quartet comes in. According to her servants, ladies rarely visit that house."

As soon as Hawk and his ladies were escorted into the *condesa*'s drawing room, he was uncomfortably aware that his relatives were the only women there. The rest of the party was made up of elderly gentlemen, who surrounded their hostess, and the *conde*, who showed more interest in Emily than Hawk liked.

"*Condesa,* may I introduce Lady Mairmount, my wife's aunt; my mother, Mrs. Josiah Hawksleigh; and my wife, Mrs. Anthony Hawksleigh?" He gave her a brief bow and turned back to the ladies he had escorted. "My dears, this is the Condesa de Ildefonso." The *condesa,* who had risen when she saw the older ladies walk in, curtsied gracefully.

Before she had time to say anything, her cousin was at Hawk's side. "Introduce me, sir. I do not wish to be thought impolite to three so charming ladies." Although the *conde*'s smile included all three, his eyes never left Emily's face.

"And this is her cousin, the Conde de Ildefonso," Hawk said curtly. His frown deepened as he watched the *conde* lead Emily carefully to a chair.

"May I offer you tea?" the *condesa* asked politely. She too glanced at her cousin, who sat smiling at Emily.

"That would be delightful, *condesa,*" Lady Mairmount said. "We simply had to come and offer you our apologies for Anthony's hasty actions the other evening. The poor boy was beside himself—his war injury, you know." The gentlemen around the *condesa* leaned a little closer. "Seeing you, someone he had known in Spain, simply made him forget everything else."

"But it was just the thing, the doctors tell us, finally to free him from the last effects of that horrible time," Mrs. Hawksleigh added. "Now he is almost the old Anthony again."

"What are you talking about, Lady Mairmount?" one of the elderly gentlemen asked.

"You mean the *condesa* has not told you of her ordeal in Spain?" She turned to her hostess. "Oh, my dear, I had not known you were keeping it a secret. But there is nothing to be ashamed of. Just because you survived and Hawk was too late to rescue your husband, you must not feel guilty." Lady Mairmount leaned forward and patted her hostess's hand. Mrs. Hawksleigh dabbed at her eyes with the softest bit of muslin and lace imaginable.

The *condesa,* her face more flushed than usual, smiled sadly. "I am trying to put all that behind me. My cousin insists." She lowered her lashes as if to shut out unpleasant memories. From under those lashes, she shot a glance at the man who sat talking to Emily, oblivious of the other conversation. "But you are so kind to think of me. These last few days I have been quite alone except for my good friends here." The *condesa* smiled at each of the gentlemen present. They each blushed like schoolboys.

"So this is where you have been each afternoon, George," Lady Mairmount said. "Missed you at Lady Godwin's card party the other day. None of the other players are your caliber." One of Lady Mairmount's passions was cards, and she was very particular with whom she played.

The elderly gentleman whom she had addressed flushed slightly and made his excuses. Soon all of the older men were gone, afraid Lady Mairmount would inquire too deeply into their activities.

"Good. Now we can be more private." Mrs. Hawksleigh nodded. Hawk, caught between wanting to stay as close to Emily as possible and knowing what his mother and Emily's aunt had planned, shifted nervously. Then he caught sight of the passionate glance that the *conde* gave Emily and moved behind her chair. "Anthony Hawksleigh has done both his wife and you a disservice. We are here to put it right," Lady Mairmount explained.

"Unfortunately, my son does not think about the social ramifications before he acts," Hawk's mother said dryly. "If you will allow us to help, we think we can smooth over the situation." She smiled sweetly at the *condesa.*

"As soon as I arrived this afternoon, I knew the situation would require my utmost concentration," Lady Mairmount said smugly. "A lovely widow like you does not need to surround herself with those old dogs."

The *condesa,* bewildered by what was happening, blinked once or twice. "But those gentleman are my friends, have been my friends even when the hostesses of the *ton* turned their backs on me," she said hastily. "I could never abandon them now."

"And we would not want you to, my dear," Mrs. Hawksleigh smiled benignly. "We simply want you restored to your rightful place in society, accepted in the proper circles. We will plan several outings, rides in the park in my carriage."

"A play or the opera. Just to show we approve of you," Lady Mairmount added.

"You are too kind," the *condesa* said. "But you must not blame the captain too harshly. If I had not allowed him to escort me home . . ." She paused dramatically, a tragic look in her eyes.

"Seeing a person you thought dead had to be a shock. Do not blame yourself. As soon as they realize that we do not blame you, the rest of society will follow," Mrs. Hawksleigh assured her. Just then the clock chimed in the background. "Emily, Julia, we must go. Anthony!" As though she were the mother hen gathering her chickens around her, Mrs. Hawksleigh ushered them out the door, giving them time for only the briefest farewell.

"I thought that went very well," Lady Mairmount said as she settled into her corner of the carriage.

"Splendidly. Shall we ask her to drive in the park tomorrow?" Mrs. Hawksleigh asked. "Perhaps I should stay in town for a few days. Emily, do you have room for me?"

"Of course." Emily leaned back, feeling that slight rush of power that every woman knows when a handsome man demonstrates that he thinks she is worth his attention.

"No!"

"Anthony Hawksleigh, I never thought a son of mine would deny his mother a room in his house," his mother said indignantly. Emily and Lady Mairmount simply glared at him.

"Mama, you live only a few miles away. Besides, Father needs you. You know he does not eat properly when you are away." And we just got rid of Emily's stepmother, he added to himself.

"Well, you may be right. Still, I think you could have been kinder. Maybe you should see if that old injury is giving you problems again." Mrs. Hawksleigh looked at her son anxiously, wanting to believe that his words were not an indication of his feelings for her.

"That is a very good idea, young man," Lady Mairmount added.

"Well, if it will make you happy," Hawk said hesitantly. And keep you from moving in with us, he thought to himself.

"I will send you the name of my doctor. Good man," Lady Mairmount said firmly. "Good idea if you could develop a headache or two, besides bad temper, before he sees you."

Emily giggled, and Hawk glared at her. "You are not to receive the *conde* if I am not home, Emily. I do not trust that man," he said firmly. "Anyone who would let those old rakes visit his cousin without another lady present must not have good sense."

"You sound like Sir Horace now," Emily said, smiling.

"For all his faults, Sir Horace knows more about society than the *conde* does. Your stepmother does not get herself talked about the way the *condesa* does."

"And whose fault was that? You were the one who walked out of that ball with her?" his wife reminded him, her amusement fast fading.

"I was not talking about that!" Hawk was almost shouting, having forgotten the other ladies in the carriage. They exchanged glances and then concentrated on what he was saying. "They are taking bets in the clubs over which of the older gentlemen she will choose as a husband."

"That is all a hum, Anthony. It must be. Most of those gentlemen are involved in government. Having a foreign wife would be a definite liability for them," his mother explained patiently. "In fact, I am not certain how discreet some of them are now. One of them was talking about how careful the government must be with their shipments to Spain. Your father refuses to discuss that type of information with me, and we have been married for thirty years, not that I would want him to do so anyway." The carriage rolled to a stop in front of Lady Mairmount's home. The coachman opened the door, but she waved him away. Shrugging his shoulders, the man went back to his perch, muttering under his breath.

"Damn, I knew I recognized some of those names," Hawk said, hitting his knee with his fist.

"You were too busy listening to the *conde* talk to me,"

his wife reminded him. She smiled sweetly. He ground his teeth together.

"Who were they, Mama?" Quickly she went through the list. He listened intently, comparing them to the names he had gone over for weeks. Several matched. "Do you ever visit Father at the Exchequer?"

"Occasionally."

"Good." Hawk noticed the open carriage door and swung it shut. "Coachman, take us to the Exchequer." Emily and her aunt exchanged glances but did not say a word. Hawk's mother protested the whole way there. "Just tell Father to come to Grosvenor Square within the hour," Hawk told his mother as the coachman helped her from the carriage. "We will wait for you here."

Her errand completed, his mother climbed back into the carriage. "He will be there," she said quietly. Something in her husband's face when she had told him what had happened had made her uneasy. They pulled away.

When they were some distance away, Hawk signaled the driver to stop. He got out of the carriage. "Emily, please take your aunt and my mother home. I will take a hackney to Grosvenor Square to meet my father." She nodded.

As soon as the carriage drove away, each of the ladies began asking questions. But no one had any answers. "I will ride with you to take Mrs. Hawksleigh home, Emily," her aunt declared. "Maybe the drive will help us come to some conclusions."

Later that evening they were no closer to any answers. Emily arrived home to find her father-in-law and husband closeted in the library. They did not emerge for hours. She had almost decided to go upstairs to dress for dinner when she heard them in the hall. "I hope you are wrong about what you suspect, son," she heard his father say.

"I wish I were too. Damn, I do not want to believe that she or they could be involved in anything like this," Hawk said, his voice tired and dispirited.

"You have to admit you know nothing about the lady except what she told you."

"You should have seen her, Father. Bruised, her clothes

ripped. No woman could have been acting. No one is that good. It has to be that cousin of hers.''

''Or it may not be them at all,'' his father reminded him.

''You are right. We will have to wait and see. Good night, Father.''

Emily heard the door close behind her father-in-law and Hawk start up the stairs. She opened the door. ''Hawk,'' she called.

He stopped, startled. Then he turned slowly, wary, as though he was not certain what to expect from her. ''Yes.''

''What was that about?'' She walked slowly up the stairs until she stood next to him.

''What do you mean?''

''That conversation between you and your father?''

''How much did you hear?''

''Just when you were in the hall.''

''Emily, don't ask me,'' he said quietly.

''Then it does involve something about the government?'' He did not even blink. ''All right. I will not ask. But I am here if you need someone to talk to.'' She looked up at him, her face serious.

The tension seemed to drain from Hawk with her words. He smiled at her and wrapped her arm around her waist, pulling her close to his side. ''I know you are, my darling.'' Emily tucked her head against his shoulder and allowed him to lead her to their suite. That evening after dinner she did not say good night outside the bedroom door. He stood there hesitantly for a few minutes. Then she took his hand and pulled him inside.

Remarkably rested the next morning, although neither of them had gotten much sleep, Hawk waited in the library for his father's message. Early in the afternoon he heard a scratching at the door. ''Come in,'' he called impatiently.

''Dr. Woodbridge, sir,'' Clarke announced. Hawk groaned, remembering his promise.

''Send him in. But let me know immediately if that message arrives,'' Hawk ordered. He watched the tall gray-haired man enter the room and stood to meet him. ''Good afternoon, Doctor. I am afraid you are here for naught.''

''Lady Mairmount told me about your case. I am interested

in the subject of blows to the head and amnesia. Even if there is nothing I can do for you, you can help me,'' the doctor assured him. "May I?'' he asked as he put his hands around Hawk's head. Interpreting Hawk's nod as agreement, he ran his hands over his head. "And the blow landed where?'' Hawk showed him. "Hmmmm.''

"Well, Doctor, have you ever heard of a case like mine before?''

"Not exactly. Although some of the same things have happened to others. At least, once you regained your memory of the time in Spain, you did not forget what had happened since then.''

"That has happened?''

"More than once. Really sad too. One man refused to believe that the babe his wife carried was really his. I do not know what would have happened if the babe had not looked like him.''

"Do you know why this happens?''

"No. Sometimes there is not even a blow to the head. Those are truly strange.'' The doctor put his fingers together and tapped them lightly. "You were very lucky.''

"Will I forget again?'' Hawk shuddered as he thought of the way he had left Emily alone on the ballroom floor, knowing that if it happened again, she might not be so willing to listen to him.

"I doubt it, but I cannot promise you that it will not. Once your memory returns, it is usually back permanently. But we know so little about the head and brain, so little.'' His voice died away as the door opened and Emily walked in.

"Clarke said you had arrived, Doctor. Can you tell us any more about my husband's injury?'' she asked, looking from one serious face to another.

"He is fine now, Mrs. Hawksleigh. You have nothing to worry about. His case is typical of others. I am certain he will be fine.''

Emily breathed a sigh of relief. She smiled, her relief sending a wave of happiness across her face. "Good.''

Hawk caressed her face with his eyes. The doctor, realizing he was no longer needed, told them, "I will send Lady Mairmount a copy of my report. Would you like one too?''

"Please," Emily said quietly, her eyes on her husband. "Thank you for coming." The doctor walked out into the hall, stopped for a moment, and then looked back. He smiled.

Inside the room, all was quiet. For a few minutes Hawk and Emily simply smiled at each other. Then they were in each other's arms. "Why are you wearing all these clothes?" Hawk asked as he tried to find a way into her bodice.

"Because your mother and my aunt will be arriving shortly. We are to take the *condesa* for a ride in the park."

"I think I shall have the groom saddle my horse and come along," he said, stepping back for a moment. He leered down at her suggestively. "If not, you will be gone all afternoon."

"You must not. Until the *ton* has a chance to hear what the doctor said, you are to remain indoors."

"But I will get bored without you."

"And I without you," she promised, running her finger down the side of his face. "But I do not want to be the center of scandal for the rest of our lives. Think of what would happen to our children then."

"Children?" he asked excitedly.

"Not yet." She looked up at him and blushed.

A scratching on the door interrupted them before he could say anything further. "Lady Mairmount and Mrs. Hawksleigh are waiting for you in the carriage," Clarke explained. He looked on with paternal fondness as they moved away from one another. After all, the man could not be held responsible when he was suffering from a war injury. All the butlers agreed on that.

"Hurry home," Hawk said as he handed Emily into the carriage.

15

Besides calling on the *condesa* and taking her for drives in the park, Lady Mairmount had carried out the other elements of her plan. Choosing the leading gossips of the town, she had entertained them when they called, telling the story she had concocted so carefully. When she was finished, all of them would dab at their eyes with tiny handkerchiefs, and the gossips would make their excuses, hoping to be the first one in their circle to tell the story abroad. So touching, they all agreed. And to think that the brave man had kept his injury a secret. So tragic. How brave dear Emily must be. No wonder she was seen with the *condesa*, poor lady. How horrible to lose everyone.

By the time a week had passed, everyone except the highest sticklers began to feel a certain sympathy for those involved. Although Emily did not accept many of them at first (she too followed Lady Mairmount's plan), she once again began receiving invitations to most of the entertainments.

Emily continued to drive out with the *condesa* at least twice a week. It took an effort, but Emily had learned to take Jonathan along. His innocent chatter did much to cover the silence between the two ladies. Emily had tried to like the other woman, but the *condesa* was too much like her stepmother. Interested only in wealth and social standing, the *condesa* ignored those who she felt were her inferiors. Had it not been necessary, the *condesa* would have refused the invitations from the Hawksleigh family. But Lady Mairmount had so many friends, and as her cousin the *conde* told her, "If you hope to make a worthwhile second marriage, you should cultivate them." She smothered her own resentment as she watched Emily garner the attention and sympathy from the London *ton.* Their acceptance of the *condesa* came more slowly, the English being very suspicious of foreigners. But as soon as they were certain that recognizing her would not spell their social doom, the émigrés flocked to her side, ready to sympathize with her over the coldness of their hosts.

While Emily drove in the park and smiled at the *condesa,* Hawk stayed at home, hoping for a message from his father. Still forbidden to return to the Exchequer or to spend much time in company, he tried to fill his days with reading and making plans for his estate, but nothing held his attention for long. Like Emily, he sought out Jonathan, finding the young boy an antidote for the boredom that plagued him. If Emily were away from home, Jonathan would come running down the stairs after his lessons, looking for Hawk. "Are the mountains in Spain really the same color as those in Russia?" he asked one day, looking at Hawk's globe carefully before giving it a twirl.

"What color are they on the globe?"

"Brown."

"I do not know about Russia, but the mountains in Spain are brown," Hawk said thoughtfully.

"If all mountains are not that color, why did they make them brown on the globe? I thought this was supposed to be a picture of the world."

"Jonathan, I think the cartographers—?"

"What's a car-tog-rafter?"

"A person who makes maps. Jonathan, these men—"

"How do they make maps?"

"They travel around the world studying the lands and shorelines," Hawk explained patiently. He sat down beside his brother-in-law and gave the globe a whirl. "Someone had to know these islands existed before they could be part of the globe," he explained as he put his finger on the islands in the Indian Ocean.

"How do they know the world is round? No one has ever traveled above it to find out," Jonathan said confidently. He looked up with trusting blue eyes, certain Hawk would have an explanation.

"People in balloons do. Have you been to the sea?"

"The sea? No." This time Jonathan's tone was wistful.

"Emily and I will take you sometime. Then you can tell that the world is round. You can watch a ship sailing away from you. At first you can see every mast clearly. Then it slowly begins to disappear beneath the horizon. Finally it is gone."

"How do you know it does not fall off the edge? Some people have said the world is flat." Jonathan stuck out his chin and dared Hawk to come up with an answer to that.

"Then how do the English ships get home from China and India?" Hawk asked quietly, enjoying making the lad think.

Jonathan screwed up his face, his brow wrinkled. "That's too hard for me." He walked toward the door, dragging his heels and toes along the carpet, watching the nap of the rug change. Before he got there, he turned around, more serious than any six-, almost seven-year-old should be. "Hawk?"

"Yes?"

"Will my mama come back to take me back with her?" Although Jonathan was trying to be brave, his voice wobbled just a bit.

"I do not know, Jonathan. I do not know." Hawk watched as the small boy's shoulders drooped even lower. "But we can ask Sir Horace when he arrives at the end of the week." At the mention of his grandfather's name, Jonathan brightened. "I will call for you when Emily returns home," Hawk promised. "You can have tea with us."

"Will Lady Mairmount be there?" For Jonathan, Emily's aunt was an irresistible magnet. He followed her around like a puppy, even though she ignored him. "She says the strangest things."

"I do not know." Hawk almost added: But I hope not. Fortunately, he held his tongue.

"When is Andrew coming back?" Jonathan asked, unwilling to return to his tutor and looking for an excuse to stay with Hawk.

"As soon as he recovers from his anger at me. I expect him almost any day."

"Who?" Andrew asked. Jonathan gave a shout of glee and ran toward him, jumping at the last minute into his arms. Andrew had only an instant to brace himself and hold them out.

"You. Serves you right, little brother, for sneaking up on

us," Hawk told him. He smiled at Andrew, noting the pleasant expression on his face. "Hmm. Very nice." He walked around his brother carefully, examining the dark blue coat with gold buttons, buff pantaloons, and the shiniest Hessians that Andrew had ever worn. His hands tucked behind his back like Hawk, Jonathan followed him.

"Well, have you looked your fill?" Andrew asked, enjoying the sight of his tall dark brother and the small blond shadow. "Will I do?"

Hawk and Jonathan looked at each other and nodded. "Need tassels on the boots, though," Jonathan decided, cocking his head to one side to inspect them more closely.

"Leave, brat. Tassels are too foppish for me," Andrew said, frowning. His bootmaker had tried to convince him to put tassels on, but he had resisted. Jonathan's face fell. "Go tell your tutor I am taking you for a ride. Change your clothes." The boy grinned and dashed from the room. "Clarke sent my things up to my room," Andrew said hesitantly, as if unsure what Hawk would say to his moving back in.

"Good! Emily and Jonathan have missed you." Hawk paused and looked at his brother fondly. "And so have I."

Andrew closed his eyes and heaved a sigh of relief. Then, as if to get the difficult part over quickly, he said, "You were wrong to treat Emily the way you did, Hawk. No, do not get angry with me all over again. I now know that you did not mean to do so. But if it ever happens again . . ." His face was serious as his voice trailed off.

"Emily will kill me, and you will have nothing further to be angry about," his brother added only half-facetiously. "No, no, remember my war injury," he chortled as he put up his hands to ward off Andrew's blows. Then his face grew serious. "I have missed you, little brother."

"And I, you." Andrew took a seat beside the fireplace, where a small fire kept the chill off the room. "Mama told me that Lady Mairmount has managed to soothe most of the indignation of the *ton*." His brother nodded as if he did not care. "How is Emily doing?"

"Very well, most of the time. At least she is talking to me." And sleeping with me, he added to himself. "I think she has been surprised by how little she cares for society's reactions. After living with her stepmother as long as she did, she was less hurt by what they were saying than someone else might have been. And having Jonathan here has helped.''

"He is something special, isn't he?" Andrew asked, as proud of his little friend as though he were his proud parent. "How long will his mother allow him to stay?"

Hawk walked over to the table where the wine sat and poured his brother and himself a glass. He took a sip before he answered. "Sir Horace is coming to London soon. With his help, Emily and I hope we can persuade Lucretia to allow Jonathan to make his home with us." Hawk looked deep into his glass, wishing he could read the future in the wine that glimmered there.

"Whew! After the way the lady shook the dust of your household from her heels, you expect her to allow you to keep her son?" Andrew drained his glass in one gulp and held it out so that Hawk could fill it.

"She left him in our care in the midst of the deepest scandal. How will it look if she takes him back now?"

"As if she wanted to care for her son herself."

"Ha! She has not cared for him since the day he was born. And if that fiancé of her plans to be saddled with him, I will eat—"

Jonathan burst into the room at a full run. He skidded to a stop. "You do not mind if I do not have tea with you and Emily?" he asked Hawk, remembering his manners. Hawk shook his head.

"Let's be on our way." Andrew took his hat and shoved his gloves into his pocket for the moment. A look of chagrin crossed his face. "This is for you. From Father." He held out a crumpled letter to his brother. "Come on, Jonathan; let's go." Like a schoolboy escaping a punishment, he grabbed Jonathan's hand and rushed from the room, a guilty look on his face.

"Andrew!" Hawk raised his eyes and sighed heavily. He looked down at the letter and wondered how long it had been in his brother's pocket. In that he did his brother an injustice, as it had been there only since morning. Hawk smoothed the crumpled paper carefully, broke the seal, and looked at the few words written there in his father's bold handwriting: "Come to dinner this evening. Bring Emily."

Thoroughly disgusted by the lack of information it contained, he wadded the paper up and threw it into the fire, where it smoldered for a few seconds and then burst into flames. "Why hasn't he told me any more? What are those agents of Perceval doing? Doesn't Father know—?"

Emily appeared in the doorway, her curls charmingly disarranged by the wind. "What?"

"Father has sent word that he needs to see us at dinner this evening," Hawk said quietly, enjoying the picture his wife made in her soft coral muslin with the matching pelisse. "What happened in the park?"

"Nothing unusual. Hawk, I am so tired of those ladies sympathizing with me, pitying me. If I hear one more word about how brave I am, I think I will scream!" He opened his mouth to soothe her, but she cut him off. "And your *condesa* is not the most exciting person to be around. The only gentleman who stopped beside our carriage today who was not elderly was the *conde*. Where does she find them?"

Hawk felt anger flare through his system. He had been told to avoid his wife's company, but the *conde*, a spy if he had ever seen one, was free to roam around London flirting with other men's wives. "I am certain it is not she who discovers them. She does not have access to the clubs. Perhaps you should look more closely at your friend the *conde*," he said bitterly.

"My friend? If it had not been for your behavior at the ball, I would never have known the gentleman." Hawk ground his teeth together in an attempt to control his temper. But he nodded to show that she had scored a hit. Emily ignored him. "If today were the last time I saw either of them, I would not cry a single tear," she said forcefully, stamping her foot to add emphasis. She turned to glare at him. "Sometimes I wonder if you did this on purpose just to see what I would do."

"Emily . . . " Hawk said, his voice low and soothing. He reached out and pulled her close. "I would never deliberately do anything to hurt you. You must know that, don't you?"

She gave a tremendous sigh and put her head on his shoulder. "Most of the time," she admitted.

"What do you mean, most of the time? What about the rest of the time?" His voice was sharp, but his arms were warm and loving.

"Then I think of you at home, and of myself with the *condesa*, smiling and answering their impertinent questions, and I begin to think of ways to get even with you," she said thoughtfully. The look on her face was not one Hawk enjoyed seeing. It was the same one she had worn during the first days after the ball, during the days when she had kept him out of her bedroom.

"Emily, you are just tired. Let's go upstairs and rest until it is time to dress for dinner with my parents." He ran his hand down the side of her face, sending a shiver through her. Then he bent and kissed her neck. She melted against him, pulling his face to hers for a kiss that revealed that her earlier complaints had been merely for show.

"Don't think you can get around me so easily every time," she whispered as they walked arm in arm toward the door. She knew in her heart, however, that all Hawk had to do was smile at her, and she was his. In spite of her anger, her frustration, she loved him from the depth of her soul. When she was away from him, her world grew dark. The door opened in front of them. Trying to regain her composure while she was in front of the servants, she asked, "Why are we going to your parents' this evening? I thought we were going to a musicale."

"Father simply told us to be there. He did not say why." Hawk sighed. Then he looked at her, his eyes dark with mischief. "I think I could beat you to our rooms," he said provocatively.

"And I think we have called enough attention to ourselves already," his wife retorted. But she lengthened her stride, gaining a few steps on him. Reaching the landing before him, she looked back over her shoulder, her eyes inviting him to hurry.

That afternoon, the two of them closed out the world, reveling in their private world of ecstasy. When they emerged dressed for the evening, Andrew waited for them at the foot of the stairs.

"I thought I was going to have to ride out and tell Father you would be late," he said accusingly, looking at the clock on the table.

Emily blushed and looked at the tips of her silk slippers that peeked out from under her sea-green gown. Hawk frowned. "Why are you going with us? I thought you had an engagement," he said, certain his father would never discuss government business with his brother around.

"And who said I was going with you?" Andrew asked. "I have something more exciting planned." He pulled on his gloves and took his cane from the footman. "Something much more exciting than dinner with Mama and Father." He gave his cane a twirl and winked at Hawk.

"So that is the way it is, little brother. Watch your step," Hawk added only half-playfully. Then he rushed Emily out to the coach before she could ask the embarrassing question he could see trembling on her lips.

"Really, Hawk," she protested, "you did not even let me say farewell. Sometimes I do not know what to do with you."

"Exactly what you did this afternoon," he whispered as he took his place beside her in the carriage. "No, do not hide from me." He lifted her chin so that she had to look at him, her face burning. "You are so wonderful."

"So are you," she said, looking deep within his eyes. The carriage started, but neither of them noticed. Only when the carriage door opened again a short time later did they move apart.

"Coo, just like they was still in their honey month, they was," the groom told the coachman as he climbed back up to his place. "Never knew anyone else was around."

"Just mind your own business, you," the coachman told him sternly. "And keep what you see to yourself."

As Hawk and Emily handed their cloaks to the waiting footman, both wondered why they were there. But for once they were so relaxed that neither really cared. Not until after dinner, when his father and he were sitting at the table with their port, was Hawk able to satisfy his curiosity.

His father poured the wine and then sat back. "Well, why am I here?" Hawk asked. Even though he realized that his mother and Emily were privy to many secrets, he had not raised the question when they were in the room because his father had told him by his manner that he did not wish him to do so.

"We investigated the *conde* and the *condesa* as well," his father told him.

"The *condesa*? She is merely a pawn in his game. What did you find?"

"Nothing."

"What? What do you mean, nothing?"

"Exactly what I said. They are both who they said they were. Oh, they are not as fabulously wealthy as they once were, but they have enough to survive on comfortably."

"He is not working for Bonaparte?" Hawk asked, hoping the answer would be different this time.

"No." His father picked up his wineglass and twirled it in his hand, watching the port swirl up the sides of the glass.

"Damn! I will have to start all over again!" Hawk slammed his hand against the table.'

"I do not think the prime minister would agree to that," his father said firmly but quietly. "Besides, there is no need."

"What do you mean? You said the *conde* was not involved."

"He wasn't, but your suggestion that we investigate him and the gentlemen who cluster around his cousin produced an interesting side effect."

"What?"

"As our agents began following them, we found one who had a very wealthy mistress. Of course, the gentleman did not know how wealthy she was." His father sat back, a smile much like Hawk's own creasing his face.

"Father, stop giving me clues. Tell me what happened," Hawk demanded. "Have you caught the ones who stole the payrolls? Were they working for Bonaparte?"

"Yes. No." Again the older man simply smiled.

"Stop being cryptic." Hawk got up and crossed to stand above his father. "Tell me what happened."

"Apparently one of the gentlemen—I will not tell you his name because Perceval has already taken care of him, banished him to his estates . . ." The elder Hawksleigh

chuckled wickedly. "He hates the country." He took another
swallow of port. Then, taking pity on his son, he hurried
on, "Apparently this gentleman told his mistress more than
he should have, and the woman and her lover decided to make
some money for themselves."

"You mean the only motive was robbery?" Hawk asked,
amazed. He had never truly considered that a possibility.

"Nothing else. Now both of them are in prison, but the
money has disappeared. They probably spent it. I hope they
enjoyed it. It will cost them their lives, or transportation at
least," the older man said thoughtfully.

"Transportation? But a theft that size is a hanging
offense," Hawk protested.

"If we are willing to let it come to trail. Perceval has
suggested that we offer them transportation for the money.
One of them will probably talk, and we will not have to face
a very public trial."

"Oh, so we are keeping it away from Parliament?"

"You have just broken the bank, sir." His father smiled
at him and nodded. "Shall we join the ladies?"

"I was so certain it was going to be the *conde*. Now how
am I supposed to get him away from Emily? Every time I
turn around, he is at her side," Hawk complained.

"Life does not always work out neatly, Anthony," his
father reminded him. Secretly the older man was pleased to
see his elder son so jealous of his wife.

While the gentlemen had their port, the ladies had their
tea. "How long must I keep escorting the *condesa* around
town?" Emily asked.

"What does your aunt say?"

"You know Aunt Julia. She said she had taken care of
the problem and that she could no longer be bothered. I plan
to try to talk to her again tomorrow, but I do not hold out
any hope for a different answer. She hates to be bored,"
Emily explained.

"None of us can complain about that this Season. For my
part, I would enjoy some boredom now and again," Mrs.
Hawksleigh said with a smile. "But tell me about the
condesa. Why are you so upset with her?"

"To begin with, she does not have two thoughts in her

head except fashion and gossip. And the way she encourages those older gentlemen to haunt her footsteps disgusts me. She is playing with them." Emily put her teacup down and got up to move closer to the fire. "Why they cannot see her for what she is, I do not know."

"Gentlemen see only the fluff, my dear, or what we choose to let them see. Obviously, the *condesa* has some reason for inviting the gentlemen's attention. Maybe she intends to remarry," the older lady suggested.

The door opened on her last words, and Hawk and his father walked in. "Good. Then maybe Emily would be rid of her," Hawk said. "Perhaps your Aunt Julia would help."

"Hawk," his mother protested, "you do not even know if the *condesa* is looking for a husband."

"She is, isn't that right, Father?"

"Josiah, how do you know about the *condesa*?" Mrs. Hawksleigh asked, her face frozen in a calm mask.

"Just something I heard the *conde* say," her husband answered, frowning at his son. "Apparently he is hoping that she will make an advantageous marriage to help restore the family fortunes."

"Well, I do not know why Emily should get involved," his wife said, still not satisfied.

"To keep from having to take her about, I would even find her a husband," Emily declared, taking a seat beside her husband on the settee. He laced his fingers with hers and nodded.

"What about Sir Horace? He is coming to town this week," Hawk suggested.

"And have her related to Jonathan? Never!" Emily frowned. "Maybe Aunt Julia could help. At least she could not complain because I was boring her with an old problem."

"I have great faith in your aunt," her mother-in-law said reassuringly. "And anything I can do, I will. Now, tell me what arrangements you have made about Jonathan."

"Nothing yet. We have to wait and talk to Sir Horace. Since my stepmother left without telling Jonathan good-bye, we are hoping she has forgotten about him."

"Forgotten her own child? The woman is a villainess."

Mrs. Hawksleigh frowned and looked toward her husband
for support. He nodded encouragingly. "The child is too
sweet to let her ruin. You have done a wonderful job with
him, Emily."

Hawk put his arm around her and gave her a quick squeeze.
Emily tried to pull away, but he would not let her. "If Sir
Horace agrees, we will keep Jonathan most of the year so
that he can grow up knowing his own estate. During the
summers, he will visit his grandfather."

"What about his mother?" the older woman asked.

Emily and Hawk exchanged glances. "He does not want
to go to her," she said quietly, a note of uneasiness entering
her voice.

"She is his guardian," Hawk added. "But her fiancé does
not seem to like the boy. Maybe that will add the weight
we need."

"Let me know if there is anything I can do," his mother
said firmly. His father frowned and nodded.

A short time later, Hawk and Emily made their way up
the stairs in their own home. "Do you think she will allow
us to keep him?" Emily asked wistfully, tucking her head
into his shoulder.

"We will not know until we ask."

That chance came before either of them was quite prepared
for it. During the middle of the next morning, Sir Horace
arrived in his big traveling coach, anxious to see his
grandson. A short time later, Lucretia Cheswick strolled into
the salon, where they all sat drinking tea.

"What are you doing in London? I thought you were
visiting that man milliner's family?" her father asked, much
more bluntly than Emily would have ever thought of doing.

"Something has come up," Lucretia said mysteriously.

"He has called it off. I told you if you played those airs
with him, that, gentleman or no gentleman, he would not
stand for it," her father reminded her.

"He did not call it off," she said angrily. She composed
herself and took a seat near Emily. "May I have a cup of
tea?"

Emily poured it and handed it to her, wondering what new
idea had crossed her stepmother's mind. She took a deep
breath.

Lucretia looked deep into her cup and then raised her head. "Hawk, will you agree to be Jonathan's guardian?"

"What?" Hawk sat up straight, his face puzzled.

"Hawk? What is the matter with your own father?" Sir Horace asked petulantly.

"Why are you doing this?" Emily cried, her hand shaking so much that she had to put down her teacup. "I cannot believe you are doing this. What has happened?"

"I am being married tomorrow, and we are leaving the country immediately, something to do with the government." Hawk and Emily exchanged puzzled glances. "And my fiancé does not want Jonathan to go with us. I knew Emily would be happy to take him, but she has less financial sense than a pea." Her stepdaughter sat up, her face set in stern lines. Hawk crossed to stand behind her, putting his hands comfortingly on her shoulders.

"You still did not explain why you did not consider me," Sir Horace said indignantly.

"You indulge him too much. Grandfather this, Grandfather that. Jonathan gets whatever he wants. He would beggar you in a month," his daughter explained, thinking of her father's investments that would someday come under her control. Although she was usually good at hiding her feelings, this time her greed was written on her face. Her father drew in his breath, ready to strip a piece of hide from her. Then he saw Hawk shake his head and caught sight of Emily's excited face. He held his tongue.

"If you are certain that you want me in charge of Jonathan, I will be happy to accept the responsibility," Hawk assured her.

"Good. I told my attorney we would be in his office by twelve, ready to sign the papers. If we hurry, we can still make it by then. My carriage is outside." She swept from the room, ignoring her father and Emily.

As soon as she and Hawk had gone, Sir Horace began to crumble. "Never thought my own daughter would dust me from her feet like that," he said with a quiver. "No more thought for me or for Jonathan than for an old pair of shoes she was throwing away." He took out his handkerchief and blew his nose fiercely.

Emily had to blink away her tears before she could go to

his side. "At least she left us Jonathan," she said softly, patting his arm.

"Left *you* Jonathan," he reminded her, wiping his eyes. "I'll be gone and not bother you," he said with a catch in his voice.

"No. We want you here. Jonathan is as much yours as he is ours. That's why we wanted you to come to London. We were afraid she would take him away, would neglect him again. We wanted to prevent that." The words tumbled out of Emily's mouth as water tumbles over a waterfall. "We thought you could persuade her."

"Now you know. My daughter has no more feeling for me than for her coachman." He took a deep, sobbing breath.

"But Jonathan loves you. And so do I. Hawk and I want to share Jonathan with you, not take him away," Emily said, tears running down her face as she realized how deeply wounded the old man was, as wounded as she had been during the years under her stepmother's care. "He will stay with you any time you wish him to come and you will visit us whenever you like."

Gradually her words began to register. They did not erase the pain, but they did give him a sense of hope, of belonging. "You won't try to keep me away?" he asked, a quiver in his voice. He patted his eyes with his handkerchief again.

"Never. Sir Horace, you are not simply Jonathan's family. You are my family, too," Emily said. She tried to smile, but ruined it by sniffing.

Sir Horace stood up and grabbed her, giving her a hug. Together they shed a few more tears, using his handkerchief to dab at both their faces. Before Emily could grow self-conscious at being in his arms, the door flew open and Jonathan hurtled in. "You came, Grandfather! You came! Emily said you would." He skidded to a halt in front of them and wrapped his arms as far around them as he could. "I am so happy to see you."

"And I am happy to see you, young man." Sir Horace stepped back away from Emily and sat down again in his chair. "Now, come here and tell me what you have been doing." Jonathan climbed onto his lap and began to explain. Sir Horace exchanged glances with Emily, humor replacing the sadness in his eyes. "Slow down, son, slow down," he told his grandson as the words spilled from the boy's mouth faster than anyone could understand them.

The three of them were still talking when Hawk returned sometime later. "I'm going to live with you," Jonathan told him importantly. "And Grandfather is going to come and see me often. He promised. And I will go see him. I am to learn to care for both estates. They will be mine someday," the little boy said pompously.

Hawk looked over Jonathan's head at the older man. Sir Horace nodded. "I will see my attorney tomorrow. Oh, I'll leave her something. But the bulk of it will go to him. But not anytime soon. I plan to be around for some time to come. Emily has told me she expects her children to call me Grandfather too." Emily smiled at her husband, hoping that he would agree with her.

"So do I," he said warmly, smiling at the family scene before him. He looked at Emily again, the thought of her carrying his children sending waves of desire through him. He sat down hastily, his eyes reminding her of shared excitement. She looked at him longingly, wishing they were alone.

Clarke opened the door to announce luncheon, but before he had a chance to say a word, Lady Mairmount rushed into the room. "Emily, Anthony, you must do something!"

"What is wrong?"

"What's happened?"

"That woman, that *condesa*," Lady Mairmount said, almost stuttering.

"What about the *condesa*?" Emily asked warily.

"She is a menace. Not to be trusted. She's stolen my favorite card partner again. We are going to have to do something about her. Maybe if we find her a husband . . ."

Emily and Hawk looked at each other and burst out laughing.